Twins of Evil

Shaun Hutson is one of the UK's best known horror writers. He is the author of more than sixty books. He lives in Buckinghamshire.

SHAUN HUTSON
Twins of Evil

Published by Arrow Books in association with Hammer 2011

2 4 6 8 10 9 7 5 3 1

First published in Great Britain in 2011 by
Arrow Books in association with Hammer
Random House, 20 Vauxhall Bridge Road,
London SW1V 2SA

www.randomhouse.co.uk

Addresses for companies within The Random House Group Limited
can be found at: www.randomhouse.co.uk/offices.htm

The Random House Group Limited Reg. No. 954009

A CIP catalogue record for this book
is available from the British Library

ISBN 9780099556190

The Random House Group Limited supports The Forest Stewardship
Council (FSC®), the leading international forest certification organisation.
Our books carrying the FSC label are printed on FSC® certified paper.
FSC is the only forest certification scheme endorsed by the leading
environmental organisations, including Greenpeace.
Our paper procurement policy can be found at:
www.randomhouse.co.uk/environment

MIX
Paper from
responsible sources
FSC® C016897
www.fsc.org

Typeset by SX Composing DTP, Rayleigh, Essex
Printed and bound in Great Britain by
CPI Group (UK) Ltd, Croydon, CR0 4YY

Foreword by John Hough, director of *Twins of Evil*

Made in 1971, *Twins of Evil* was my one and only Hammer film. Later I was to direct three episodes of *Hammer House of Mystery and Suspense* (*Czech Mate*, *A Distant Scream* and *Black Carrion*). During my time at Elstree Studios I had the great pleasure of seeing the legendary Roger Corman at work. I was directing *The Avengers* TV series and then made a feature film called *Wolfshead: The Legend of Robin Hood*. This screened in UK cinemas alongside Hammer's *Hands of The Ripper* as a double feature. Later Hammer was to buy *Wolfshead* and I was given *Twins of Evil* to direct.

I had always wanted to do a Hammer film. The screenplay was by Tudor Gates and I found it an exciting read. *Twins of Evil* was made at Pinewood Studios with all the exterior locations next door in Black Park, which was used for several Hammer projects due to the Transylvanian-style trees that give the park a mysterious, Gothic atmosphere. I wanted to add an atmosphere of tension to the horror, so I tried to imagine what it had been like in the days of witch burnings, with any woman a possible suspect and the witch hunters out for blood whether their victims were guilty or not.

Casting the twins at first proved difficult. I played around with the idea of using one actress for both roles and utilising a split-screen technique, but I didn't want the limitations this would have imposed on the camera so soon ruled this out. The main problem with casting the twins was that they would both have to do nudity freely, so would have to have identical bodies. When I met and tested the Collinson twins the search was over. They each had the perfect balance of innocence and daring, and their Maltese heritage gave them an added quality. Could I tell the difference? Most of the time, no! They both had genuine charisma and certainly made an impact that was in tune with the film's title. If CGI technology had been available back then, I suspect Hammer would have missed-out on the Collinson twins altogether!

The twins were surrounded by stars and very good character actors, some of whom I brought with me from *Wolfshead*. At this time Christopher Lee had stated he would not play Count Dracula any more, so Damien Thomas played the vampire lead Count Karnstein. I thought he was excellent and would go on to do more, but Hammer went in a different direction. Peter Cushing played Gustav Weil. His wife had died just two months earlier and he quietly concentrated his grief into an outstanding performance. Dennis Price was his usual class act as Dietrich. The hero, Anton Hoffer, was played by David Warbeck who later tested for James Bond – as a substitute for Roger Moore if he should retire. He got the job, but Roger didn't retire so he never got the chance to be 007. David died in 1997 at age of just 55 after having achieved star status in Italy.

My director of photography Dick Bush did everything I could have asked for. Harry Robinson wrote a superb score that was laced with impending doom. There was top-class art direction from Roy Stannard and outstanding editing from Spencer Reeve, as well as innovative visual effects from Bert Luxford and striking makeup by George Blackler. Indeed all the cast and crew were first class and contributed to the great success the film became.

August, 2011

Author's Introduction

Hammer Films were always synonymous in the minds of movie fans with words like class, integrity and quality. When you went to see a Hammer film you knew that the performances, photography, direction and everything else was going to be top-notch. They had a Gothic splendour to them that perfectly reflected their subject matter, and was also a tribute to the absolute professionalism of the cast and crew.

The first film that ever gave me nightmares was a Hammer Film. Normally this wouldn't be viewed as an endorsement, obviously, but with Hammer producing some of the finest horror films of the Fifties and Sixties I think this is praise indeed. The film responsible was the 1963 remake of *The Phantom of the Opera*, starring Herbert Lom. I saw it when I was about six (and no, my mum didn't take me because she was an irresponsible parent, she took me because I pestered her!). It was showing with another Hammer film called *Night Creatures* and it was my first introduction to the wonderful world of Hammer.

In the years that followed I was lucky enough to see all their films and, with a growing interest in films in general, and horror films in particular, I became a huge fan of Hammer and their productions. Most of them I sampled via late-night TV and I can remember sitting through classics like *Dracula*, *The Mummy*, *Brides of Dracula*, *Curse of Frankenstein* and many more over the years. I even had a copy of *The Quatermass Experiment* on Super 8! (Younger readers are now searching Wikipedia to find out what the hell Super 8 was!) Hammer films captivated me as a viewer when I was younger, and they influenced me as a writer when I was older, and I still make a point of watching any of their films on TV when they're shown.

There was a style and panache about Hammer films that's missing from modern-day horror movies. A dignity that the multiplex dross we're faced with today just doesn't have. Admittedly, as the years progressed they were overtaken by what was happening in the film industry in America, and some of their efforts look pretty tame compared to the hack-and-slash bloodfests that overwhelm cinema-goers now, but what these modern movies will never have is the subtlety and pure class with which Hammer imbued all their productions.

I viewed the chance to do this novelisation of *Twins of Evil* as an opportunity to try and recreate in print what Hammer had presented on the screen. I didn't want to update it or 're-imagine' it or whatever buzzword Hollywood is using these days for ripping off old classics. I wanted to do something that was faithful to the memory of Hammer in that decade. The fact that it was a vampire film was also a great attraction, because I personally believe that some of the studio's greatest creations over the years were its bloodsuckers. The most obvious is Dracula, who was played more ably on screen by Christopher Lee in seven outings for Hammer than by any other actor in film history. He was the personification of everything vampires are supposed to be: powerful and frightening, but also attractive and insatiable. Lee's portrayal of the King of Vampires puts to shame any of the lifeless cinematic ciphers that pass for vampires in modern-day cinema (especially the teenage 'vegetarian' ones in a certain well-known franchise!).

But Hammer's other vampires were also memorable. Probably none more so than David Peel's supremely evil Baron Meinster in *Brides of Dracula*. Over the years there would also be notable contributions from Noel Willman as Doctor Ravna in *Kiss of the Vampire*, and, of course, from Ingrid Pitt as Mircalla Karnstein in *The Vampire Lovers*, the first of the trilogy about Mircalla that culminated in *Twins of Evil*.

Of course, now they've added a new vampire to their catalogue of classic bloodsuckers in the shape of Abby in *Let Me In*, one of the first films to mark the emergence of the New Hammer. Along with *The Resident* and *The Woman in Black* these films mark a fresh and vibrant chapter in the evolution of Hammer, and I can't express how excited I am to be involved with this rebirth, and why I was so happy to be a part of Hammer's re-emergence. I think there is an entire generation that has missed out on everything associated with Hammer and I'm delighted that they are now going to discover what they've been missing.

So, it's Hammer's bloodsuckers that I wanted to pay

homage to with this novelisation of *Twins of Evil*, and I hope I've managed that.

Those of you who've seen the film will no doubt be wondering why there are scenes in the book that never appeared on screen, but all I've got to say on that point is: artistic licence. There were things I wanted to expand and extend, and this wasn't me taking liberties with the script it was just my attempt to broaden and enlarge some of the ideas presented. I did the same when I novelised the screenplay of *The Terminator* back in the Eighties, if that's any consolation.

So, here is *Twins of Evil*, my homage to Hammer and their vampires. Hope you like it.

SHAUN HUTSON

Prologue

Karnstein Castle stood on the highest point of the hills that surrounded the village below.

It dominated the skyline with its black outline. Like a bird of prey poised to drop on its next meal it sat there on the hilltop. A huge monolithic reminder to all those who saw it of the power of the family who had been resident there for so long.

The entire structure looked as if it had been hewn from one enormous lump of rock, rather than constructed from many separate bricks. Its turrets and spires thrust upwards to the sky like accusing fingers, threatening at times to tear open the cloud that often lay so low over the hills in that area, particularly in the winter months.

The castle's black outline was visible no matter where anyone roamed in the village or surrounding forests. It was a symbol of the splendour of the family that had ruled this area of Styria for longer than anyone remembered. Some said the castle was more than seven hundred years old, the seat of the Karnstein family ever since it had been presented as a gift to one of their distant ancestors by a grateful Emperor.

What any of that family might have done to be granted such a gift no one knew. All that mattered to the residents of Karnstein village, Vaseria and the other nearby villages was that the castle on the hill was the home of their masters. The men who worked the fields around the villages did so because they had been granted that land generations before. They would till and plough that soil until the day they were finally laid to rest in it. And whichever Count or Countess of the Karnstein dynasty held court in the castle decided whether or not they were allowed to continue dragging a living from land that would never be theirs. They ruled with the kind of absolute power any aristocratic family would wield.

It was a power that caused them to be feared and sometimes even reviled by those beneath them, but there were many things about the Karnsteins that caused consternation and not all were to do with abuses of power and wealth.

They were feared for other reasons, too.

Some said this fear was down to mere superstition, to the stupidity or gullibility of the peasants who had lived in this area all their lives. Many in this part of Europe shared the same beliefs and mistrust of anything out of their sphere of experience. As religion dominated their lives, so too did stories told by their fathers, grandfathers and unknown generations before of some of the events that had tainted their homeland.

Many of the residents of Karnstein and its neighbouring areas had never been more than fifteen miles from their homes. During their entire, sometimes brief but always hard and uneventful lives they would never even visit neighbouring villages, let alone the bigger cities they had heard of. These distant places were unimaginable to the peasants of the area. Farmers grew their crops and sold them within the confines of the village. The innkeepers saw the same faces every day. Women who made clothes found buyers among their neighbours. Anyone who ventured too far beyond the village – or, indeed, who visited it – was viewed with mistrust.

But few ever visited Karnstein. Perhaps a merchant with cloth to sell or someone passing through briefly on the way to a more distant destination, but apart from that there were rarely new faces to be seen in the narrow streets among the familiar inhabitants of the village. And, if truth were told, that was the way the residents of Karnstein liked it. They didn't care for outsiders anyway. They didn't court the attentions of anyone who wasn't born and raised within the confines of the place they called home. Familiarity had bred not contempt for these humble people but rather a sense of security. Outsiders threatened that comfortable state of affairs.

Sometimes they passed through Karnstein to reach the building perched on the hilltop. And when they did, those who lived in the village eyed them with distaste and suspicion.

And fear.

No one knew what went on inside the high walls of the castle, but many were prepared to offer their own thoughts on the kind of antics that were perpetrated there. Some from the village had worked for the family in days gone by. Carpenters, blacksmiths and wheelwrights had all plied their trades up at the castle when summoned. Even some of the local girls had served as maids or housekeepers in days gone by. But no one from Karnstein had been inside the castle for more than six months now.

Not since the last disappearance.

Of course, no one had questioned the Karnstein family about the whereabouts of one simple peasant girl. No one had the power and, if the locals were honest, no one had the courage to enquire of those who lived at the castle what had become of her. Many had their own ideas as to her fate – linked inextricably to the way the aristocratic family sought its pleasures. How the rich and privileged passed their time, how they sought their thrills and satisfaction was something the peasants in the valley could only speculate on.

There had been talk of ancient rites. Of obscene rituals to be spoken about only in hushed tones. Some had used words like 'sacrifice'. Many more had murmured of evil happenings and even devil worship. Rumours grew and spread like poison in an open wound and, as time passed, the fear that the villagers felt for their masters became tinged with anger too. Resentment sat alongside rage when some looked up towards the gaunt edifice that was Karnstein Castle.

Each night, as darkness fell upon Karnstein and its surrounding hamlets, lights could be seen glowing in the windows and turrets of the castle.

And those in the valley below looked up at those lights and wondered.

And feared.

One

Clad from head to foot in black they rode along one of the many dirt tracks that cut through the woods around Karnstein.

Mud flew up from dozens of churning hooves as large horses carried these black riders through the night and along the narrow track that had been turned to little more than liquid mud by recent torrential rain, and by the passage of other horses and wheeled vehicles during the past two or three days.

With their long capes flying out behind them and black hats pulled down tightly over their faces the riders looked not so much like men but like pieces of the night which had detached themselves and were now hurtling along, as if propelled by some unknown force.

In the branches of a tree high above an owl looked down at the swiftly moving body of horsemen, then shrieked loudly and took to the wing, as if anxious to be away from this group of black-clad figures.

They rode on, moving with a speed and singleness of purpose reflected in their eyes. They knew what they sought and nothing would distract them from that goal. Even their horses seemed to move with a fleetness of foot and a determination that made their passage over the sodden ground effortless.

As the land sloped upwards gently the trees on either side of the track also began to thin out, and the leader of the riders saw more easily the low wooden fence up ahead. It surrounded a cemetery.

The entrance was little more than a wooden archway, roughly built and sporting a large wooden cross at its pinnacle. Graves inside the cemetery were scarcely more than mounds of earth, the type they called burrens in some European countries. Some were marked with wooden crosses, others with little more than sticks rammed into the dark soil to mark the last resting place of whoever occupied the coffin beneath.

A hundred yards from the cemetery entrance there was a small wooden hut, a thick plume of smoke rising from its chimney into the night air. A single dull yellow glow lit the nearest window.

The leader of the horsemen raised his hand, tugged hard on the reins of his horse and called loudly: 'Halt!'

The other horsemen also reined in their mounts, the animals blowing heavily after their long ride.

The leader looked around at his men, studying the faces that were now fixed upon him, awaiting his next instruction.

'Wait here,' he said, quietly, his hand still raised, as if to reinforce his words.

As the others watched, he walked his horse slowly towards the wooden hut.

*

Rolf Kessler looked across at his daughter and smiled reassuringly.

He reached for the lamp and turned the small screw at the base, raising the height of the flame.

Inside the hut it was smoky. The fire they had lit earlier had been made with wood, some of which was still damp, but despite that, he and his daughter had not complained as they had sat around the leaping flames eating the rabbit stew she had prepared.

There wasn't much that Rolf Kessler ever did complain about, if truth be told. He was a simple man and much about his life was simple too. He had been a woodsman for as long as he could remember. The forest had been his home these past thirty-two years and he felt comfortable among the trees that he felled for a living.

It had been easier for him before his wife had died two years earlier, taken by smallpox and now buried in the cemetery close by. Raising a daughter had been difficult, but she had grown into a fine young woman and Kessler now looked across at her again and smiled.

Sophie was nineteen in just two weeks and, when Rolf looked at her he could see her mother in her deep-blue eyes. She even had the same long dark raven-coloured hair her mother had sported. He felt a twinge of sadness, but it passed rapidly.

Sophie shifted uncomfortably in her chair, her head turned towards the door of the hut.

'What's wrong with you tonight?' Kessler asked. 'I think you're hearing things.'

Sophie shook her head.

'I heard a noise,' she told him.

'There are lots of noises in the forest at night, you know that,' he reminded her.

'Listen.'

'There's no one.'

'I hear them,' Sophie insisted. 'Please, father.'

'And what would you have me do?' Kessler enquired.

'Just see if there's anyone out there.'

Kessler smiled to himself and shook his head gently.

'Your imagination is running away with you,' he chided.

Nevertheless, he got to his feet and crossed to the small window set next to the main door of the hut. Kessler squinted through the gloom outside, trying to pick out any shapes or movement in the almost impenetrable blackness beyond. It was like looking into a sea of black ink.

'There's nothing there,' he told his daughter.

Sophie shifted uncomfortably.

'What do you think you heard?' Kessler persisted, still squinting out into the blackness.

His daughter only shook her head.

Kessler hesitated a moment longer, then turned to move back into the room.

As he turned he heard a sound from outside. It was the unmistakeable whinnying of a horse.

'I knew I heard something,' Sophie said.

Kessler didn't speak, he merely grabbed for the large axe that stood by the front door. The tool of his trade. It was razor sharp and would have been difficult for most men to lift, but for Kessler gripped the axe in his power-ful hands with effortless strength and headed for the door of the hut.

'Be careful, father!' Sophie called after him, watching as he tugged open the front door and stepped a couple of feet across the threshold.

'Who's there?' Kessler called, his voice echoing in the stillness of the forest.

There was no answer.

'What do you want here?' he called again, hefting the axe before him as he took another couple of steps into the enveloping night.

Silence.

'Just leave us alone,' Kessler continued. 'Whoever you are. I'm warning you.'

Still there was no answer.

Kessler shook his head.

He was about to turn back into the hut when something struck him hard on the back of the head.

The blow was of such power and savagery that it opened a wound just above the base of his skull, splitting the flesh there. As Kessler fell to the ground blood was already running freely from the wound. His body shuddered once, then was still.

Inside the hut, Sophie heard the thud as her father hit the ground and she rose to her feet, her back now to the fire.

When the black-clad man entered the hut she screamed.

He looked at her appraisingly, his cold grey eyes taking in every detail. He looked from her bare feet upwards at her slim figure, his gaze eventually fixing on her terror-stricken eyes. He was a gaunt, thin-faced man and it looked as if the flesh barely covered his bones, and yet there was a power in his gaze and also in his demeanour. When he looked at her it was with something close to contempt.

'What have you done to my father?' Sophie blurted.

The black-clad man didn't speak.

'What is it?' the girl went on, the fear she felt now growing uncontrollably inside her. 'I know you,' she said, quietly. 'I know what you are.'

As she spoke the words, she ran past the black-clad man and out into the night.

He made no attempt to stop her.

Gustav Weil pulled hard on the leather gauntlets he wore, then followed the girl out into the blackness.

He saw her running for the safety of the trees, slowing her frantic pace momentarily as she saw the body of her father lying motionless close by. Weil moved after her with measured steps, his pace unhurried. It was as if no matter how quickly the girl fled he would still catch up with her. She could not escape him and his brethren, and that knowledge filled him with satisfaction.

Two more dark shapes emerged from the trees and grabbed the girl.

She screamed in terror and Weil stood motionless now as he saw more of his companions grab the girl, one of them ripping her dress in several places, tossing the material aside contemptuously.

They half-lifted, half-dragged her towards where Weil stood, his hands planted firmly on his hips. She struggled violently for a moment, but then realised her struggles were futile. The four black-clad men who held her captive threw her to the ground, where she lay still, her eyes fixed on Weil's boots.

'Look at me,' he said, quietly.

She raised her head reluctantly, hauling herself up on to her knees.

Tears were running down her cheeks now.

'You said you knew who I was,' Weil intoned. 'Well, we know what you are.'

He took a step forward, glaring down at the helpless girl.

'Witch!' he said through clenched teeth.

'I'm not a witch!' Sophie gasped. 'I'm not! You have to believe me!'

'There is no hiding what you are,' Weil went on, venomously. 'How else do you think we found you? God led us to you.'

Sophie dug inside her dress and pulled something metallic free, brandishing it before her. It was a gleaming silver cross on a thin chain, and she held it up so Weil could see it.

'Would I be wearing this if I was a witch?' she challenged, tears still streaming down her face. 'Please believe me! I'm not a witch! I swear in God's name!'

'Do not dare to use His name in your defence!' Weil snarled. 'We know what you are.' His hand shot forward and he grabbed the cross, tearing it from her neck.

Again Sophie screamed.

Weil, the cross still gripped in his fist, raised both hands above his head.

'Oh God have mercy on this poor unfortunate creature,' he began. 'She is a child of the Devil!'

Three of the other black-clad men dragged Sophie to her feet and dragged her towards the nearest tree. The first of them hurried to his horse and pulled out a long thick length of rope from the saddlebag. As his companions held the girl he quickly wound the rope around her, securing her to the thick trunk. Despite her struggles she could not escape, and she felt the rope biting into her wrists and ankles as the man pulled tighter.

Others now gathered around her, piling pieces of wood at her feet.

'Oh God, no!' Sophie cried at the terrible realisation of what they intended to do. 'You can't do this to me! Please! In God's name!'

'I have told you before not to use His name in vain,' Weil snapped. 'Do not try to escape your fate. We do this to help you. To purify your soul.'

Sophie screamed.

Weil merely turned his gaze skyward.

'Oh God, we ask Thee in Thy great goodness to save the soul of this girl,' he called.

'I haven't done anything!' Sophie shrieked.

More wood was piled around her feet and she strained frantically against the rope that held her, helpless, against the tree.

'Help me!' the girl screamed. 'One of you must know I have done nothing!'

The other black-clad figures merely moved nearer, their gaze fixed on the struggling girl.

'Please, help me!' Sophie moaned, her head lolling against her chest.

'We commend unto Thee her earthly body,' Weil continued, his face still upraised. 'And we see to purify its spirit. God guide us in our work.'

One of the other black-clad men approached and Weil nodded, taking from him a burning torch.

He held it before him for a moment, watching the dancing flames.

'No!' Sophie shrieked.

Weil took a step forward and jammed the torch into the pile of wood that had been built up around the girl's feet.

Sophie screamed even more loudly as the flames took hold with incredible swiftness.

'The fires of purification burn so brightly because they are fanned by the breath of God himself,' Weil said, watching as the flames flickered, then rose more furiously. He turned and looked at the other black-clad men. 'Brothers, let us pray.'

All of those watching clasped their hands together, some closing their eyes; others content to gaze at the leaping flames. They seemed untroubled by Sophie's harrowing cries. Screams of pain as well as fear. The fire was searing her flesh now. On her legs and arms patches of skin were already turning bright red, blistering as the fire burned her. Again she struggled against the rope, but it was useless and now even the screams began to die in her throat.

The black-clad men watched as the fire devoured her, ignoring the stench of burning flesh that was beginning to fill their nostrils as surely as the odour of charred wood.

Weil looked at the blazing pyre and the incinerated body within and smiled.

'Thy will be done,' he murmured.

The flames rose higher.

When he woke, Rolf Kessler struggled to his feet, his head filled immediately with a throbbing pain. The wound at the back of his skull had stopped bleeding, but the legacy of the blow was the ache that distorted his vision and made each step an effort. Despite that, Kessler sucked in a deep breath and forced himself onwards through the forest, following the hoofprints of many horses, using them as his guide. On more than one occasion he had been forced to stop, fearing that the pain was going to overcome him completely. He had leant against tree trunks or squatted on the dark earth until his vision had cleared enough for him to continue.

Kessler had been tormented not just by the pain and his unsteadiness but by the thought of what he might find at the end of his trek. He knew that the Brotherhood had taken his daughter, and he had a good idea where. The tracks of the horses seemed to confirm his suspicions. He also had an idea of what they might have done to her once they reached the appointed spot, but he tried to force those thoughts from his mind. Along that road lay madness. However, as he approached a slight rise in the ground he stopped again, not because of the pain he was feeling but because of the smell that assaulted his nostrils. Kessler had smelled it once before and it had stayed with him, seared into his consciousness. It was the smell of burnt flesh.

He saw a thin plume of smoke rising into the night air, too, and he hurried his pace, almost stumbling over some fallen branches in his haste. As he reached the top of the gentle rise he looked down into the hollow beyond, his eyes bulging madly as he surveyed the sight before him.

What was left of his daughter was still secured to the tree in the middle of the clearing. The smoke still rose around her body, despite the fact that the flames had obviously gone out some time before.

Kessler shook his head and advanced falteringly down the slope towards the remnants of the pyre, his gaze fixed on the blackened shape at the centre.

'Sophie,' he murmured, his voice cracking and tears flowing freely down his cheeks.

He moved to within a few feet of her, transfixed by the sight of his child hanging there, her skin like charred paper barely attached to calcified bones. Her mouth was open in a silent scream and Kessler's only thought was what agonies she must have endured as she died.

'Sophie,' he said again, dropping to his knees, his whole body now shaking violently as the word dissolved into sobs, but as he gazed at her those sobs turned slowly into another sound. One of pure, undiluted fury and despair. Kessler threw his head back and screamed, a sound torn raw and bloody from the base of his spine. A shout so loud it seemed to reach to heaven itself.

Rolf Kessler collapsed.

Two

The boys heard the coach before they saw it.

Both of them no older than twelve, they were hanging from one of the lower branches of an oak tree, laughing to themselves as the thick bough swung earthward under their weight, before springing back up again. It had creaked menacingly a couple of times and the boys had wondered if it was going to snap, but they held on, the element of danger only adding to their enjoyment.

They had left the village early that morning, running happily through the fields and woods, enjoying the feeling of warm sun on their faces as they played.

The gloom and rain of the previous night had given way to a glorious sunlit morning and the boys were taking full advantage of the improved weather conditions. They'd skimmed stones on one of the streams that snaked through the countryside, and when they'd tired of that they'd watched farmers working in the fields for a time. But their own energy had forced them on into the woods where they had climbed and where they now clung to the oak branch like two clothed and exuberant monkeys.

There was a crossroads nearby, signposts showing

the location of Vaseria, Karnstein and the other small villages round about, and it was near this signpost that they now played.

It was towards this crossroads that the coach came thundering.

Drawn by four large grey horses, it moved along the road swiftly, the animals coaxed to greater speed by an occasional flick of the driver's whip.

The boys weren't the only ones who watched the progress of the coach. Farmhands working in the fields on either side of the road also turned to stare as the vehicle moved along. They wondered who was inside, who was passing through or visiting their village. Some looked on with interest, others with suspicion.

Two men repairing the broken wheel of a cart also ceased their labours for long enough to wave in the direction of the coach. The driver nodded in recognition of their gesture, but nothing more. He checked his pocket watch and noticed that he was actually well ahead of time for the arrival in Karnstein, so he tugged gently on the reins and slowed the pace of the horses considerably.

The animals seemed to appreciate this and settled into a trot, pulling the coach effortlessly in their wake, even at slower speed.

Seeing the coach slow down, the two boys both dropped from the branch of the tree, landing effortlessly on the ground beneath.

The first of them pointed in the direction of the coach and ran towards the road.

'Come on!' he called to his companion who scurried after him.

'I wonder if there's anyone important on it?' the second boy said as they ran towards the road.

'Like who?' the first boy grinned.

'A soldier coming home from war,' the second offered. The two boys laughed.

'A beautiful lady,' the first boy suggested.

'A judge, coming to the court to sentence a man to hang,' the second offered and again the two boys laughed.

'Hey look, it's slowing down,' the first boy noticed and the two of them increased their pace in order to reach the coach. They ran alongside it, keeping up without effort.

'Hello!' they called in unison.

There were small green curtains at the window of the coach and the boys were delighted when one of these was pulled aside. They were even more delighted to see the face of the person who looked out.

Maria Gellhorn was beautiful. That had been the considered opinion of all those who had seen her since the day of her birth twenty-one years earlier. She had grown from an angelic-looking child into a gorgeous teenager, and then into a quite stunning young woman.

Both boys looked at her, open-mouthed, as she waved at them from inside the coach.

'Hello!' she called to them, smiling warmly. The gesture only served to enhance her appearance.

The boys seemed dumbstruck by such a gorgeous presence and merely waved without speaking.

Maria sat back inside the coach, giggling to herself.

'What is it?'

The question came from her sister, Frieda.

Born just minutes apart twenty-one years ago, the sisters were identical. It was as if each were the mirror image of the other. Impossible to tell apart, their perfect features were like porcelain. Over the years their incredible similarity had made it hard for anyone, including their parents, to tell them apart. Now Frieda looked questioningly at her sister.

'Who were you waving to?' she asked again.

'Just a couple of little boys,' Maria said, still smiling. She pulled the curtain open and Frieda could see that the boys were still running alongside the coach.

Both girls laughed.

The sound was met with a somewhat disapproving look from the couple sitting opposite.

The woman was in her fifties, her husband a little older.

Maria became aware of the woman's scornful glance and looked back evenly at her.

The woman was glaring at Maria's all-too prominent cleavage.

'You may wish you had dressed more appropriately for these parts,' the woman said waspishly.

'What do you mean?' Maria challenged.

The woman merely glanced frostily first at Maria and then at the similarly dressed Frieda.

'We know your type,' the woman proclaimed, turning her head.

'What are you trying to say?' Maria went on.

'Never mind, Maria,' Frieda said, quietly, placing a hand on her sister's arm.

The coach suddenly came to a halt and the occupants heard the driver shouting something to someone ahead.

Maria peered out of the window and saw that two farmhands were driving some cattle across the road, prodding them with sticks to hasten their passage.

'Get out of the way!' the coachman shouted, but the farmhands merely ignored him, ensuring that every one of their bovine wards got safely across the road.

'Peasants,' the man in the coach grunted dismissively.

Maria, who had been staring at the cows, now looked upwards, her eyes widening. She touched Frieda's hand, beckoning her to the window, so that she, too, could see what had so transfixed her.

'Look!'

Frieda followed her sister's pointing finger and saw the outline of a castle perched high up on top of the hill.

'It's beautiful,' Maria went on. 'It must be Karnstein Castle. It looks like something from a fairy tale.'

Frieda nodded, a broad smile on her face as she regarded the imposing fortress high above them.

'Whoever owns that must be rich,' she said quietly. 'Who lives there?' she asked the woman opposite. 'Do you know?'

The woman nodded.

'Count Karnstein lives there,' she said, without looking at Frieda.

'Who is he?' Frieda asked politely.

'He owns that castle and most of the land around here,' the woman told her. 'How do you not know?'

'We've never been here before,' Maria explained. 'We come from Venice.'

'That would explain a lot,' the woman snorted.

'Are you visiting?' the woman's husband asked, as if anxious to defuse the growing antagonism between his wife and the two girls.

Frieda looked first at the man, then at her sister, but she didn't speak.

'We're going to live with our aunt and uncle in Karnstein,' Maria said. 'They're our guardians. Our parents died six months ago.'

'In a fire,' Frieda added, quietly.

The couple opposite nodded in unison.

'I'm sorry to hear that,' the man said, gently. 'No one should have to go through that kind of loss, especially not girls of your age.'

'I don't know how I would have managed if it wasn't for my sister,' Maria said, smiling in Frieda's direction. 'She was there for me whenever I needed her.'

Frieda looked coyly at the couple.

'You helped me, too,' she said to Maria.

'There is no bond like that between sisters,' the woman pronounced.

'Well ours is stronger than normal, then,' Maria told her. 'I don't know what I would have done without Frieda's love and kindness.'

Frieda reached over and squeezed her sister's hand gently, smiling lovingly at her.

The coach continued on its way, lurching from side to side on more than one occasion as it struck ruts in the road. Those inside were buffeted mercilessly, forced to hold on to the leather straps that hung on the sides of the coach to steady themselves.

The coach driver guided the vehicle past more watching villagers, who glanced briefly at it as it rumbled on towards the centre of Karnstein along narrow streets, until it finally reached the village square. Like the roads leading in and out of the village, the square was unpaved and, because of the heavy rain of the last few days, it was little more than a quagmire in places. Some straw had been scattered over the worst patches, but nevertheless it still contained many deep potholes that had filled up with dirty water. The buildings that surrounded the square were simple, white-washed constructions. There was an inn, a baker's, a cooper and several other small businesses all interspersed with houses.

As the carriage came to a halt Maria poked her head out of the window once more to see what kind of surroundings they had finally been deposited in.

She wrinkled her nose and frowned.

'Karnstein!' the coachman shouted, as if reminding his passengers where they were.

The man inside the coach was the first to emerge, clambering down and sinking almost up to his ankles in the thick mud.

Maria saw this and did her best not to smile, watching as he helped his wife down from the coach. The two girls followed, careful to avoid the same glutinous ooze that had almost sucked the man's shoes off as he walked away.

The coach driver had descended from his seat by now

and he helped each of the girls alight, affording himself a long glance at each of them in the process.

He wasn't the only one who was gazing. A group of men stood outside the inn, watching intently as the twins clambered from the coach. One of them muttered something to his companions and several nodded, smiling lecherously at the girls.

Others were watching, too.

In one corner of the square there were several black-clad figures looking in the direction of the coach, watching each new arrival climb down. They waited until all of the occupants had emerged, then slipped away down one of the narrow streets that led off from the square.

The two girls glanced around at their new surroundings, watching as the coachman lifted their luggage down from the rear of the coach and deposited it in one of the drier areas of the square. He nodded in the direction of the two girls, then clambered back up on to his seat.

'Maria! Frieda!'

The calling of their names made both girls turn in the direction of the voice.

'Aunt Katy!' Maria beamed as she saw an older woman advancing happily towards them.

Katy Weil was in her early fifties, but looked older. Her skin was pale and her face thin, yet there was a warmth and welcome in her eyes that belied the weariness of her expression. She looked at both girls and shook her head, still smiling warmly.

'I swear I'll never be able to tell the difference

between you,' Katy said. 'You were both about that high when I last saw you.' She held her hand flat and level with her hip.

Both girls laughed.

'We've grown up a bit since then, Aunt Katy,' Maria said, happily.

'You certainly have,' Katy echoed. 'Your parents must have been very proud of you.' Her smile faded a little and she felt a stab of sadness as she spoke the words. She motioned to the girls' luggage that they retrieved. 'Come on,' Katy went on. 'Let's get back to the house.'

The men outside the inn continued to look on, eyes fixed on the two girls. Again one of them spoke, licking his lips as he watched the twins.

And, as before, as they left the square, other eyes also watched them go.

Three

The house that Katy and Gustav Weil lived in was simple both inside and out. Everything was functional. Everything had a place and a purpose. It was as if anything that did not was viewed as an extravagance, and that was something that was never tolerated in the Weil household.

Extravagance was to be frowned upon. Indeed, in this house most things were frowned upon if they went against the thinking and beliefs of Gustav Weil.

Now Katy poured some wine into the mug in front of Maria and regarded her new wards evenly.

The girls had eaten the meal she'd cooked for them and they'd thanked her for her troubles. They were well brought up, polite young women, as Katy had expected. For that she was grateful.

'Perhaps you'd like to go to your room now and change,' Katy offered.

'Change?' Maria echoed, looking a little puzzled by the statement.

'Your uncle will be back soon,' Katy explained, looking down as if to avoid Maria's questioning gaze.

'Of course,' Frieda said. 'You'd like us to look our best for when uncle arrives.'

Katy drew in a sharp breath.

'It's not that,' she said, almost apologetically. 'Well, it's just that the way you're dressed.' She nodded towards the low-cut green dresses the girls wore. 'We do things differently from Venice, you see.'

Frieda frowned.

'No, I don't see,' she said, puzzled.

'What I mean is, had you lived in Karnstein you would still be wearing black,' Katy went on.

'But Aunt Katy it's not a lack of respect,' Frieda said, softly. 'We wore black for more than two months.'

'Until last week,' Maria said, a little sharply. 'How long are we supposed to remain in mourning so that people will know how much we miss our parents? We loved them and we miss them more than anyone does, but wearing black for the rest of our lives isn't going to bring them back is it?'

'I understand that,' Katy admitted. 'But, as I said, we do things differently here. Your uncle would expect it of you. He's a very religious man.'

'We didn't bring any black,' Frieda said, sharply.

'Well perhaps something more sober then,' Katy insisted.

'Yes, of course,' Maria said, smiling. 'If you'd like it.'

Frieda looked sternly at her sister for a second, but said nothing.

'Thank you, Maria,' Katy said. 'I'll show you to your room and you can change.'

Katy headed towards the staircase and, after a moment's hesitation, the two girls followed.

They were actually on the first step when the front door opened.

Gustav Weil stepped across the threshold and froze as he set eyes upon his twin nieces.

He ran an appraising and increasingly disapproving eye over them, the muscles at the side of his jaw pulsing.

'What kind of plumage is this?' he said, quietly. 'For birds of paradise?'

The two girls met his gaze, but only Frieda could hold it for longer than a moment or two. Maria looked at the floor, her cheeks colouring. Katy cleared her throat awkwardly, looked first at her husband and then at the two girls.

'Maria, Frieda,' she began. 'This is your Uncle Gustav.'

Both girls curtsied, but Weil seemed unimpressed, his eyes still ranging over them disdainfully.

'Do you know the Fourth Commandment?' he said quietly, his features set and stern.

'Which one is that?' Frieda asked, waspishly.

'Honour thy father and thy mother,' Weil snapped. 'That thy days may be long upon the land which the lord thy God has given thee.' He sucked in a deep breath. 'You would do well to remember it.'

'We didn't mean to offend you,' Maria offered.

'Your parents are not yet cold in their graves,' Weil snapped. 'And yet you display yourselves like . . .' He clenched his teeth as if unable to finish the sentence.

'Like what, Uncle?' Frieda said, challengingly.

'Those dresses you are wearing would be more suited

to a brothel than to a good God-fearing house like this!' Weil snapped.

Frieda thought about saying something else, but Katy stepped in front of her, anxious, it seemed, to get the girls away from their uncle as quickly as possible.

'Your room is at the top of the stairs,' she said. 'The door is open.'

The twins hesitated a moment longer, then hurried up the stairs, their footsteps echoing on the bare wood as they ascended.

Weil shook his head as they disappeared from view, then stalked into the kitchen, took off his shoes and pulled on a pair of riding boots.

'Gustav, I'll get you a meal,' Katy said.

'There is no need,' he told her. 'I'm going out.'

'Gustav,' Katy continued. 'Try not to be so hard on the girls. They don't know our ways.'

'Then the quicker they learn them the better for everyone. Do you expect me to look the other way while they parade around like prostitutes? They are living in my house now. They will abide by my rules and by the rules of God, and the first of those rules I demand be obeyed is respect. They must show respect for themselves, for their dead parents, for us and for God. Otherwise I will not have them under this roof.'

'But Gustav, they have nowhere else to go.'

'Then they had better learn to behave correctly.'

Weil got to his feet and headed for the door.

'Where are you going?' Katy asked.

'There is a meeting of the brotherhood,' he told her.

'What time will you be back?'

'I don't know. Perhaps while I'm gone you might find the time to speak with those girls and remember what I said. I meant it.'

He swept out of the house, closing the door behind him.

Katy waited a moment, then made her way wearily up the stairs.

Gustav Weil paused outside his front door, glancing up at the night sky and the clouds that scudded across it. Behind him he saw the light from one of the upstairs bedrooms and he paused to gaze at it, shaking his head gently. It was the room where the two girls were to stay. He stroked his chin thoughtfully, realising that they were going to have to adjust – and quickly – to their new surroundings, otherwise they would have to leave. He had a reputation to consider and no one could be allowed to sully it, least of all the offspring of his dead sister-in-law. He shook his head once more and headed towards the small barn next to the house where his horse was tethered.

'Weil.'

The sound of his name made him turn, and he saw a large figure lurch from the bushes nearby.

'You bastard!' the figure snarled. 'You murdering bastard!'

Weil frowned, but held his ground as the figure advanced upon him. Only when the dark shape was a few feet away did he recognise it.

Rolf Kessler stood before him, his hands clenched into fists, his teeth gritted. Even from such a distance Weil could smell the odour of dried sweat and unwashed clothes, and he wrinkled his nose and took a step back.

'I should kill you for what you and your Brotherhood did to my Sophie,' Kessler snarled.

'And I should warn you that I am armed and will not hesitate to protect myself if I have to,' Weil said, evenly.

'You killed my daughter, why not kill me, too?'

'You have committed no crime, as far as I know,' Weil said.

'And neither had she!' Kessler roared furiously. 'She was innocent!'

'So you say, but we had evidence to the contrary. You were blinded by your love for her. You couldn't see the evil in her.'

'There was no evil, you bastard! That girl would have harmed no one. She thought none harm, she did none harm and yet for that you and your Brotherhood burned her.'

'We purified the evil that was inside her,' Weil announced.

'I should kill you now,' rasped Kessler.

Weil stepped back, pulling the pistol from his belt. He aimed it at Kessler's head and thumbed back the hammer.

'We were doing God's work,' he said, flatly.

'What kind of God demands the murder of a young girl?' Kessler wanted to know. 'You won't get away with this, Weil. Not you and not your Brotherhood.'

Weil regarded him dispassionately.

'I saw those girls,' Kessler said, quietly. 'The two who arrived at your house today. I saw them.'

'My nieces.'

'They looked the same age as my daughter when you murdered her.' He moved a step closer to Weil. 'I want you to feel the pain I felt, Weil. Perhaps if something happened to your nieces you would know what I have to live with every day.'

'Is that a threat?' Weil challenged.

Kessler sneered, hawked and spat on the ground in front of Weil, before turning and heading back towards the enveloping darkness of the bushes.

'You won't escape, Weil!' he called as he strode away. 'I will have my revenge! I will make you suffer as I did! Mark my words!'

And he was gone.

Weil waited a moment, then slowly lowered the pistol, pushing it back into his belt.

Four

The building where the Brotherhood met was owned by one of their number. A merchant named Franz. He had a successful tree-felling business just outside Karnstein itself, and the building had been his gift to his fellow members. It was a short ride or a brisk walk from the centre of the village itself. Close enough to be convenient for members to reach, but far enough away to give them the privacy they wanted. The place where they met had a high vaulted ceiling and wooden floors. It was not designed acoustically for such meetings, but they had been using it since their foundation and it had the kind of austerity about it that these men appreciated. What they spoke about inside this building was their business and no one else's.

The wooden floor descended in tiers, each tier holding a long wooden bench. It was upon these benches that the black-clad members of the Brotherhood now sat.

There was a long table at the far end of the room, a huge wooden cross suspended on the wall behind it. It formed a suitable backdrop for the words they spoke and the beliefs that governed their lives.

Outside, darkness had fallen. Inside candles flickered

and danced in the breezes, casting long deep shadows as they lighted the room.

There were between twenty and thirty members of the Brotherhood, their number having grown since their formation. Most of them were present now, gazing down from the tiered benches towards the table where Gustav Weil, Franz and Hermann now sat.

Hermann was a magistrate. A tall, powerfully built man with short grey hair that was hidden beneath the black hat he wore. At the other end of the table, Franz could not have been more different. He was short and slim with dark eyes that were constantly darting this way and that, as if anxious not to miss anything. He had a long hooked nose that gave him the appearance of some kind of bird of prey.

Now he steepled his fingers and looked around the room at his companions, his gaze moving from face to face, as if checking they were all listening intently enough to what was being said.

Weil was on his feet, his fists pressed against the tabletop as he stood waiting for the words he had just spoken to register with his brethren.

Murmurs of agreement and approval filtered around the room, the babble dying swiftly as Weil raised his hands again when he wished to continue.

'Two young men have been killed within the last ten days,' Weil said. 'And each victim bearing the mark of the Devil.'

There were loud calls of agreement, some of the Brotherhood standing to show their assent.

'We know this to be true,' Weil went on. 'We also know what must be done.'

Again the other members of the Brotherhood shouted their agreement or punched their fists in the air to accompany their exhortations.

'This place has been cursed,' Weil went on. 'This village and everyone who lives in it.'

Franz nodded sagely and glanced at Weil.

'Who among us does not know why this evil has been visited upon us?' Weil asked.

More shouts of agreement.

'He speaks the truth!' Hermann shouted, getting to his feet momentarily.

Weil nodded, waited for the noise to die down, then continued.

'But the signs are plain,' he said. 'God is calling on us who believe in His holy word to stamp out that evil. To seek out the devil-worshippers and to purify their spirits. Only by this fate may they find mercy at the seat of the Lord. Only burning these heathens will save them.'

'And where are we to find these devil-worshippers?' one of the Brotherhood called.

'I know of one,' Franz said, leaning forward in his seat.

'Speak, brother,' Weil said, looking at his companion.

A hush fell over the room as the other members of the Brotherhood listened to Franz as he spoke.

'There is a cottage in the woods,' he began. 'A young girl lives there. Alone. She refuses to take a husband.'

'Why?' one of the Brotherhood called.

'Because she does not need one,' Franz intoned.

'They say she has many husbands,' Hermann added.

'Many men have been seen going to and from that cottage,' Franz continued. 'Why would so many visit her, unless she was offering something they wanted?'

'Whore!' one of the Brotherhood called.

'She's a creature of the Devil!' Franz said. 'She is wicked!'

'Immoral!' Hermann added, sharply.

'There are many without morals around here!' one of the others shouted.

'And they will pay!' Hermann cried.

'And this girl?' Weil said. 'What should we do with her, my brethren?'

'Burn her!' shouted one of the other puritans.

'Yes!' another added. 'Let her roast in the flames! Purify her!'

Weil smiled.

'We know what we must do, brothers,' he called.

'And we shouldn't wait,' Franz insisted. 'As long as she is free to continue her witchcraft and heresy, then others will be in danger.'

'Burn her!' another of the puritans roared.

The cry was taken up; filling the room until it seemed the sound would shatter the windows.

'Burn the witch!' Franz called, raising his voice so that he was heard over the baying throng. He and Hermann rose to their feet and joined Weil, who was pulling on his gauntlets.

'Let us do God's work!' Weil shouted. 'This is what He wants us to do. Let us not disappoint Him.' He turned to Franz. 'Lead the way, brother. This witch must not live another night.'

Like a black tide, the Brotherhood poured towards the doors of the building. Outside their horses waited.

And high above, in a cloud-choked sky, the moon looked as though it had been obscured by smoke as it was engulfed by thick cloud.

Weil swung himself into the saddle and, with the others following, he spurred on his mount. As he rode, Weil felt a curious mixture of pride and excitement. It was a feeling he had come to know well these past few months and he urged on his horse to greater speed, the animal responding as he snapped the reins.

The time had come once again.

Rolf Kessler watched them leave and he felt the hatred filling him. It was a feeling he had come to know well since the death of his daughter. He was comfortable with it now. Not all men could live with such feelings, but Kessler did. He had no choice. She had been his world and now she was gone, because of those men in black. The men he had been watching. Men like Gustav Weil, Franz and Hermann. And their accomplices. Those self-appointed guardians of morality and religion who had tied his Sophie to a stake and burnt her alive.

'Bastards,' Kessler murmured under his breath.

He gripped the hilt of the long-bladed knife he carried, his knuckles gleaming white in the darkness.

They would pay. All of them. The time would come when he would watch them die, just as they had watched Sophie die. They had taken from him that which was closest to him. He would repay that debt if it was the last thing he did.

Five

'Put to bed at nine o'clock. You'd think we were ten years old.'

Frieda spoke the words angrily. She was sitting up in bed, gazing towards the window of the bedroom, and the candles flickering gently on the windowsill. Others burned on the bedside table, lighting the room with a warm, yellow glow.

Like the rest of the house the bedroom where the girls now found themselves was functional but hardly welcoming. They had hung their clothes in the small wardrobe, and neatly folded the others before placing them in the drawers provided. Their shoes were lined up on either side of the bed.

Maria, who was lying beside her, looked around the small room, then glanced at her sister.

'I know, Frieda,' she said. 'But there's nothing we can do about it. We're living in someone else's house now. We have to do as they say.'

Frieda looked briefly at her sister, then continued gazing towards the window and the darkness beyond.

'We might have to do as they say, but it doesn't mean we have to like it,' Frieda offered.

Maria considered what her sister had said for a moment, then touched her gently on the arm.

'You'd better put out the candles. Uncle Gustav might be back soon,' she said, softly.

'Let him come,' Frieda snapped. 'I don't care.'

'I'm thinking about Aunt Katy.'

'Yes I know, she's terrified of him. God, how would you like to be married to a man like that?'

'I feel sorry for her.'

'She must have known what he was like when she married him. He must have always been as puritanical. She knew what life with a man like that was going to be like.'

'I still feel sorry for her. She must love him or she wouldn't have married him.'

'She's probably too afraid to tell him what she really thinks. You heard what she said to us – that they do things differently here. She doesn't want us here any more than he does. We don't belong here, Maria. It's just that you can't see that.'

'I don't believe you. Aunt Katy is a good woman and I'm sure Uncle Gustav means no harm. He's just very religious.'

'The worst kind.'

'What do you mean?'

Frieda didn't speak for a moment. Instead she kicked the blankets back irritably. She stretched her shapely legs out before her.

'He's a man of God,' she went on. 'Too good to be true. I know his kind.'

'What do you mean?' Maria asked.

'I can just imagine if he came back now and saw the lights on in here,' Frieda continued. 'That would give him an excuse to come in.'

'Frieda!' Maria gasped.

'Don't you know men like that?' Frieda went on, vehemently. 'Didn't you ever notice them in the park when we were little girls? The ones who watched us with their funny staring eyes. And when we got older they watched us even more closely. I know men like that and I'm telling you that Uncle Gustav is just the same. He hides his true feelings behind his beliefs. Everyone thinks he's so good and upright. If they knew how his mind worked they wouldn't be so forgiving.'

'Frieda, stop it!'

'You see if I'm not right. He'd love to find us doing something wrong, just to punish us.'

Maria shook her head.

'He'd probably make us strip naked first,' Frieda said, easing her nightgown from one shoulder and rubbing it gently. 'He'd want to look at us. Didn't you see the look in his eye when he first saw us? I know the way his mind works.'

'I'm not going to listen,' Maria protested.

'All right, don't listen, but let me tell you, it's going to be hell living in this house.'

'But we've got nowhere else to go. What can we do? Uncle Gustav is our guardian now.'

'He may be yours, but he's not going to be mine. Not for long. I'm not going to live with that religious old fool.'

43

'You shouldn't say that, Frieda. This is our home now, for better or worse.'

'If you had any sense you'd come with me.'

'I wouldn't want to leave Aunt Katy.'

'You have to think about your own life, Maria. You can't live your life for others.'

'But she loves us.'

'That may be, but I'm going away from here.'

'How?'

'I'll find a way,' Frieda proclaimed. She swung herself out of bed and crossed to the window, blowing out the two candles there. She gazed out into the night, her eyes drawn to the silvery orb of the moon. She smiled to herself. 'Somehow I'll find a way.'

Six

He watched them from deep within the woods.
Horsemen.

Each one dressed the same. Black tunics and capes.
Black hats and black trousers.

He counted twenty at least as they swept past him, the
thunder of their horses' hooves shaking the ground as
they passed. If they saw him they didn't acknowledge his
presence, but then again he doubted if they were aware
of him, hidden as he was in the blackness of the trees,
enveloped by the impenetrable gloom of the night.

He was a big man. His skin was the colour of burnt
wood and his neck was as thick as a tree stump. Tall and
muscular, he had hands the size of ham hocks, which
looked capable of easily crushing the head of a child.
That particular task had never been asked of him, but if
his master had so wished, then he would have done it
willingly. Whatever his master ordered him to do, he
complied. Not for fear of retribution, but because he
knew there was no other way for him.

All his life he had known only to obey and he did it
unquestioningly. He served and he protected, and it
was in that capacity that he now watched the black-clad
men sweep past.

He knew where they were going and he had to reach that place before they did. His master was there and he had to protect him.

Unseen, he slipped back into the enveloping shadows.

Gustav Weil saw the woodsman's cottage a hundred yards or so ahead, just off the narrow track that cut through the forest. He urged his horse on, then tugged hard on his reins, bringing the animal to a halt. As he did so he raised his hand and those following him also reined in their mounts.

'I'll go first,' Weil told his companions.

He swung himself out of the saddle, leading his mount by its reins, the animal walking along obediently behind its master. Weil tethered it to a tree and stood gazing at the small cottage, his hands planted firmly on his hips.

'This is the place,' Franz assured him, joining Weil in front of the building.

'Let us see what this witch is doing tonight,' Weil hissed. 'It is time to do the Lord's work again.'

Franz nodded, watching as Weil walked briskly towards the cottage.

As he drew nearer he saw movement at the window.

The girl was in her mid-twenties. A mane of blonde hair cascaded as far as her shoulders, which were bare, Weil noted with something approaching distaste. He moved towards the window and looked through, able to see the girl more clearly now.

She was not alone inside the cottage.

There was a man lying on the bed, his shirt open to the waist. As Weil watched the girl climbed on to the bed beside the man, one hand gliding across his broad chest. They kissed deeply. Weil sneered as he saw the man's hand slide between the girl's legs. She moved closer to him, murmuring encouragement.

'Is she in there?' Franz asked, appearing beside Weil and also peering through the window.

'Look for yourself,' Weil said, venomously. 'She lies in the filth of her own corruption even now.'

'The man with her . . . ,' Franz said, allowing the sentence to trail off.

'What does it matter who he is?' Weil snapped, and moved towards the door of the cottage.

He paused for a second, then pushed it open. The door slammed back on its hinges and the two occupants of the cottage swung round to see who was intruding.

The man stood up, rising to his full imposing height. He had jet-black hair and it seemed to match his eyes as he glared at Weil.

'What's the meaning of this, Weil?' Count Karnstein demanded.

Weil hesitated for a moment, his initial show of bravado receding. Franz took several steps back, surprised by the presence of Karnstein, who also glared disdainfully at him.

'Are you and your little band out witch-hunting again?' Count Karnstein sneered.

Weil held his gaze.

'Well, you've come to the right place,' the Count went on.

'We seek the servants of the Devil,' Weil countered.

'Well you've found one,' Count Karnstein insisted. 'Me. Now get out. I have other business to attend to.'

Karnstein turned and looked at the blonde girl, who was sitting up on the bed, observing the scene. Weil watched as the Count returned to the bed and sat down beside the girl.

'Do you want to watch, Weil?' the Count chided.

He smiled and kissed the blonde girl, his hand moving to her left breast, which he squeezed firmly.

'Don't let them bother you, my dear,' Karnstein purred to the girl. 'Some men like a musical evening, but Weil and his friends find their pleasure burning innocent girls.'

'Innocent?' Weil snapped. 'You do not know the meaning of the word.'

'Well I know the meaning of the word "intrusion",' Karnstein replied. 'Do you?'

Weil regarded the aristocrat with barely suppressed fury.

'You are arrogant, Count Karnstein,' he said between gritted teeth. 'Because you have the protection of the Court and the Emperor himself. But there is a higher authority.' He pointed skyward with one gloved hand.

'Tell that to the Emperor,' Karnstein said, dismissively. He was looking down his long aquiline nose at Weil with undisguised contempt.

'God will have his revenge!' Weil snapped.

'Be careful he doesn't have it on you,' the Count growled. 'Now get out.'

From inside the cottage the blonde girl laughed. The sound jabbed into Weil like a blade into soft flesh. The colour rose in his cheeks and he could feel himself shaking with suppressed rage. For long moments he hesitated in the doorway of the building.

'Well, what are you waiting for?' Karnstein challenged. 'I told you to get out. You and all of your sad little followers.'

The Count walked to the door and the blonde girl joined him, moving close to him.

'Look at them, Gerta,' Karnstein chided, sliding his arm around the girl's waist. 'Gustav Weil and his brave band in search of women. Not that they would know what to do with a woman if they needed her for anything other than burning.'

Karnstein and the girl laughed.

Weil could barely contain his anger now. Franz looked at him and gently pulled the pistol from his own belt. He handed it furtively to Weil, who took the weapon.

Franz nodded. Weil merely stood with his back to the Count, glancing down occasionally at the pistol.

'Wait,' Karnstein called. 'If you want a woman then take this one.' He pushed Gerta before him. 'Have Gerta if you like. If you want some excitement. I'm sure she could teach you much that you do not know.'

The Count suddenly pushed the blonde girl towards Weil. Surprised by the sudden movement, she tripped and went sprawling, looking first at the Count and then up at Weil who was standing beside Franz looking down at her.

Karnstein strode over to where she was kneeling and he place one hand on her blonde hair, stroking gently.

'She could show you so much, Weil,' he chided.

Karnstein gently stroked one long index finger across the girl's cheek' finally pushing it towards her mouth. He allowed the digit to glide over her lips before finally pushing it between them.

'See,' Karnstein smiled. 'You and your brotherhood would feel better then. You won't go around burning pretty girls.'

Weil turned slowly to face the Count and, as he did, he extended his arm.

The pistol was gripped tightly in his fist, aimed at Karnstein's chest.

The Count merely smiled.

Weil looked at him with hatred in his eyes. He was shaking with rage now, his finger crooked around the trigger of the pistol.

'Go on then, Weil,' Karnstein said, flatly, the smile fading from his face. 'Pull the trigger. If you have the stomach for it.'

Weil raised the weapon slightly, so that it was aimed at the Count's face.

'Do it,' Karnstein taunted. 'Show all your little followers how brave you are.'

Weil thumbed back the hammer of the pistol, the metallic click reverberating through the night.

The large black man chose this moment to step in front of his master. Weil regarded him evenly, the barrel of the weapon now aimed at his face instead of that of his master.

'Let him shoot, Joachim,' Karnstein said. 'The Emperor will hang them all.'

Weil hesitated, aware of the stares not only of Karnstein and his manservant, but also of his companions, who were looking on intently at the scene unfolding before them.

'Come on, where is your courage, Weil?' Karnstein said, mockingly. 'You're brave enough when you're dealing with young women. One pull of the trigger and that would be it. Go on. Do it or are you as much of a coward as I think you are?'

Weil eased the hammer of the pistol forward then turned and handed the weapon to his nearest companion.

'You are not worth a bullet, Count Karnstein,' Weil said as he moved towards his horse.

'Are you sure, Weil?' the Count called after him. 'You wanted to kill me a moment ago. Afraid of what the Emperor will do to you and your little organisation?'

The other members of the Brotherhood also hauled themselves into their saddles.

'The whole village would turn out to see you and your brethren hang,' Karnstein continued, as Weil and the others turned their horses and prepared to ride away. 'A public hanging in the square, Weil. You mustn't have all the pleasure yourself. Everyone enjoys a good hanging.'

Karnstein stepped out from behind the black manservant, shaking his fist in the direction of the Brotherhood as they rode away.

'Pray for me, Weil!' he bellowed. 'That's what you're supposed to do, isn't it? That's what you're supposed to do for sinners! Pray for me!'

Gustav Weil could not hear the words that taunted him. He was riding away from the cottage, swallowed once again by the forest and the night.

Seven

Even above the pounding of horses' hooves they heard the scream.

Weil reined in his horse, holding up a hand to bring those who rode behind him to a halt, too.

Franz and Hermann joined him, shock and concern etched on their faces. To their right lay the entrance to the cemetery and it was from that direction that the scream had come. Weil hesitated for a moment, then swung himself out of the saddle.

'We must see what is happening,' he said, taking several steps towards the cemetery entrance.

Franz and Hermann dismounted somewhat reluctantly and followed Weil.

'The rest of you stay here,' Weil called to the other members of the Brotherhood who remained in the saddle, their eyes and ears alert for the slightest sound or movement. Horses whickered and pawed the ground nervously. Riders tugged hard on the reins to keep their mounts still.

There was a large wooden carving of Christ himself above the entrance to the cemetery, and the lifeless eyes seemed to look down upon Weil, Franz and Hermann as they prepared to enter the necropolis.

Inside, gravestones and crosses stood in untidy lines like unruly soldiers awaiting orders.

There was a light mist that night and it hung over the ground like a white shroud, the passage of the men through it causing it to swirl and dance like some living thing. High above, in one of the tall trees, an owl screeched loudly as it looked down upon the figures making their way through the cemetery. Its talons were red with blood. It had already killed once that night. Now it took to the wing, flapping into the black sky, away from the men picking their way through the gravestones.

Weil was at the front, glancing to right and left, wondering what could have caused the scream. It had been human, of that he was sure, but exactly where the piercing sound had originated he could not tell.

Something moved just ahead of them. Something large that scuttled away through the long grass and the grave markers. Weil assumed it was a rat. He moved a little deeper into the cemetery, then stopped next to a moss-covered gravestone, glancing around him. The silence was oppressive. It was as impenetrable as the night here among the graves.

Franz and Hermann also looked around them. Their hearts were beating a little faster, the breath clouding before them when they exhaled.

'Who would be out so late?' Franz asked, quietly. 'Who could have made that sound?'

'Were we mistaken?' Hermann added.

Weil shook his head and took a step forward.

It was as he did that a hand closed around his ankle.

His heart thudded hard against his chest, the shock forcing him back two or three paces.

His two companions also gasped and retreated rapidly.

Only then did they look down towards the ground.

There was a man lying there. He was in his early thirties, his body hidden behind two gravestones. His hand was stretched out beside him, the fingers flexing gently. His lips were moving soundlessly. But it was his eyes that the three men gazed at with such awe. They were staring wide, bulging in their sockets until they threatened to burst from his skull. He was shaking.

'Look at his face,' Franz murmured.

The man's skin was the colour of fresh milk. Even in the gloom of the cemetery Weil and his companions could see that his flesh was so pale it was almost translucent.

'Drained of blood,' Hermann said, watching as Weil knelt beside the man.

'Who did this to you?' Weil said.

The man opened his mouth to speak, but no words came, only soft panting breaths. A loud gurgling rattle deep in his throat followed these as his last breath left him. Weil touched the man's face and felt how cold it was. Then he gently took hold of his chin and turned his head.

There were two large puncture wounds on the throat; both of them still weeping blood.

Weil crossed himself.

'The Devil has struck again!' he rasped.

Franz and Hermann also saw the savage wounds.

'Not the Devil,' Hermann said. 'But his servants.' He sucked in a deep breath. 'Vampire.'

The words reverberated in the air like a gunshot.

Weil looked at his companion and then back at the dead man before him.

'Servants of the Devil,' Weil proclaimed. 'They will pay for this.'

'She lives not two kilometres from here, you see, I warned you,' Franz added, vehemently.

Weil leaned forward again and crossed the hands of the dead man on his chest, then with one thumb he gently drew the sign of the cross on the man's forehead. When he got to his feet Weil's face was set in hard lines.

'The Lord will light our path. Let us ride,' he said, angrily. 'This evil cannot be allowed to continue. Let us strike in God's name!'

He turned away from the corpse and strode back to where the other members of the Brotherhood were waiting. Franz hesitated a moment, his gaze fixed on the dead man, then, as Hermann pulled at his arm, he, too, hurried out of the cemetery, behind Weil.

'The evil we feared has struck again!' Weil called to his companions as he swung himself into his saddle. 'We ride to destroy it!'

The others shouted their agreement and the black-clad men put spurs to their mounts and set off once again through the forest. Weil rode ahead of his companions, his hands gripping the reins tightly, his knees digging into his mount, guiding it along the narrow forest roads. The animal responded and increased its speed to such a degree that some of the other riders had trouble keeping up. Weil glanced over his shoulder and saw that Franz and Hermann were close to him now. Franz guided his horse up alongside Weil and pointed towards a fork in the road just ahead of them.

'That way!' he shouted, indicating the left-hand path.

The horses moved as one in the direction that Weil and Franz took, hooves pounding on the forest floor.

'There!' Franz shouted, pointing to a figure moving among the trees. 'The servant of the Devil!'

The girl was in her early twenties, dark-haired and slightly built, dressed in simple garb that she had probably made herself. She was carrying a basket filled with wood that she had been collecting for the last hour or so. Now she stood motionless as she saw the horsemen thundering through the forest.

Only when she realised they were riding towards her did she drop the basket and turn.

'Ride her down!' Weil shouted, bending forward over the neck of his horse.

The girl screamed and spun around, running as fast as she could along the narrow path that wound through the trees. The path was wide enough to accommodate a horse and Weil urged his mount on towards the fleeing girl. The others followed him, shouting angrily as they saw her run. They were now less than fifty yards away.

The girl ran for her life, chancing another look behind her. Her breath caught in her throat when she saw that the leading horses were less than forty yards away now.

She stumbled and almost fell.

Thirty yards.

Already the muscles in her thighs and calves were throbbing with the effort of running from these men who seemed intent on galloping over her.

Twenty yards.

She screamed again. As she put out a hand to steady herself, one fingernail caught against a tree trunk. The girl winced in pain as the nail was bent backwards and almost ripped free, but she continued running, all too aware that the leading horseman was nearly upon her now.

Ten yards.

The trees were starting to thin out a little, the path widening. The girl realised with horror that it would allow the horsemen more room for manoeuvre. She had no chance unless she could reach her cottage.

She was still thinking that when she felt herself grabbed and lifted into the air. Strong arms dragged her bodily from the forest floor and up on to the saddle of the leading horse.

She screamed again, kicking and punching at the pilgrim who had grabbed her, but he did nothing except growl something angrily at her.

'Keep still you whore!' he hissed.

'We have her now!' Franz smiled, reining in his mount, watching as the leading pilgrim brought his horse to a halt and swung himself out of the saddle, dragging the girl with him. He threw her to the ground, the impact knocking the wind out of her. She looked up imploringly at him, but there was no pity in his eyes, only hatred and anger.

'Let us act swiftly!' Weil called.

Even before he'd finished the others were dismounting, running in all directions to retrieve pieces of wood, while three or four members of the Brotherhood dragged the girl towards the nearest tree and lashed her to the trunk with thick rope.

'What are you doing?' she wailed.

'God's work,' one of the Brotherhood snarled, grabbing her by the chin and glaring into her wide eyes.

'I've done nothing to you,' the girl whimpered.

'How many others have suffered because of your witchcraft?' Hermann snapped, joining his companions, who were piling wood around the girls' bare feet.

'You left your mark on the man you killed,' Franz hissed. 'The mark of your master, the Devil.'

'I have killed no one,' the girl protested. 'I don't know what you're talking about.'

'The Devil hides inside those no one would suspect,' Hermann told her. 'But we can see his evil. We cannot be misled by his trickery.' He glared at the girl, who was struggling helplessly. Her dress had been torn in several places and when she twisted to one side her breasts were clearly visible. 'Even now you try to tempt us,' grunted Hermann.

Weil joined him, the burning torch clutched in one gloved hand.

'Look at her,' Hermann went on. 'Even at the moment of her purification she tries to flaunt herself.' He pointed at the girl, his eyes now fixed on her slender legs. 'She would tempt us the way she has tempted so many before.'

'Whore!' Franz breathed.

Weil stepped forward and jammed the torch into the stacked-up wood, waiting while the flames caught, licking over the kindling until the blaze took hold more strongly. Yellow and orange flames began leaping high into the air.

The girl screamed.

Weil smiled thinly.

'Please!' the girl shrieked as the flames began to sear her flesh.

'She should call on her master for help,' Franz muttered. 'Perhaps he could cast a spell and dampen the flames.'

Hermann laughed loudly.

Weil stood silently watching the fire as it grew. The girl screamed more loudly, but the sound was drowned by the roaring blaze. The stench of burning flesh began to fill the air.

'Happy with your latest kill?'

The words rang out across the clearing and several members of the Brotherhood turned in the direction of the shout.

'More innocent blood!' the voice bellowed again. 'Spilled in the name of God?' There was a harsh and sardonic laugh to join the vehement words.

Gustav Weil looked in the direction of the shouts and saw the source of them. He recognised Rolf Kessler immediately and fixed him with an icy stare.

'Who is that?' Franz asked, standing at Weil's side.

'A woodsman,' Weil said, quietly. 'He's insane. A madman.'

'If I'm mad it's because you've made me that way,'

Kessler snapped, lurching towards Weil. 'You and your kind.' He looked around contemptuously at the other Brotherhood members.

'What are you doing here?' Franz wanted to know.

'Watching you murder another young girl, as you murdered my daughter,' Kessler rasped. 'How long will you continue? There won't be anyone left in Karnstein at this rate. How many more have to die needlessly before you fools stop?'

'Go home, Kessler,' Weil said, dismissively.

'I have no home,' Kessler snapped. 'Not since you killed my Sophie. It isn't a home without her there.'

'Then go back to wherever you came from and keep your nose out of our business,' Franz added. 'You have no right to be here.'

'Why? Because you bloody butchers would rather carry out your murders without interference?'

'We are doing God's work,' Franz said.

'You are no better than the evil you claim to fight,' Kessler sneered.

'Stay away from us, Kessler,' Weil insisted.

'Or what? You'll burn me like you burned my daughter and so many others?'

'It may be easier to find evidence against you than you think,' Weil told him.

'And what about your nieces, Weil? What do they think of your activities? Or your daughter, Franz? And your son, Hermann? Do your children know what you do?' Kessler said, challengingly.

'They know we do the Lord's work,' Hermann interjected.

'Scum,' Kessler snapped. 'That's what you are. Spineless, cowardly scum.'

'Be careful who you insult,' Weil taunted.

'And you be careful,' Kessler said, defiantly. 'All of you. Watch yourselves and your families. There will be a reckoning.'

'If you go anywhere near my nieces I will kill you,' Weil snapped.

'He wouldn't dare,' Franz sneered. 'He's just an ignorant woodsman. A madman.'

'Driven mad by his daughter's evil,' Hermann added.

Kessler shot Hermann a withering glance.

'Get away from here,' Weil insisted. 'Do not bother any of us again.'

'I will be watching you,' Kessler rasped. 'All of you.' He turned and stalked off back into the woods. 'And your families.' The words echoed on the still night air.

'We must deal with him before he carries out his threats,' Hermann said.

'Idle threats,' Weil offered.

'And if you're wrong?' Franz wanted to know.

Weil didn't answer.

Eight

The storm had been building steadily throughout the night, rumbles of thunder rolling across the sky like warnings. Now those rumbles had turned to deafening waves of sound that shook windows in their frames when they came. Accompanied by the cracks of lightning that lit the heavens it sounded as if the sky itself was exploding.

Gustav Weil stood gazing out at the celestial display for a moment longer, then turned to face his wife.

'The aristocracy of this country is decadent,' he snapped. 'Their whole lives are devoted to sinful pleasures, the pursuit of lust.' He shook his head and wandered across to the table where Katy Weil sat sewing. 'But God's will shall prevail.'

'Amen,' Katy murmured.

'They think themselves above the law,' Weil continued. 'Because they have important friends they fear no one and no one dare challenge them.'

'Is there nothing you can do, Gustav?' Katy wanted to know.

'How can I? I am helpless against them when they are protected the way they are.' Weil drew in a deep breath. 'They are not protected from God, though. He sees their debaucheries. He sees how they defy Him and He will act. He will act through his servants.'

'Like you.'

'I and many more like me. Their wickedness will not be tolerated long. The day of reckoning will come for them both on earth and when God decrees. They will not stand against Him. Not they or their master Satan.'

Katy listened to his words silently, her gaze fixed on his face. He was staring off into the distance, as if his attention was caught by something she couldn't see. It was almost as if the words her husband spoke were addressed not to her but to someone she wasn't aware of. A presence she was oblivious to.

'Why are there not more who feel as I do?' Weil went on. 'Why are so many willing to stand by and let this debauchery continue unchallenged?'

'Perhaps others think they can do nothing to stop it, Gustav.'

'The Lord will send word to his servants, do not doubt it,' Weil snapped, raising his voice.

Upstairs with the bedroom door slightly ajar, Frieda heard the words clearly, and she leaned closer so she could make them out as Weil spewed them forth like a litany.

'Frieda,' Maria whispered.

Frieda put her finger to her lips.

'Sshhh!' she snapped. 'I'm trying to listen.'

Downstairs, Weil moved to the end of the table and picked up the large Bible that lay there. He held the sacred book close to his chest almost lovingly.

'The time is coming when the wicked and the evil will

be forced into a reckoning,' he said. 'And Count Karnstein will be the first to answer.'

'Gustav, be careful. The Count has important friends,' Katy reminded her husband.

Weil laid the Bible gently on the table once again, stroking his hand over the cover.

'And sinners every one of them,' he said through clenched teeth. 'They meet at the castle and hold debauched gatherings. Men and women strip naked, they say, and indulge in pagan rites.'

Upstairs, Frieda opened the door wider, then finally stepped out on to the landing, padding barefoot across to the wooden rail at the top of the stairs.

Maria looked at her and shook her head reproachfully, but her sister merely advanced nonetheless. She peered cautiously over the banister, but couldn't see her uncle or aunt. Weil's words were clear enough, though, as she remained where she was, listening to what he said.

'They practice the black arts. They worship the Devil,' Frieda heard. 'They are all slaves to Count Karnstein and he is their evil master.'

Outside, a particularly loud rumble of thunder shook the house. A flash of silver lightning that threatened to rip the sky in half followed it immediately.

Frieda started at the sound and retreated towards the bedroom, but she left the door open wide enough so that she could still hear Weil's ranting.

'They must be stopped!' Weil said, his voice barely less than a shout.

'Gustav, the girls, please,' Katy pleaded.

Weil gritted his teeth.

'The sooner Karnstein is exposed for what he is the better it will be for everyone,' he said angrily. 'His evil practices cast a shadow over our countryside and our lives.'

Frieda strained her ears to hear her uncle and, when she couldn't she advanced a step or two on to the landing.

A floorboard creaked beneath her.

She froze momentarily, but the sound was drowned out by another massive clap of thunder. Again she moved towards the banister rail and leaned over in an effort to pick out the words her uncle spoke.

'Young girls from the villages are abducted by Karnstein's lackeys and initiated into unspeakable ceremonies,' Weil went on, doing his best to control the tone and volume of his voice. 'What if something were to happen to the girls? How would you feel then?'

Katy looked aghast at her husband.

'Karnstein would be only too happy to get his hands on them,' Weil went on. 'To force them into God alone knows what kind of depravity.'

'The girls would never let themselves . . . ,' Katy said, but Weil cut her short.

'It isn't what they would let themselves do,' he snapped. 'You have no idea what Karnstein is like.'

Frieda retreated back into the bedroom and this time she closed the door behind her. She crossed to the window and peered out. More lightning lit the sky, and Frieda looked up towards the hills around the village that were clearly visible in the wake of each blinding flash.

On the top of the highest hill, lit up by the cold white light of the lightning was Karnstein Castle.

'How it must hurt Uncle Gustav to have to live in the shadow of the man he hates so much,' Frieda said, smiling.

Maria looked on silently.

'Come and look, Maria,' Frieda urged, still gazing out of the window. 'You can see the lights of the castle from here.'

'I don't want to look,' Maria assured her.

'I wonder what's going on up there right now?' Frieda purred. 'One of those meetings Uncle Gustav was talking about? Men and women stripping naked?' She breathed heavily. 'Drinking? Touching each other?'

'Don't speak like that, Frieda.'

'I'm just imagining what they're doing at the castle. It's exciting.'

'No it isn't. And if Uncle Gustav heard you speaking like that he'd punish you.'

'I don't care about Uncle Gustav,' Frieda snapped. 'But I'll tell you something. Do you know what I want more than anything? I want to meet Count Karnstein.'

Outside, the storm raged on.

Nine

The girl was naked.

Strapped to the top of the stone tomb, she struggled helplessly, straining against her bonds periodically, but only too aware of how firmly they held her.

At the long table on the far side of the main hall of Karnstein Castle, the Count sipped wine from his goblet and gazed across in the girl's direction. The look he afforded her was only cursory, however, and the expression on his face as he regarded the men moving around her was nothing short of derisory.

The men, despite the fact they were most certainly not holy men, were all wearing priests robes, but not of the customary black. These long gowns that brushed the floor when they walked were a rich purple colour, as were the hoods they wore, which obscured their faces. Their garb was as fake as their supposed calling. There were white crosses sewn on to the material of these garments, but they were upturned, the apex of the crosses facing the ground. The leading man was holding a silver bowl that he had taken from the end of the table where Karnstein now sat. As the Count watched, the chief priest turned and headed back towards the girl tied to the tomb.

He placed the silver bowl close to her head. The girl shot him a nervous glance, and then also looked worriedly at the silver bowl. The priest looked at her from under the hood of his robe, then he reached out with one hand and squeezed first one of the girl's breasts and then the other. Squeezing so hard he left the imprints of his fingertips on her flesh. She whimpered in pain, but the priest merely continued with his ministrations. He was murmuring something that sounded to Karnstein like Latin, but the exact origin of the language was a mystery to the Count. Neither did he care for its true meaning.

He looked from the priest to the walls of the hall instead. Flaming beacons lit the hall, casting long shadows and illuminating the high-ceilinged room. It was vast, the walls decorated with old weapons, hunting trophies and the portraits of his ancestors. The Count regarded these old paintings with something approaching envy. The eyes of each subject seemed to focus on him, their expressions mocking. As if they, too, were tired of the pathetic spectacle being presented to him.

Karnstein shifted in his seat and exhaled wearily. What had his ancestors seen in this hall during their hundreds of years of residence here, he wondered? Things of which he could never even dream? Thrills and excitement that seemed to elude him, no matter how fervently he searched for them? He doubted if any of them had ever sat through the kind of sham spectacle he was now witnessing.

The Karnstein family had a proud heritage. Warriors,

rulers and sometime confidantes of emperors. They had learned and experienced things that the Count feared he would never sample. Pleasures and delights that seemed to elude him. He felt a stab of anger amidst the envy and longing.

He looked again at the priest who had now been joined by two assistants who were holding a white sheet. They slowly covered the girl's naked body with the sheet, then one of them handed the priest a small chamois bag, before retreating a few steps from the tomb.

The priest slid a long, double-edged knife from his robe and held it before him.

Karnstein sat up slightly, hoping that something interesting was about to happen.

The priest lifted the bag above the girl's head, then he pressed the point of the knife against it, his incantations growing louder.

He drove the knife into the bag, splitting it effortlessly. Blood burst from it, some spattering the girl's face.

She let out a cry of disgust and turned her face to one side, as the priest now held the chamois bag over the silver bowl. Blood dribbled into the receptacle, some of it dripping on to the cold stone of the tomb.

Karnstein took another sip of his wine as he watched.

'Your Excellency is pleased with the entertainment?'

The question came from the Count's right, the words spoken by a chubby man with flabby cheeks and a receding hairline. What little hair he possessed was swept over the top of his bald pate in wispy strands. The jacket he wore was too small for him, the buttons straining to remain closed over a stomach that jutted forward, threatening to burst the garment. His flesh was mottled, especially on the cheeks and nose, the legacy of too much alcohol and rich food over the years.

Karnstein didn't answer. He was still watching the priest, who was squeezing the chamois bag like a cow's udder, coaxing the last of the blood from it into the silver bowl that still sat atop the tomb next to the girl's head.

'He is calling up the Devil,' the fat man went on excitedly.

'Well so can I or you,' the Count said, wearily. 'But will the Devil come?'

The priest dropped the chamois bag on to the stone floor of the hall and picked up the silver bowl in both hands.

'Fresh blood,' the fat man said, moving his chair closer to that of Count Karnstein.

'The guts of a chicken or a suckling pig. The Devil won't be cheated as easily as that, Dietrich,' the Count grunted. 'You may be a fool, but the Devil is not.'

The fat man frowned, his own attention now fixed on the tableau around the tomb. He was more concerned with the girl than the robed men. Dietrich watched as she writhed beneath the sheet. He had preferred it when she had been uncovered. He had found it more pleasing to gaze upon her naked body than to have it shrouded by this sheet.

'Your Excellency is pleased with the girl?' Dietrich asked.

'A peasant bought for a few gold coins,' Karnstein sneered.

'But a shapely one, Excellency,' Dietrich insisted. 'More shapely than last time, and more willing, I'll wager.'

'Can you never find anything new?' Karnstein chided. 'Anything different?'

'I try, my lord.'

Karnstein took another sip of his wine then stroked his chin thoughtfully.

'They say that Gustav Weil has two pretty nieces staying with him,' he said, finally.

Dietrich nodded.

'So I've heard, your Excellency,' he said.

'Twins,' the Count murmured. 'That would be something different.'

'Your Excellency is pleased to joke,' Dietrich said. 'We do not want trouble with a man like Weil.'

'Why not? What can that old fool do to me? He has no power, Dietrich.'

'He has the Brotherhood behind him, Excellency.'

'And I should fear them? A bunch of religious fanatics?'

'Weil has the ear of the villagers, Excellency.'

'Those villagers care nothing for him or his brethren, Dietrich. In these parts I am the one with the power, not Gustav Weil.'

The Count got to his feet.

'I don't know why I employ you, Dietrich,' he said, dismissively, walking to the end of the table and seating himself on it. 'You bore me and everything you do for me I find tedious, including this charade.'

He nodded towards the robed figures that were now busily pulling the white sheet from the girls' body, exposing her nakedness once more. Dietrich moved closer to his master, his attention caught again by the girl. He gazed raptly at her slender legs and lissom body.

As he watched, the priest dipped his fingers into the chalice of blood. He withdrew the stained digits and drew them across one of the girl's breasts, pausing at her nipple, which he rubbed. He then repeated these movements on the other breast, smearing more of the blood on her belly and neck.

'Oh, this is all so tiresome,' Karnstein remarked walking towards the hooded figures.

The priest was now holding the knife above the head of the girl. She looked up at him with terror in her eyes.

'Look, Excellency, he is possessed!' Dietrich insisted, pointing at the priest, who was now babbling away almost uncontrollably in his indistinguishable language.

Karnstein stood glaring at the priest for a moment longer then he shot out both hands, grabbed the man and practically lifted him off his feet.

'Is this your manifestation of the Devil?' he snarled.

He hurled the priest to the ground.

'Are you still possessed?' Karnstein rasped, looking down at the man. 'Or have I exorcised your demons?' The Count looked at the other robed figures. 'You are charlatans, all of you! Get out!'

The robed men hurried towards the archway that led out of the main hall. Karnstein glanced in their direction, then looked back down at the girl.

Dietrich appeared beside him, his gaze also drawn to the helpless young woman tied to the tomb.

'Forgive me, my lord,' Dietrich said. He reached out and began to untie the rope around the left wrist of the girl. 'I will get rid of her, too.'

'No,' Karnstein snapped. 'Leave her.'

Dietrich backed away.

'Oh, of course,' he murmured.

'And now go.'

'Yes, at once. Your Excellency knows that I endeavour to do my utmost to please him.'

Dietrich was standing next to the girl, one pudgy hand gently stroking her long blonde hair.

'They knew,' Karnstein snapped, pointing at the portraits of his ancestors that adorned the walls of the hall. 'They didn't play at being wicked.' He stood next to the bust of one of his female ancestors looking into the sightless stone eyes. 'They worshipped the Devil and he taught them delights that you will never know.'

Dietrich listened obediently, one hand still stroking the girl's long blonde hair. The other hand he was gently rubbing against his crotch. The girl turned her head towards him, revolted by his actions, but helpless to do anything about it.

'Delights of punishment inflicted,' Karnstein went on. 'And punishment received. Of torture and death.' The Count moved towards Dietrich, gazing into his eyes. 'Yes, of death and pleasures beyond the grave. Something you could not even comprehend.' The Count held his gaze. 'But I know.'

Dietrich opened his mouth to say something, but Karnstein merely shook his head to silence him.

'Go, Dietrich,' he snapped.

The fat man nodded and a little reluctantly let go of the girl's soft hair. He took one last look at her, then backed away.

'Good night, my Lord,' he offered, retreating from the hall through a door at the foot of the stone steps that led up to the first floor of the mighty building. The door slammed shut behind him. Karnstein and the girl were alone in the hall.

'And how could you ever know of such pleasures?' the Count said, softly, leaning over the girl who was shaking from a combination of fear and the chill in the room. 'You might know of the common touch of some peasant on your body,' he breathed, placing his hand gently on the girls left thigh. 'The delights of an uneducated fool's fumblings,' the Count continued as he slid his hand between the girl's legs. 'But what else could you ever understand?'

He touched her cheek with his other hand, then allowed himself to paw softly at her breasts, ignoring the blood that had congealed on them.

The girl sighed and smiled at the Count.

'I can show you pleasure, my lord,' she told him, hoarsely.

'Yes, I know. Would you do anything I wanted?'

The girl nodded.

Karnstein smiled.

'Then die for me,' he breathed and, as he spoke he lifted the double-edged knife into view.

'No!' the girl gasped.

The Count held the knife in his right hand, both his arms extended on either side of him, his head tilted backwards.

'Oh, Lord of Darkness!' he called, his voice reverberating around the great hall. 'I am weary of this world and its pathetic pleasures! Teach me to reach beyond the flesh! Reveal yourself to me that I may bow down before you and be your servant! Give me the power to do your evil!'

He looked down at the girl, his eyes blank.

'No, no, please!' she babbled, struggling against the ropes that held her in place.

'In token of my faith,' Karnstein went on, 'I offer you this woman.'

'No!' the girl wailed. 'Please don't!'

The Count raised the blade in both hands.

'In God's name, don't!' the girl, screamed.

'God has nothing to do with this,' Karnstein snarled at her. The girl screamed again, a high-pitched sound that echoed inside the hall and throughout the entirety of the castle, while outside the storm raged ever more fervently.

'Accept this offering!' Karnstein roared.

He brought the knife down with all his strength.

Ten

The blade buried itself in the chest of the girl, and Count Karnstein put all his weight behind it as the metal sheared effortlessly through bone and lung.

A huge gout of blood erupted from the wound and Karnstein leant forward on the weapon, more jets of crimson exploding from the savage wound he had inflicted. For what seemed an eternity he stood there, both hands still clenched around the hilt of the blade.

The girl thrashed madly for a second or two as the knife snuffed out her life, then her body spasmed once. She lay still, her eyes open wide. The Count watched as a single mote of dust drifted down and landed on one of the bulging orbs. He was breathing heavily, as if the exertion of killing the girl had drained him, but slowly he straightened up, stroking the girl's cheek as he did so.

Using both hands again he tugged the knife free.

More blood pumped from the deep rent in her chest, much of it spilling onto the cold stone lid of the tomb, trickling down the cracks in the time-worn stone.

Karnstein held the knife high, the blade coated with crimson.

'Satan!' he roared.

Outside the thunder rumbled loudly, and a fork of lightning exploded across the sky.

'Satan!' he bellowed again.

He looked down at the body of the girl, and at the blood that was coursing over the stone tomb, a good deal of it oozing through cracks in the sarcophagus.

Inside the tomb the blood dripped steadily on to the shroud that was beneath. Hundreds of years old, it absorbed the red fluid easily.

In the hall, Count Karnstein looked at the blood that stained his hands then at the body of the girl. He wiped his hands on the sheet and moved back a pace, before finally turning and heading back to the huge open fire that had been raging in the great stone fireplace all night. He stood before the leaping flames, gazing into them, his mind spinning.

'Satan,' he whispered. 'Was the offering not enough?'

He sat down and reached for the goblet of wine closest to him, draining much in one large swallow. He re-filled the receptacle and drank again.

'What must I do?' he murmured. 'Whatever I have to do, I will.'

He ran a hand through his hair, exasperatedly.

Behind him a thin white mist was seeping from the stone tomb that the dead girl lay upon. Like ethereal tendrils, the mist crept from the sarcophagus and spread slowly across the stone floor roundabout, growing thicker and denser by the second.

Karnstein slumped back in his chair and swallowed more wine.

The white mist was now pouring from the tomb like

smoke from a burning building. It covered the floor, spirals of it rising a foot or so into the air, then dipping again as the whole boiling mass of heaving mist twisted and turned and spread ever further across the floor of the hall.

The Count looked up at a painting of one of his ancestors and studied the outline of the man's face. Were the eyes mocking him somehow?

'What did you have to do?' he whispered to himself. 'What offering did you give that allowed you the secrets you knew?' The Count sucked in a deep breath, the knot of muscles at the side of his jaw throbbing angrily. 'What did any of you have to do?' He regarded each portrait and bust in order, but none, it seemed, was willing to give up its secrets. What more could he offer than a human life? What had his ancestors offered to bring them the kind of rewards he sought for himself? He could butcher hundreds, thousands of animals in Satan's name, but no matter how many he sacrificed, surely they would never amount to as much as one human life.

The Count exhaled wearily. Perhaps it was the kind of human life that was offered that made the difference, he pondered. He had given the life of a young girl, but perhaps there were greater offerings he could produce. Perhaps a child, he thought, sitting up slightly in his chair. A young child barely into pubescence might be more appreciated. He smiled slightly as he thought of how easy it would be for Dietrich or Joachim to bring a child to the castle. If grown women could be bought for a handful of gold pieces or could be abducted with ease, then surely a child should be a much easier proposition. Yes, that had to be the answer. A child was the kind of offering required to bring him what he sought. He could picture himself standing in this great hall with a small child beside him. In his mind's eye he could see the child looking up at him trustingly, even as the blade was drawn across its throat or its heart was ripped from its chest.

Count Karnstein shook his head. No. Not a child. Not a young woman. He realised there was one kind of life he could take that would cause such affront and outrage that Satan would most definitely accept it.

A baby.

Yes, to take a newborn baby and sacrifice it to Satan, to call upon him, while its blood still dripped and poured from the wounds that had killed it. That would bring him the kind of pleasure his ancestors had enjoyed. He was certain of it. It would be more difficult to obtain a baby, of course, but then that was not his problem. That was Dietrich's province or Joachim's. The Count would tell them to get a baby for him and they would do so. How they did it he didn't care. Again he imagined himself in the great hall holding a baby this time, perhaps driving the knife down into its body or even simply dashing its brains out against the cold stone floor. It would be so much easier to kill. He could even throw it into the air and impale it on a sword as it fell to earth again.

The Count sat up, excited by his own thoughts. That had to be the answer. Then all his longing and frustration would be gone, and he would possess the same knowledge his ancestors had enjoyed. He would sample delights unlike any other man alive.

A powerful wind blew suddenly through the hall of Karnstein Castle, extinguishing several candles and one of the flaming torches near the fire. The Count paid it no heed, but merely sat slumped in his chair his gaze still fixed on the portraits of his predecessors.

Behind him, the white mist was rolling inexorably across the floor towards him.

The Count looked up when he heard a particularly loud crash of thunder and lightning, but otherwise he was still seemingly transfixed by the array of portraits before him. Their blank eyes stared down on the hall impassively as the rolling white mist grew thicker, some of it still spilling from inside the tomb. Like a living thing the mist made its way across the floor, bringing with it a chill that cut to the bone.

The Count shivered involuntarily in his seat and reached for his wine once again.

There was another strong blast of wind and more candles were blown out, but Karnstein didn't stir.

Had he turned, he would have seen the figure standing at the foot of the tomb.

Surrounded by the swirling white mist it looked as if it had grown from the ethereal matter itself. It was swathed in a hooded robe that obscured its face and the colour of the robe only served to reinforce the appearance that the garment was actually woven from the mist that had given birth to the figure. When it moved it seemed to glide with infinite slowness across the floor towards the table where the Count sat, still oblivious to the presence of the shrouded figure. It was within feet of him now, looking down upon him, just as the sightless eyes of the paintings of previous Karnsteins looked down. The figure came to a halt behind his chair.

Karnstein felt the incredible chill penetrating his flesh and boring into the marrow of his bones. He felt as if he had been enveloped in ice as he sat motionless before the still raging fire. He was about to take another swig of wine when the figure reached out and touched him.

The Count spun round, almost falling from his chair in surprise. He let out a gasp and scrambled to his feet, backing away from the figure, which remained motionless, its features hidden by the cowl of the hood it wore. For long seconds it stood gazing at him, then it moved forward, one hand outstretched towards him.

For an instant, Count Karnstein felt an emotion he had not experienced for many years. Fear lanced through him as the hand reached out. The cold seemed to intensify, and even though he had backed up close to the open fireplace, he felt as if his blood had been turned to ice.

The hand touched his right cheek.

As it did, the cowl of the hood slid back to reveal the face of the figure.

Karnstein's eyes opened wide, his jaw dropping as he stared incredulously.

The figure moved nearer.

Eleven

Count Karnstein stood transfixed, his heart pounding against his ribs.

His lips moved silently, but no words came. He was gazing directly at the figure before him that now extended a hand towards his face. The Count recoiled, wondering what fetid and decaying appendage was going to be revealed when the hand had reached beyond the folds of the hooded shroud that enclosed it. He closed his eyes momentarily as the figure touched his flesh.

He didn't feel the expected touch of wrinkled or decaying skin, but instead the soft gossamer caress of beautifully smooth flesh. The hand that had been placed against his cheek was cold, but it felt like marble when he raised his own hand to touch it.

The Count opened his eyes and looked more clearly at the figure before him, holding the hand in his own, inspecting it for flaws but seeing none.

The figure gently lowered its hood.

Again Count Karnstein gasped.

She was beautiful.

Her face, framed by long blonde hair, looked as if it had been carved from alabaster. Her skin was flawless, so pale it was almost translucent. Even in the gloom of the hall, Karnstein could see the piercing blue of her eyes as she held his gaze unblinkingly.

'Mircalla!' the Count whispered.

The figure nodded almost imperceptibly, turned and motioned for him to follow her. She moved gracefully across the hall to the tomb where the dead girl still laid, her life fluid now everywhere on the sarcophagus and the stone floor. As Karnstein joined the figure beside the tomb he looked at what one of the long fingers was indicating.

It was an inscription, carved into the stone.

COUNTESS MIRCALLA KARNSTEIN
DIED 1574

'Mircalla,' the Count murmured again.

The figure merely looked evenly at him.

'He sent you?' Karnstein asked.

'Yes,' Mircalla told him. 'To show you the way. To point you along the path you seek.'

'You died over two hundred years ago,' the Count said, quietly. 'And yet . . . '

Mircalla put an index finger to his lips.

'That is the way it is,' she murmured. 'Only flesh is corrupted by time. Is that what you want, too?'

'Must I give my life?'

'Your soul. Your body remains on earth. You will be of the undead.'

'When?'

'Now.'

She took his hand and led him back towards the fireplace, where she lay down on the large fur rug in front of it. The Count stood gazing down at her as she undid the fastenings on her robe, finally pulling it open to reveal her nakedness beneath.

'The flesh remains uncorrupted,' Mircalla told him as he looked at her.

For long moments he stood transfixed by her, then he knelt beside her on the rug, feeling her hands on his face once again as she pulled him closer. They kissed and the Count slid one hand onto her right breast, kneading the pale flesh there for a moment before dipping his head to her stiff nipple. He flicked his tongue over the swollen bud, then transferred his attention to the other. She gasped beneath his touch and when she parted her legs he slid one hand between them.

He stroked his fingers along her smooth thigh as they kissed, lost in his own pleasure now as well as hers. Karnstein broke the kiss and slid slowly down her body, flicking his tongue across her smooth flesh as he went, moving lower and lower until his head was close to her mound. He could feel the warmth from between her legs and he kissed her there, causing her to gasp. It was a warmth that he had not expected, but one he welcomed. He kissed the small triangle of tightly curled hair between her legs, then allowed his tongue to travel lower, tasting her. She gasped her pleasure and opened her legs wider for him.

Mircalla sat up and pulled him towards her, wrapping her slender legs around him and pulling him closer. She ran her fingers over his lips then his cheeks.

'Would you give your soul?' she murmured to him.

'I would give anything,' the Count told her.

Mircalla got to her feet, shrugging the hooded robe off in the process. It fell to the floor and Karnstein stepped on it in his eagerness to follow her as she made her way across the hall. She paused beside a bust of herself, her long fingers once more trailing over the inscription beneath.

COUNTESS MIRCALLA KARNSTEIN
DIED 1574

'Stand there,' she told him, indicating the large mirror that hung on one wall.

Karnstein obeyed and moved in front of it, glancing at his own reflection and that of the fire, which he could still see dancing behind him in the glass.

'Look at your reflection,' Mircalla told him and the Count obeyed.

When he felt her arms on his shoulders it startled him. He looked into her eyes and then at the mirror.

Mircalla cast no reflection.

'I can't see you,' Karnstein murmured.

'We are the undead,' she told him. 'And the mirror sees only the living.' She stroked his face with one pale hand. 'We walk the earth, but we exist only in hell.'

Mircalla's lips slid back venomously and Karnstein saw the two long wickedly sharp canine fangs protruding from her upper jaw. She snapped her head forward, her eyes widening as she saw the vein in his neck throbbing.

The fangs cut through flesh and vein effortlessly, and Mircalla pressed her mouth around the twin wounds, milking them with her lips and tongue as she tasted blood.

Karnstein felt pain searing through him as she pulled him more tightly towards her, but there was no passion in her grasp now, only the animal desire to feed on his blood. He felt the strength in her grip and did not resist.

She finally pulled away and he saw his own blood smeared over her teeth. It also trickled down her chin. Her top lip curled and her nostrils flared, her eyes still fixed on the two raw puncture wounds she had inflicted on him. Karnstein turned towards the mirror to inspect the twin gashes, touching them tentatively with his fingers.

Even as he watched his reflection began to fade. It was as if he were dissolving, his image slowly receding from sight, until finally all he could see in the glass was the flickering flames of the fire and the rest of the hall behind him.

Mircalla smiled at him, his blood still smeared on her mouth.

The Count looked back once again at the mirror, at where his reflection should have been, then he, too, smiled.

Twelve

The wagonette lurched violently to one side as one of its wheels slid into a deep rut in the road, but the driver flicked his whip and the single horse battled on down the rain-drenched track.

The driver glanced over his shoulder and apologised to his passengers for the uneven passage.

'That storm last night has turned all the roads around here into swamps,' the driver said, cheerfully. 'But don't worry, ladies, we'll soon have you there, even if you are a little shaken up.'

'A little?' Frieda said, haughtily. 'We'll all be shaken out onto the road at this rate.'

She touched a hand to her hat, which had slipped slightly, then looked at her sister and Aunt Katy, who were also seated in the wagonette.

'He's doing his best, Frieda,' Maria said.

'We're not far from the village now,' Katy added.

Up ahead, just off the road, a cart was waiting, and as the driver of the wagonette watched a woodsman swung himself from the vehicle and walked along the edge of the road towards them, one hand held before him to slow their advance.

'Hold up, there!' the woodsman called.

'Morning,' the driver replied cheerfully, tugging gently on the reins to bring the wagonette to a halt.

The woodsman nodded in the direction of the passengers.

'Good morning, ma'am,' he said to Katy, deferentially.

Katy smiled back at him.

'Why have you stopped us?' Frieda wanted to know. 'We're in a hurry.'

Katy put one hand on her niece's arm to silence her.

'There's great events,' the woodsman began. 'The boar-hunters are coming through this way.'

'There's a hunt?' the driver enquired.

'It's traditional,' the woodsman told him.

There was a loud grunting sound from somewhere in the woods and all heads turned in that direction. Seconds later, as they watched, something large hurtled across the road. It was a wild boar. A big specimen that squealed loudly as it ran, its fur spattered with mud, its tusks gleaming in the early morning sunlight.

'It's horrible,' Maria said, watching as it ran across the road and disappeared into the undergrowth on the other side.

Several horsemen suddenly burst from the woods, too, thundering along in pursuit of the fleeing boar. The leading man was carrying a long lance in his hand. Hunched low over the neck of his horse he dug his heels into the animal, urging it to greater speed. Those following him copied his example.

'They'll kill it if they catch it, won't they?' Maria asked, quietly.

'It's a tradition in these parts, miss,' the woodsman told her. 'A sport.'

'The boar will be used for food, Maria,' Katy explained.

There was a sudden ear-splitting squeal.

Maria put her hands over her ears, trying to shut out the sound.

'They've got it,' the woodsman grinned. 'Skewered it by the sound of things.'

'That's horrible,' Maria insisted.

'There's nothing to be afraid of,' Katy told her.

'But that awful sound,' Maria went on, only reluctantly removing her hands from her ears.

'They're killing the boar, you see,' Katy said, reassuringly. 'Don't worry.'

As if to reinforce her words a mounted man emerged from the trees, gripping a long lance in his right hand. The end was stained thickly with blood. He nodded amiably in the direction of the wagonette.

'Good morning, ladies,' he proclaimed, smiling.

Katy, Frieda and Maria all nodded demurely.

Frieda, in particular, ran appraising eyes over the man and then smiled playfully at him.

'A good hunt?' the wagonette driver asked.

'Very good,' the man with the lance said then he turned as someone shouted to him from the woods behind. He turned his horse and guided the animal back into the trees out of sight.

The wagonette driver flicked his whip and the horse pulling the vehicle moved on along the road towards Karnstein.

'Not long now, ladies,' the driver called over his shoulder. 'Sorry about the delay.' The wagonette moved on, bumping over more ruts and potholes in the road as it moved towards the village. Thrusting upwards towards the sky, visible above the treetops was the church spire, the weather vane turning gently at the top, buffeted by the breeze that had sprung up.

'I think hunting is very cruel,' Maria said quietly, gazing at the trees on one side of the road.

'It's a sport, Maria!' Katy exclaimed. 'The men around here like it.'

'I still think it's cruel,' Maria intoned.

'Life is cruel, Maria,' Frieda said, without looking at her sister.

They rode the rest of the way in silence. Only when the wagonette finally came to a halt outside the school building did Katy finally speak again.

'This is the school,' she announced, motioning towards the whitewashed building decorated with window boxes. It was set back a little from the main square of the village and straw had been laid on the mud leading up to the door to offer some kind of pathway, and also to protect the shoes of visitors. Katy led the way up the small flight of stone steps to the solid oak front door. Once open, they found themselves inside a spacious entryway. There were doors to the left and right, but it was the one to their left that Katy knocked on. From inside a voice called to her to come in and Katy did as she was instructed, ushering the girls in behind her.

They found themselves in a large and very welcoming room with a large wooden table at its centre and a glowing open fire at one end. All four sides of the room bore long bookcases, and they were so filled with volumes both ancient and modern that it seemed they might collapse under the weight of so much knowledge. There were several smaller desks set around the room, too, one of which bore a globe, another of which displayed a human skull. There was a stuffed fox in a glass case perched on another, the beady eyes of the animal gleaming when the dancing flames from the fire were reflected there.

In one corner of the room there was a harpsichord atop which lay a flute and two recorders. Every kind of lesson seemed to be catered for in the room and the eight young women who were seated around the long wooden table, drawing or reading, were suitably involved in their work, all of them under the watchful eye of a woman in her early thirties.

Ingrid Hoffer moved around the table slowly, pausing beside each of the girls to inspect their work, nodding approvingly on occasion as she looked at what they had produced. Sometimes she would lay a gentle hand on the girl's shoulder, as if to reinforce her delight at the quality of the work on show. She had been a teacher all her life and had always found that pupils responded better to encouragement and praise than they did to the kind of strictness and regimentation that she had encountered herself when learning. She had promised herself that her approach would always be nurturing and that her pupils would work because they wanted to, and not because they were afraid of the consequences if they didn't.

When Ingrid heard the knock on the door she turned to see who had just entered.

She smiled warmly when she saw Katy and the two girls.

'Hello, Ingrid,' Katy said.

'Hello,' Ingrid echoed.

'This is Maria and this is Frieda,' Katy went on, gesturing to each of the twins in turn. 'My nieces.'

Ingrid looked at each girl, then shrugged good-humouredly.

'I shall never be able to tell one from the other,' she remarked, smiling.

'This is Ingrid Hoffer, who runs the school,' Katy told the girls, both of whom curtsied politely.

The other girls in the room had stopped their tasks and were also glancing at the twins, taking in the details of their dress and appearance.

'Ingrid's brother Anton is the choirmaster,' Katy added, frowning slightly as Frieda moved away from her and towards one of the windows in the room. It looked out upon the town square and there was movement out there. Several horsemen had just galloped into the wide expanse and Frieda was watching them intently. Especially the leading man on the big grey horse, who carried a lance in his hand.

'I'm sorry that Anton isn't here,' Ingrid said, apologetically. 'He's hunting.'

'We passed him on the way,' Katy told her.

'I expect he won't be long,' Ingrid said.

'They're coming now,' Frieda informed them, still

gazing out of the window. She watched as the leading rider drove the lance into the ground, then swung himself out of the saddle and led his horse away, patting the animal's neck as he did. The grey tossed its head, but the rider patted it again to quieten it.

The other girls, following Frieda's example, had also crowded around the other windows of the room and were looking out excitedly into the square, watching the other hunters milling about among the usual inhabitants of the square.

Ingrid clapped her hands.

'Girls,' she said, sharply. 'Back to your places. What is there to look at? You've seen the men coming back from hunting before.'

The other girls turned and returned to their seats a little reluctantly.

'Sit down,' Ingrid insisted, watching as they seated themselves and continued with their work.

Ingrid smiled and shook her head.

'The girls are always happy for any excuse to stop work for a few moments,' she said. Her gaze moved towards the two twins. 'I expect you two are just the same.'

Maria smiled guiltily.

Ingrid looked at them for a moment longer, then shook her head.

'I've seen twins before,' she said. 'But never as alike as you two. It really is remarkable.'

'Even I have a problem telling them apart sometimes,' Katy told the teacher.

'Perhaps I should ask you to dress differently,' Ingrid

joked. 'I think that's the only way I'll ever be able to tell you apart at first sight.'

'Oh we're quite different once you get to know us,' Frieda said.

'I'm sure you are, Maria,' Ingrid answered.

'No, that's Frieda,' the other twin corrected. 'I'm Maria.'

Ingrid shook her head again and laughed.

'You'll probably find it very different here to what it was in Venice, girls,' she went on. 'That is where you're from isn't it?'

Both girls nodded.

'We've already seen how different it can be,' Frieda told her.

'But we're quite harmless here in Karnstein once you get to know us,' the teacher went on.

They all turned as the door to the schoolroom was opened.

Anton Hoffer walked in and looked around at the gathering and smiled. He moved to his sister's side and Ingrid took his arm, smiling at him.

There wasn't a striking family resemblance, but both of the Hoffer's boasted strong features and lustrous dark hair.

Ingrid looked down at the mud on her brother's boots and frowned.

'Must you bring most of the forest back inside with you after you've been hunting, Anton?' she said, trying to feign irritation, but failing miserably. They both laughed.

'I apologise,' he said, squeezing her arm.

'Come and meet our new pupils,' Ingrid said, and she motioned towards the twins who both stepped forward. 'This is Frieda and this is Maria.'

'No, no,' Frieda said. 'I'm Frieda and this is Maria.'

'I'm Maria,' her sister added.

Anton looked at each girl in turn and smiled. His attention, however, seemed focused upon Frieda. She smiled playfully at him and he held her gaze, seemingly transfixed by her beauty. Well aware of his interest, Frieda flicked her hair with one hand. Anton nodded slowly by way of a greeting.

In the centre of the room, their voices lowered, two of the other girls were watching the scene of introduction.

'I can't tell the difference between them,' Vivien Steiner said, quietly, watching the two twins.

'Nor can I,' Maxine Stransky echoed, keeping her voice low. 'But it seems Anton can.'

'What do you mean?' Vivien wanted to know.

'Well, just look at him,' Maxine insisted.

Anton Hoffer had ushered the twins and their aunt towards some high-backed chairs close to the fire, and he seated himself in one, moving it a little closer to Frieda, who smiled demurely at him and allowed her leg to brush against his briefly.

'I saw you ride by,' Anton said.

'While you were hunting?' Frieda asked.

'Yes.'

'It seems to be everyone's occupation around here,' Frieda told him. 'Hunting of one kind or another.'

'What do you mean?'

Frieda raised her eyebrows.

'Boars in the morning and witches at night,' she said, flatly.

The smile slipped from Anton's face.

'Who told you about that?' he enquired.

'No one told me anything. I listened.'

'To your uncle?'

Frieda nodded.

'Well don't blame me for that,' Anton said, sharply. 'I take no part in it.'

'Don't you?' Frieda challenged. 'Don't you like dressing up in black and frightening helpless young girls?'

'There are enough men in and around Karnstein who agree with your uncle,' Anton continued. 'He has no need of help from men like me.'

'And what kind of man are you?' she wanted to know.

'Not the kind that follows your uncle. I know some of those men and I'm nothing like them.'

'So you don't agree with what they do?'

'No, I think it's barbaric. But superstition dies very hard here.'

'What are they afraid of?'

Anton lowered his gaze momentarily

'You'd have to ask your uncle that,' he said, quietly.

'How well do you know him?' Frieda enquired.

'I don't know him. I know what he believes, though. Perhaps you just don't understand.'

'I don't want to,' Frieda snapped leaning forward. 'I hate it here.'

Anton smiled gently at her.

'Your uncle is misguided perhaps,' he said, softly. 'But he's a good man.'

'Really?' Frieda said, raising her eyebrows. 'Does persecuting helpless young girls make him good?'

'He thinks he's doing God's will.'

'Then he's a fool,' snapped Frieda.

'As I said, deep down he's a good man,' Anton reassured her.

She licked her lips slowly and leaned closer to Anton.

'Perhaps I don't like good men,' she breathed. A faint smile flickered across her face.

'Anton.'

He turned as he heard his name. Ingrid was standing at his side now, smiling down at him. Anton got to his feet. Frieda watched him, her gaze moving slowly up and down his frame.

'Maria was asking about the history of Karnstein,' Ingrid said. 'I told her you were the expert.'

Anton looked at Maria and she blushed. He smiled to himself and turned to the bookcase closest to him, retrieving a large leather-bound tome that he held with something close to reverence.

'It's all in here, Maria,' Anton said, holding the book before him. 'The history of the village, its inhabitants and those who have ruled it for more than five hundred years.'

'Is there anything in there about Count Karnstein?' Frieda wanted to know.

'There's information about his family and his ancestors,' Anton informed her.

Frieda turned away and walked across the room

towards one of the windows that looked out on to the village square. Anton glanced at her for a moment, then turned his attention to her sister.

'Anything you want to know about the village and its history is in here,' Anton announced, opening the book. 'Look, I'll show you.' He laid the book on the table close to the fire, and Maria moved nearer to see more clearly what he was indicating in the large tome.

Frieda yawned and did little to disguise the gesture. However, seconds later she peered more intently out of the window, a slight smile spreading across her face.

She saw the coach pull up and she watched as its occupant climbed out.

Count Karnstein stood motionless next to his coach.

Thirteen

Frieda watched as the Count stood, glancing around the square at the villagers with barely concealed contempt.

Frieda studied his features and then his clothes, the black garments and the long cloak that hung from his shoulders like the folded wings of some gigantic bat. When he walked his cloak seemed to glide with a life of its own, inches above the filth and mud of the village square. A man wearing a grey uniform clambered down from the driver's seat of the coach. He was a huge black man and Frieda watched him with interest as he faced the Count. She saw Karnstein's lips moving and wondered what he was saying to the coachman. Everything about the tall aristocrat fascinated Frieda, and she glanced over her shoulder into the classroom to see if anyone else had noticed the arrival of the Count and his manservant.

Apparently they hadn't. The other girls were still seated around the large table in the middle of the room; Aunt Katy was speaking with Ingrid Hoffer and Maria was listening intently as Anton pointed out something in the large book he held. Frieda returned her attention to the Count, who was glancing up at the sky for some reason. She could see him watching the thick, slowly moving clouds as if searching for something in their dense shapes. He stood motionless for a moment longer, his attention still fixed on the heavens then he strode away from the coach towards the school itself. Frieda felt a sudden stab of excitement.

Behind her in the classroom she could hear Anton's voice as he showed Maria more of the book that seemed to fascinate him.

'And its still a mystery,' Anton said. 'There are so many mysteries about this part of the country. Some are intrigued by them, others are uneasy.'

'I want to learn about Karnstein if I'm to live here,' Maria told Anton. 'And the legends that surround it.'

'You'll have plenty to learn then,' Anton assured her, smiling.

Frieda frowned, then looked back at the town square and Count Karnstein. Again she glanced over her shoulder into the classroom and she saw that everyone was still deep in conversation. Moving quietly and quickly, Frieda slipped out of the room and headed for the front of the building. She paused at the top of the small flight of steps leading to the front door and leaned on the metal rail there, watching Count Karnstein, who was now only a yard or two away. He stopped as he noticed Frieda, who smiled at him.

'Good morning,' the Count said, eyeing her appreciatively.

'You're Count Karnstein, aren't you?' Frieda asked, but it came out more as a statement than a question. 'I saw the crest on the door of your coach.'

'And you are a very perceptive and very beautiful young lady,' the Count told her. 'Do you go to school here?'

'My sister and I have just arrived from Venice.'

'A beautiful city. People in Venice know how to enjoy life's pleasures. Do you?'

'I don't expect I shall get much pleasure here. My sister and I are living with my uncle. He doesn't approve of things like that.'

'He doesn't approve of pleasure? What kind of man is he?' The Count smiled. 'You must find and take pleasure wherever you can, my dear.'

'Is that what *you* do, Count Karnstein?'

He nodded.

'I could show you the meaning of pleasure if you would allow me,' Karnstein told her, a crooked smile on his face.

'My uncle would never allow it. He has rules that must be obeyed.'

'I've always found that rules are there to be broken.'

Frieda giggled and playfully ran a hand through her long hair.

'If you come to the castle one night I will show you,' the Count went on, moving closer to the steps where Frieda was standing.

'I would never be allowed to do that,' Frieda told him.

'Why, because it's breaking a rule? Come and see me. Let me show you things you have never even dreamed of.'

'Sir!'

The voice made them both turn and Frieda backed off slightly when she saw its source.

Astride his horse, not more than three or four yards away from Karnstein's coach, Gustav Weil was glaring fixedly at the Count.

'This is my niece,' he went on, sternly.

'It's a pleasure to make her acquaintance,' Karnstein said, smiling mockingly.

'My words were not an introduction, but a warning,' Weil said through clenched teeth. He shot Frieda a harsh look. 'Go back inside.'

Frieda hesitated.

'At once!' Weil snapped.

As if to lend weight to his command, Frieda felt a hand on her arm and she looked to see that Aunt Katy had emerged from the school and was pulling her gently back towards the building entrance. She smiled one last time at Karnstein, then allowed herself to be escorted back inside. The Count watched her go, then he turned and strode towards Weil's horse. The animal snorted and backed away slightly.

'Sir, you are impertinent,' the Count hissed.

'I am not a peasant and I acknowledge only one Lord,' Weil told him, defiantly. 'Both my nieces will be instructed never to speak to you again.'

'Instruct. Command. Threaten all you want, Weil,' Karnstein said. 'Girls of that age are very wilful. You can't control them completely and you can't be with them every hour of the day and night. They will speak to whom they wish.'

'Not if I have my way.'

'And what if they defy you?'

'They will be punished.'

The Count smiled.

'Trying to control girls like that is like trying to catch quicksilver, Weil,' he said. 'It will take someone with more control than you to do it.'

'You keep away from them, Count Karnstein, I'm warning you.'

'Do not presume to warn me about anything, and remember what I said, Weil, you cannot be with them every single hour of the day and night.'

'Is that a threat?'

'I am just telling you that if you are not with them, then someone else might be.' Again the Count smiled.

Weil glared at him for a moment longer, then he turned his horse and guided it out of the village square. The Count watched him go, that same thin smile still fixed on his bloodless lips.

Weil urged his horse onwards, away from the square, affording himself one brief look back at Count Karnstein. He shook his head in anger then glanced ahead once more. The path of the horse was blocked by a large figure standing in the middle of the narrow street.

Weil recognised him instantly.

'I saw you speaking to Count Karnstein,' Rolf Kessler told him. 'I saw your niece speaking to him as well.'

'Who I or the members of my family speak to is no concern of yours,' Weil sneered, peering down from his saddle.

'At least you have a family, Weil,' Kessler snapped. 'For now.'

Weil tried to turn his horse away from Kessler, but the big man reached out and grabbed the bridle.

'Not yet! You're going to listen to me,' Kessler insisted.

'Get your hand off!' Weil said, threateningly.

'I hope your girls are settling into the school,' Kessler said evenly. 'You should be careful they don't come to any harm.' He smiled.

'You have threatened me once too often, woodsman,' Weil warned, and he jerked his reins, causing the horse to snap its head to one side violently. Kessler let go of the bridle and stepped back slightly, the smile still on his face.

'And with good cause, Weil,' he said, angrily. 'What are you going to do? Come to my home and burn me as you burned my daughter?'

'I will speak to the magistrate if you continue to threaten me. He will have you arrested.'

'For what? Speaking the truth? For letting everyone in this village know that you and your Brotherhood are murderers? I don't think so.'

'I've told you before, I don't want you anywhere near my house or my nieces.'

'I can come and go freely in this village, Weil. You are not the law here.'

Weil snapped his reins and dug his heels into the horse's sides, urging it forward. Kessler stepped back to allow him to pass.

'I warned you before,' Kessler snapped. 'Judgement is waiting for you and those close to you.'

Weil shot him one more defiant glance, then rode off.

Kessler watched the mounted man leave, then spat violently after him.

'Bastard,' he rasped under his breath.

Fourteen

'What does he want in the village?'

The innkeeper's wife peeked cautiously through the curtains of the window overlooking Karnstein's main village square. She murmured the words to herself as much as to her husband or the other occupants of the inn, two of whom were standing at the bar, drinking.

'Close the curtain woman!' the innkeeper snapped. 'Before he sees you!'

'I don't care if he sees me,' the innkeeper's wife proclaimed, defiantly. 'I've a got a right to look out of my own window, haven't I?'

'You're spying on Count Karnstein, Zena,' her husband reminded her.

'I was just looking. There's no law against that is there, Carl?' she demanded of her husband. 'Everyone is always so afraid of him. I was only looking.'

'People are afraid of him for good reasons, Zena,' the innkeeper said, reproachfully.

'Well, I'm not,' she insisted.

'Perhaps you should be,' the innkeeper grunted.

Carl Spengler shook his head and finished pouring a stein of ale for one of his customers. He pushed it across the bar to the man, who nodded appreciatively and shoved a couple of crowns back as payment, pointing in the direction of his companion, who accepted the brandy Spengler poured him with gratitude.

Spengler had been a part of the inn for his entire life. Either living in it when his father ran it or, as for the last thirty years, running it himself. He had even been born upstairs in one of the bedrooms, and remembered the boys at school teasing him about it, saying that he drank ale instead of his mother's milk when he was a baby. He smiled at the recollection, thinking how many of those he went to school with were still here now in the village, working their way to premature and untimely graves chopping trees or tilling soil every hour God sent. Life wasn't easy for the men of Karnstein, but they seemed to make the most of their lot and, Spengler was pleased to say, they were happy to spend their meagre earnings in his establishment supping ale and spirits. Local business made up the bulk of the earnings for the inn. There were three guest rooms, but few people ever came to Karnstein to stay for what passed as a holiday and Spengler could count on the sausage-like fingers of one hand the number of paying guests they'd had during the last year. There had been a priest a few months back travelling to Carlsbad on horseback and he'd been forced to seek refuge for the night because of the atrocious weather. Father Sandor had been his name, the innkeeper thought with a smile. He prided himself on his memory for names and faces.

Before that there had been some foreigners. English people with expensive luggage who had been touring this part of the country on their way to Budapest. They had stayed for a night and, Spengler remembered, they had left a very generous tip for himself and his wife when they'd left. He frowned as he tried to remember their names, too, nodding to himself when he did. Kent, they had been called. Mr and Mrs Kent.

A doctor had also partaken of the inn's hospitality shortly before that. Spengler couldn't quite remember his name for some reason. It had a Dutch ring to it, but he couldn't quite place it. Doctor Van something or other, but the last name still escaped him. He'd been a quiet, solitary man who had spent the entire night in his room rather than sit in the bar itself and enjoy the warmth of the fire. He had even requested his evening meal in his room for that one night he had been a guest. There had been nothing unusual or strange about his behaviour, Spengler just found it hard to understand the man's desire to be alone. He himself had always been the most gregarious of people and he hated being alone, so it was difficult for him to understand when others required only their own company and shunned the presence of others.

Spengler was convinced he would have gone insane if he'd had to spend his life alone. When his first wife died eight years earlier he was sure that madness was his only path. For days on end he'd been unable to get out of bed. Not because of the physical demands, but because there didn't seem to be any point without his wife around. The days had turned into a week and he had still found no reason to go on. On more than one occasion he had thought of killing himself. He had nothing to look forward to any more. Without her around there was no sense in living. He was just a shell of the man he used to be. Why carry on? If he'd had children it might have been different, but all he had was the inn. Somehow he'd made it out of his room one morning and that had been his salvation. The knock on the door that he had thought about ignoring had changed his life. It had given him his life back. A new and sometimes better life, he thought. Not the life of misery he had envisaged. Not the life of loneliness he had dreaded.

Zena had saved him from that. He was sure of it. Yes she was fourteen years younger than him, and he knew what some of the other villagers said about them behind their backs. That she was only with him because she wanted the inn when he passed on, and also that she sought her pleasure not just with him but with the younger men of the village. But Spengler was prepared to overlook the rumours, because he loved her and he was sure that she loved him, too.

She had arrived at the inn seeking work and he had allowed her to serve behind the bar and cook for his customers and, as she'd had no money, he had let her have one of the rooms upstairs to live in. It had been four months before he had realised his true feelings for her, and he'd been delighted when those feelings were reciprocated. They married two weeks later and Spengler had found happiness again, when he had thought that only misery awaited him in life. So, he ignored the rumours and the scornful glances from some, and he lived his life with her and that life was happy for the most part. And, Spengler told himself, how many people could say that about their lives. He felt he was a lucky man and even fewer could say *that* with any conviction.

Zena watched the Count for a moment longer, then moved back behind the bar and continued drying the glasses and steins she'd been occupied with before Count Karnstein's coach pulled up.

'He was talking to one of Gustav Weil's nieces,' she went on.

'I don't blame him,' one of the men at the bar offered and his companion laughed.

'They're beautiful girls, both of them,' Hoffman added. He was a well-built, balding man in his forties and had been the village baker for more than fifteen years now, his business thriving just off the main square of Karnstein.

'And so alike to look at,' intoned his companion, Zoll, the apothecary. He was the complete antithesis of the man he stood next to. Tall, thin and gaunt with a small moustache that looked as if it was clinging to his thin top lip for fear of falling. He adjusted his round glasses on his nose and sipped at his brandy.

'Gustav Weil won't like Count Karnstein talking to one of his relatives,' the innkeeper noted, wiping his hands on the apron he wore as he began moving wine bottles from a wooden case under the bar to a more prominent position behind it.

'What can he do about it? Hoffman asked, taking a large swallow of his ale. 'He can't stop every single person in the world from talking to his nieces.'

'He would if he could,' Zoll added. 'You know Weil.'

'I wouldn't want Karnstein talking to *my* daughter,' the baker added.

'That's probably why he's in the village,' Zena offered. 'To look for some young girl to take back to the castle.'

'Zena!' the innkeeper snapped. 'Mind your tongue!'

'Why?' she challenged. 'Who's going to hear me in here? No one's going to report me to the Count are they?'

'You should just be careful what you say about him,' the innkeeper reminded her.

'If he's looking for young, pretty women you should be careful, Zena,' Hoffman grinned. 'He might decide to take you up to his castle for some fun and games.'

The baker and Zoll laughed loudly. Spengler frowned and shook his head.

'Why would I want to go with him when I have my Carl?' Zena said, stroking Spengler's cheek with one slender index finger.

Spengler smiled triumphantly at his customers and squeezed Zena's taut little backside as she moved away from him. She lifted her skirt playfully to reveal that she wore nothing beneath it. Spengler raised his eyebrows and smiled broadly.

'You should still be careful what you say about him,' the innkeeper advised. 'Powerful men like him have ways of finding things out.'

'Rich and powerful,' Hoffman pointed out, nodding.

'Rich, powerful and evil,' Zena snorted.

A heavy silence fell over the inn and the three men looked at her almost accusingly.

'Come on,' she said, reproachfully. 'You know what he's like. Him and his whole family. They've always been the same.'

Zoll nodded.

'If half the stories about the Karnsteins are true then none of us would sleep soundly in our beds at night,' the apothecary murmured. 'And you know the stories I mean.'

He drained what was left in his glass and pushed it towards the innkeeper, who refilled it.

'Some say that the women of the family were the worst,' Hoffman offered. 'That the Countess Mircalla Karnstein was more evil and corrupt than any of the men.'

'Word has it that two men killed her inside the castle itself,' Zoll announced. 'One of them claimed that she had murdered his daughter.'

'That wasn't all he claimed,' Hoffman added. A hush fell over the bar and all eyes turned towards the baker, who took another sip of his ale before continuing. 'There had been a number of strange deaths in this area, all the victims killed the same way, and then it happened to this man's daughter, too. She was found with two puncture marks on her throat and breast. Her body had been drained of blood just like the others and this man said that Countess Mircalla Karnstein had been responsible. He and a man they called the General travelled to Karnstein Castle and one drove a stake through her heart, while the other cut off her head.' Hoffman took another sip of ale. 'The killings stopped after that. Make of that what you will.'

'Mircalla Karnstein was a vampire,' Zena breathed, but it came out more as a statement than a question. 'Mircalla or whatever she called herself. Some said she went by a different name.'

'What do you mean?' Spengler asked.

'I heard that, too,' Zoll agreed. 'Zena's right. There were some killings a few years back at a girl's boarding school near Innsbruck. Those bodies were found drained of blood; so were two of the teachers at that school. Some said that one of the other students had committed the murders. That other student's name was Carmilla.'

The baker looked vague.

'Carmilla is an anagram of Mircalla,' Zoll went on. 'Mircalla Karnstein became Carmilla Karnstein in order to continue killing.'

'And you believe that?' the baker grunted.

'I heard that story,' Zena confirmed. 'I believe it. She was a vampire.'

'Some would say that,' Hoffman admitted.

'Aye, and some would invite trouble from the Count if he heard stories like that,' the innkeeper offered.

'Do you think he doesn't know what people say about him?' Zena grunted. 'I think he enjoys it that people are afraid of him. It makes him feel more powerful.'

Zoll nodded.

'That's why he won't fear the wrath of Gustav Weil and the Brotherhood,' the apothecary noted. 'Why would a man like Karnstein be afraid of people like Weil? They can do nothing against him. They are not agents of the law, and even if they were, as far as we know Karnstein has broken no laws.'

'He might not have broken any laws set down by man, but you can be sure he's broken God's laws more than once,' Hoffman said.

Zoll nodded. He pushed his empty brandy glass across the bar, watching as the innkeeper re-filled it once again.

'How long are Weil's nieces staying in Karnstein for?' Hoffman enquired. 'Does anyone know?'

'I heard they are here to stay,' Zena told him. 'Moved here from Venice.'

'They'll find a difference,' Zoll observed. 'I visited Venice once when I was at University as part of my training to become an apothecary. They had some brilliant doctors there and three of us were sent to study under one of them for a time. It's a beautiful city, but it has its dark side. So much beauty cannot exist without darkness.'

'No good without evil,' Hoffman added.

'No God without Satan,' Zena intoned.

The innkeeper shot her a ferocious glance.

'I've already told you to mind your tongue, Zena!' he snapped.

'Oh, Carl, stop worrying,' she chided. 'You don't mind what I do with my tongue when we're alone.'

The men at the bar cheered and banged the wooden counter appreciatively.

'You tell him, Zena,' Hoffman chuckled. 'He should be glad to have a woman like you.'

'I keep reminding him of that,' Zena remarked, using

a cloth to wipe down and polish the far end of the bar. 'But he'll be grateful enough tonight when we've locked up and we're alone together in our nice comfortable bed.' She winked at her husband as the other men cheered once again.

'What does she do to you, Carl?' the baker asked, still grinning. 'Go on, tell us.'

Zoll banged the counter once more and nodded.

'Tell us,' the apothecary echoed.

Spengler smiled.

'What we do in our bedroom is our business and no one else's,' the innkeeper announced.

'I wish I had a woman like you, Zena,' the baker said, wistfully. 'I love my wife, but she's nothing like you.'

'That's because she's twenty years older than Zena,' Zoll reminded his friend.

'True,' the baker agreed. 'But I'd be happy to swap with you, Carl, just for one night. I'd show her how glad I was to be with her.'

'I am glad I've got her. That's why I don't want to lose her,' the innkeeper said.

'Then keep her away from Count Karnstein,' Zoll said, flatly. 'And if Gustav Weil has any sense that is what he will do with his nieces, too. Keep them well away from that man. For their sakes and the sakes of every man, woman and child in this village. The last thing any of us need is for Karnstein to have someone to share his perverted pleasures with.'

He took another sip of his brandy, cradling the glass in his hands as the amber fluid burned its way to his stomach.

Fifteen

In the dull light cast by the flickering candles, Frieda moved towards the wardrobe and opened it. She ran her fingers across the dresses hanging there, feeling the material of each before she finally took out a diaphanous yellow garment that reached to just above her ankles. She held it up against herself, admiring the colour and the cut of the garment. She wondered if Count Karnstein would approve and smiled.

Beside her, Maria watched with a combination of irritation and fear.

'Haven't you got us into enough trouble?' Maria said. 'No supper and early to bed.'

Frieda ignored the words; instead she pulled off her nightgown and tossed the garment away. For a moment she stood naked before her sister, who merely shook her head and walked back to the bed as Frieda pulled on the yellow dress, admiring her reflection before the mirror and the way the material hugged her perfect figure.

The candles in the room flickered as a breeze from the open window caught them.

'Did you hear what I said?' Maria persisted.

'Is that all you ever think about – yourself?' Frieda snapped. 'Don't be so greedy.'

'But if anyone comes and finds you gone there will be a terrible scene,' Maria insisted.

'It won't be *anyone* who comes, will it, Maria? It will be Uncle Gustav and you know what he will say.'

'He'll punish us both for what you're doing.'

'No one is going to notice, stupid. I don't know what you're complaining about.'

Frieda moved back to the dressing table, where she retrieved a hairbrush, and then to the mirror where she set about brushing her long brown hair, more than satisfied with the image that smiled back at her from the mirror. Maria stood behind her looking down angrily at her. Frieda glanced at her sister in the mirror and let out a weary sigh.

'All you have to do is go to sleep,' she said, irritably. 'I'm not asking you to come with me.'

'I wouldn't dare,' Maria told her.

'I know you wouldn't. You're scared of your own shadow. You always have been.'

'Why are you being so horrible to me, Frieda? Just because I'm trying to protect you.'

'Protect me from what or from whom?'

'I don't know. I'm just frightened for you.'

'And for yourself. You're terrified of dear Uncle Gustav.'

'Yes I am.'

'Well I'm not. I don't care if he does find me gone. The Count will protect me.'

Frieda got to her feet, crossed to the wardrobe once more and took out a pair of boots. She pushed her feet into them and began fastening the buttons at the sides.

'I beg you, Frieda,' Maria said, moving close to her again. 'Think about what you're doing. Everyone says he is a wicked man.'

'Uncle Gustav says he's wicked, but he thinks everyone in this world is wicked except him and his beloved brotherhood,' Frieda hissed angrily. 'He even thinks we're wicked. And even if Count Karnstein is wicked, what about it? Who wants to be good if being good is singing hymns and praying all day long?'

'Uncle Gustav is doing what's best for us I'm sure,' Maria countered.

'It might be best for you, but it's not for me.'

The two girls stood gazing at each other for long moments. Maria could see the defiance in her sisters' eyes as surely as she could hear it in her words and see it in her actions. She knew when Frieda was in this kind of mood there was no reasoning with her. It had always been the same, ever since she could remember. Even their parents had struggled to control her at times, and they had been able to both offer love and command respect. Here, in this house, neither it seemed were available. Frieda had moved towards the bedroom window now and she pushed it open and peered out.

There was a drainpipe close by and a foot or so below was the wooden roof of the porch to the rear of the building. Frieda knew that if she could lower herself on to the porch, then it was just a matter of jumping a few feet to the ground.

'I'm going now and you might as well stop arguing about it,' she said, rounding on her sister, one index finger jabbing towards her face. 'And I warn you, if you dare tell on me.'

'Frieda I wouldn't do that,' Maria assured her. 'You know I wouldn't.'

Frieda shot out both hands and clamped them around Maria's throat, pushing her backwards towards the bed.

'I'm telling you,' she snarled. 'I mean it. You know what will happen if you do.'

Maria tried to push her sister's hands away, but she couldn't. Frieda was now kneeling on the bed, looking down at her, oblivious to the tears that were coursing down Maria's face.

'Stop it,' Maria whimpered. 'You're hurting me.'

'Not half as much as I will if you don't keep quiet!'

Frieda pulled her hands away and glared at her sister for interminable seconds. The fury in her eyes was unsettling. To Maria it looked like pure undiluted hatred. Maria rolled over onto her side, her body racked by sobs.

'They're all in bed now,' Frieda said, crossing to the door and standing there for a moment, listening for any sounds of movement from the rest of the household. 'No one will notice. And don't lie awake waiting for me and don't worry. I won't be long.'

Maria sat up and shook her head as she saw Frieda moving towards the bedroom window once again.

'Frieda, I beg you, don't go,' she said, swinging herself off the bed and moving after her sister.

Frieda raised one hand threateningly and Maria took a step backwards.

'I've warned you once!' Frieda hissed. 'You know what I'll do to you if you make any trouble, don't you?'

Maria nodded.

'Don't you?' Frieda snapped again. 'Now get into bed, go to sleep and forget about what's just happened. I told you, I'll be back soon.'

'But how will you get to the castle?' Maria wanted to know.

'There's a pathway that leads through the forest. One of the other girls at the school told me about it. It leads to the foot of the hills where the castle is built. Once I get there it'll be easy to find my way.'

'Please be careful, Frieda,' Maria echoed.

'If you're so concerned about me, why don't you get Uncle Gustav to say a prayer for me?' Frieda sneered.

She swung herself over the windowsill and out into the night.

Maria waited a moment, then crossed to the window and peered out into the gloom. She could see the faint outline of Frieda as her sister hurried through the trees, swallowed by the forest in a matter of moments.

What little moonlight there was lit her way as she moved through the trees, keeping to the narrow path that wound through the forest like a knotted rope through a maze. The ground was soft in places and Frieda slipped more than once, sinking up to her ankles in thick, glutinous mud. However, eventually she found herself on a more solid pathway and she hurried on, eager to reach the castle but wondering how long her little adventure was actually going to take her. She guessed that it might be over a mile to Karnstein Castle from the village, but she told herself that as long as she was back at the house before dawn then she would be safe. Besides, the element of danger and the possibility of being discovered only heightened her excitement. She wished she could see the look on her Uncle Gustav's face now. If he only knew that she was on her way to see the man that he hated so much, the shock might be enough to give him a heart attack, and as far as Frieda was concerned that was a good thing.

She paused momentarily as she came to a road. Using a tree trunk for cover she peered right and left, then, satisfied that nothing was moving along the road, she ran across to the other side into the welcome embrace of some bushes. She ducked down and listened for any sounds, but there were none.

As she emerged into a clearing a little further on she looked up and a smile flickered on her face. The outline of Karnstein Castle loomed at the top of the hills ahead of her, its turrets and domes thrusting towards the black sky like beckoning fingers. Frieda moved on, lifting her dress as she clambered over some fallen tree trunks that had been cut down that very day.

There was movement off to her left.

She froze, ducking back behind a tree, wondering if the woodsman who had felled this mighty timber might still be around, even at such a late hour.

She waited, trying to control her breathing. Just some woodland predator on its nightly prowl, she told herself. Nothing to worry about. No interfering peasant or woodsman to delay her. High above an owl screeched loudly, then flew off in search of prey, barely visible against the blackness of the sky.

A twig snapped somewhere close by and she spun around again, her eyes searching the gloom for the source of the sound.

She could see nothing.

Frieda moved on into another small copse, glancing up again at the gaunt and imposing edifice of Karnstein Castle.

She was still looking at it when the hands grabbed her.

Sixteen

Frieda had never felt such strength before. The arms that enfolded her and swept her effortlessly from her feet gripped her with the same ease a cat holds a dead mouse.

She managed one scream, but then the sound died in her throat as she saw the face of her captor. He looked familiar. Something in her mind told her that she'd seen this man before. His black skin and massive build were not alien to her. As he carried her towards the road the recollection hit her like a thunderbolt. The man mountain who now held her under his arm was Count Karnstein's coachman, the man she had seen the Count speaking with that morning.

For reasons that even she didn't fully understand, Frieda suddenly felt less afraid and, as Joachim reached the road still carrying her, she saw the black outline of the Karnstein coach waiting on the road, the crest on the door gleaming, even in the darkness of the night. The four powerful horses that drew the vehicle waited patiently, one of the leads pawing the ground every now and then. Frieda stopped struggling against his enveloping grip and relaxed slightly as he pulled open the coach door and shoved her somewhat unceremoniously inside.

She scrambled up on to one of the velvet-covered seats and saw Joachim close the door behind her. The next sensation she felt was that of movement as the coach lurched away. She was flung backwards, but recovered her balance as the coach began to build up speed. Even from inside the vehicle, Frieda could hear the swish and crack of the whip as Joachim drove the horses on, coaxing them to even greater speed.

Frieda looked around the inside of the coach as it hurtled along. Everything was velvet and gilt. Everything signalled that this was the property of a man with wealth and power. She felt a curious thrill run through her. A frisson of excitement mixed with the apprehension and uncertainty that she was still experiencing. For all her desire to meet Count Karnstein, she was still frightened by this current situation. She knew that the black man was the Count's coachman, but as yet she couldn't be sure of their final destination; and now one terrible thought began to circulate in her mind, sticking like a splinter in soft flesh: what if she wasn't being taken to Karnstein Castle? Whither was she bound? Fear began to fill her once again.

Maria woke from a fitful sleep with a start.

She sat up in bed, the memory of the nightmare fading quickly in her mind. Details didn't linger for her; she couldn't remember what had frightened her into wakefulness. However, as she sat there, her breath coming in gasps and her heart beating hard against her ribs, she had no recollection of a dream. She had been woken suddenly by a feeling. A stab of fear that had lanced so deeply through her it had caused her to waken.

She put a hand to her chest and managed to slow her breathing a little. Not even knowing why, she swung herself out of bed and crossed to the bedroom window, squinting out into the blackness of the night, not sure what she was looking for. She felt as if someone had wrapped her in a freezing blanket, and she shivered as she stood before the window with one single thing now on her mind.

Maria was suddenly enveloped and consumed by the unshakeable feeling that her sister was in terrible danger.

Gustav Weil exhaled deeply and tapped his fingers lightly on the cover of the large Bible that lay before him.

'What I do, I do for the good of all,' he said, quietly. 'And I am even more aware of my duties to God now that we have the two girls living here with us.'

Katy Weil regarded her husband evenly as he spoke. She thought how weary he looked. It was as if age had suddenly caught up with him all in the space of one night. His face was pale in the candlelight and the shadows beneath his eyes looked even deeper than normal. When he spoke there was a weariness to his tone that she had not heard for a long time.

'But mark my words,' Weil went on, his voice acquiring some of its old edge once more. 'I will not tolerate disobedience or disrespect from either of them.'

'It will take them time to settle in, Gustav,' Katy told him. 'Remember what they've been through. Just think how dreadful it must have been for girls so young to suffer the loss of their parents.'

'Were the girls in the house when the fire began?'

'Maria was, but she was downstairs, thank the Lord. She got out easily.'

'And Frieda?'

'She wasn't in the house. No one knows where she was when the fire began.'

'I use fire to purify. Someone used it to destroy the night your sister and her husband were killed. Didn't the authorities in Venice say that the fire could have been started deliberately?'

'They weren't sure. What are you saying, Gustav?'

'Only that life is fragile and that we should thank God for it. It should not be treated as a right, but as a gift from the Lord. When anyone dies it serves to remind us of our own mortality. Both your sister and her husband are in a better place now, thank God.'

'Maria and Frieda might not see it like that. I'm sure they'd rather have their parents alive and still with them.'

'Well they are going to have to come to terms with their loss and embrace their new life here in Karnstein with us. There is nothing else for them now.'

Weil poured himself some water from the large copper jug on the table before him.

'They seem to have settled in at the school,' Katy told him. 'I think Maria has taken a shine to Anton.'

'The schoolmaster?' Weil snapped. 'What has he been saying to her?'

'Maria said she wanted to learn about the history of

132

the village, and he said he would help her,' Katy smiled.

'I'm sure he did. He's a man, isn't he? I'm sure the attentions of a pretty young girl flattered him. Be careful that his interest in either of the girls extends only to the imparting of knowledge.'

'Anton isn't like that, Gustav.'

'Every man is prey to temptation, whatever form it may take. Anton Hoffer is no different to any other man in that respect.'

'But Maria and Frieda are pupils at his school. He knows that there are boundaries that must not be crossed. I'm sure he would never think the way you suggest, Gustav.'

'You are so naïve at times,' Weil said, a slight smile on his lips.

'I'm just more trusting of people than you are, Gustav,' Katy told him, quietly.

'I have seen too much in this world to allow myself the luxury of trust in anything other than God,' Weil said, sternly. 'Man is inherently bad, the Bible teaches us that.' He tapped the cover of the book in front of him. 'Anyone may stray from the path of righteousness at any time in their life. We must see to it that the girls are protected from those who would corrupt them.'

'I don't think Anton intends to corrupt them, Gustav.'

'Perhaps not, but there will be those who would. Maria and Frieda themselves must be made aware of this. I will speak to them.'

'Let them settle in first, Gustav. They will learn our ways. They're sensible girls.'

'I hope so,' Weil intoned. 'For all our sakes, I hope so.'

Seventeen

Frieda looked disinterestedly at the boar's head as it was set down upon the table in front of herself and the other three people seated there.

She was more interested in her surroundings than the other guests. The main hall of Karnstein Castle fascinated her, and she had spent much of the time since her arrival gazing around at the portraits on the walls, the statues that decorated the hall, the weapons hung on the walls and the other paraphernalia that surrounded her, a constant reminder of the grandeur that had enveloped her since she first entered the castle. Her other source of fascination was Count Karnstein himself. Her initial fear upon arrival at the castle had given way quickly to excitement and expectation. She had found him charming and darkly attractive, and his attentiveness to her throughout the evening had both flattered and aroused her. Even now he gently touched her hand as he looked at her, and she felt a tingle run through her. Whatever consequences she may have to face, she assured herself, were worthwhile, when weighed against the experience she was enjoying. How different to her uncle this aristocratic man was. He seemed to embody everything that Frieda longed for so badly.

The other occupants of the room had said little to her, especially the blonde girl who sat opposite. She had been introduced somewhat curtly as Gerta, and Frieda had guessed from her attire that she was little more than a peasant. What she was doing at the castle Frieda had no idea, but she was content to think that the girl was merely a plaything of the Count.

The chubby man who sat on the other side of the table had been introduced as Dietrich and, throughout her time in the hall, she had been aware of his gaze upon her. Sometimes he would look away quickly if he realised she had seen him staring, but, at others, he would merely continue to stare at her, despite the fact she was aware of his lecherous glance. He reminded Frieda of a slug someone had clothed and propped up at the table.

She smiled at her own flight of fancy and sipped from the crystal wine glass before her, looking around the hall once again.

'To Satan.'

Frieda turned as she heard the words and saw Count Karnstein with his glass raised in the air in a toast. He smiled and clinked glasses with Frieda.

'Do you like my home, my dear?' the Count said, gazing at her over the rim of his glass.

'Very much,' Frieda told him.

'I wonder what your uncle would think if he could see you now?' Karnstein sneered. He took another sip from his goblet and looked across at Dietrich, who was gazing down at the remains of the food on his plate.

'Dietrich,' the Count said and the other man raised

his head. 'You're not amusing us tonight. What's wrong?

'It is nothing my lord,' Dietrich answered.

'It must be something,' Karnstein persisted. 'Don't make a secret of it. Tell us.'

'Perhaps a little later, my lord,' Dietrich murmured. 'In private. It is a personal matter.'

'Ah, a young lady, I'm sure,' Karnstein went on, smiling. He glanced at Frieda briefly and reached for her hand, holding it in his own powerful one. Frieda looked back at him and smiled, moving her chair slightly closer to him, enjoying the feel of his flesh against hers. 'Did this young lady run away from you, Dietrich?'

The other man didn't speak. His cheeks were bright red with embarrassment now and he looked uncomfortably at Frieda, then at Gerta and finally at the Count.

'Come,' Karnstein went on. 'Tell us. Did she run when you told her what you wanted her to do for you?'

Frieda laughed.

Dietrich lowered his gaze once more.

'She disappeared a few nights ago, my lord,' he said, quietly. 'I do not know what happened.'

'Disappeared?' Karnstein mused. 'You really should keep a closer watch on the women you entertain, Dietrich.'

'You know the girl of which I speak, my lord,' Dietrich said. 'The one who was here the other night.'

'Oh, that young girl,' Karnstein chided. 'Then it must have been your magicians who made her disappear. Perhaps their spells really did work.' The Count turned to Frieda, stroking her hand gently as he spoke.

'Friedrich attempted, in his bumbling way, to entertain me the other night by bringing a troupe of charlatans into the castle who presumed to summon the Devil. Can you think of anything so ridiculous?' He smiled and Frieda shivered as she returned the gesture. 'She was very pretty, though. A worthy offering. But the fools that Dietrich brought here had no idea what they were doing. They did things to this girl.'

'What kind of things?' Frieda breathed.

'Oh, they stripped her,' the Count went on. 'They touched her. One of them smeared pig's blood on her. All over her pretty little body. Everywhere.'

Frieda nodded almost imperceptibly.

'They tried to use her to summon Satan,' Karnstein said, his voice barely more than a whisper as he leaned close to Frieda. 'They failed, needless to say.'

'Her parents blame me,' Dietrich said, a little too loudly. His words reverberated around the hall for a moment and Karnstein looked venomously at the chubby man.

'You must have a very bad reputation, Dietrich,' the Count chided.

'They are threatening to report it to the authorities.'

The expression on the Count's face darkened. He leaned forward towards Dietrich.

'They had better not do that, Dietrich,' he threatened. 'It might be very bad for you.'

Dietrich nodded.

'Tell them she ran away,' Karnstein went on. 'After all, girls go missing all the time, don't they?' His smile faded as he glared at Dietrich.

'I will take care of it, my lord,' he assured the Count, who now sat back in his chair, his mood lightening again.

'Pay them,' Karnstein said, squeezing Frieda's hand. 'Just give them some money and they will forget all about their daughter. The only thing peasants are interested in is money. All peasants are insatiably greedy.' He looked at Gerta, who frowned. 'Aren't they, my dear?'

The blonde girl held his gaze for a moment, then looked down.

'Gerta's only interest is money,' Karnstein went on. 'If I give her enough money, then she will do whatever I ask of her. Isn't that true, Gerta?'

It was Frieda's turn to laugh. The other girl shot her an angry glance.

'Come, no more of your love life, Dietrich,' the Count said. 'It's too boring.' He turned and beckoned to his servant. 'Joachim, more wine. I need something to enliven my evening other than the presence of the lovely Frieda.' Again he stroked her hand, his eyes boring into her.

Across the table, Gerta shot them both furious glances.

Frieda noticed the other girl's angry look and smiled at the Count, who sat back in his chair once more and sighed.

'Really, everyone is so dull this evening,' he announced. 'This is hardly the way to entertain our guest is it?' He looked contemptuously at Gerta. 'Gerta, you're worse than Dietrich.'

'If it's your pleasure, my lord, I'll go,' Gerta said, getting to her feet.

'No!' Karnstein snapped. 'It is not my pleasure. You'll stay. Sit down.'

Gerta did as she was told, and Karnstein leaned towards her, reaching out to touch her hand, as he had done Frieda's. It was Gerta's turn to smile.

'I want to know what you think of Frieda,' he murmured. 'Don't you think she's beautiful?'

Gerta's expression darkened.

'She's all right,' she said, grudgingly.

The Count let go of Gerta's hand.

'That's not a very handsome compliment,' he snapped. 'You're not jealous, I hope.'

'I am a simple peasant girl, my lord,' Gerta said. 'We can be bought for a few pieces of gold.'

'Now you are being insolent, girl,' the Count hissed. He grabbed her hand once again, but this time he closed his fingers around her index finger, bending it backwards against the joint. Gerta let out a gasp of pain.

'My Lord . . . ,' Dietrich began, seeing the look on the blonde girl's face.

'Silence, Dietrich!' the Count snapped, still bending Gerta's finger backwards until it seemed that it would snap. He suddenly released it, allowing her to cradle the digit with her other hand. She looked at him with pain in her eyes, but Karnstein's expression didn't change. In fact, a thin smile spread across his lips. 'You need to be taught a lesson,' he breathed. He glanced at Frieda. 'Don't you think so?'

Frieda looked at Gerta and nodded.

'Yes,' she said, smiling, her excitement almost uncontrollable now.

'Then we will punish her together,' the Count announced, getting to his feet.

'No!' Gerta gasped and leapt to her feet, knocking her chair over in the process. 'I apologise, my lord, if you will permit me to leave.'

'But you can't leave now, Gerta,' Karnstein said, flatly. 'You must be punished.'

Gerta ran for the archway that led from the main hall, but it was useless.

'Joachim!' Karnstein shouted and the black man-servant appeared from the shadows as if by magic, his huge arms sweeping Gerta off her feet. She cried out in fear and anger, but her struggles against him were useless. Joachim carried her back across the room, slamming her down on to a fur-covered sofa with such force it knocked the breath from her. As she lay winded he grabbed her hands and swiftly tied them, securing her completely. She struggled against her bonds, but it was useless. She looked across the hall to where the Count now stood behind Frieda's chair.

'You don't mind, do you, if we play with Gerta?' the Count asked, looking at Dietrich.

The chubby man looked first at the Count and then at Gerta, who was whimpering quietly on the sofa, helpless in the grip of the ropes. Karnstein stroked his fingers softly across Frieda's cheek and she squirmed in her seat.

'You are very beautiful,' he said, quietly. 'For you all

pleasures should be supreme. And one supreme pleasure is to take a human life.'

It was then that Gerta understood and she screamed.

Eighteen

Frieda felt the hair at the back of her neck rise. She looked at the Count and then at the blonde girl, who had stopped struggling against her bonds and now lay motionless on the sofa on the other side of the room.

Frieda's heart was thumping against her ribs so hard she feared it might burst free, but she controlled herself and began to enjoy the feeling rather than being afraid of it. Her breathing was ragged. She had never felt excitement like this in her life. It was overwhelming and intoxicating. She looked at the Count again and saw that he was smiling at her. A smile of encouragement and cajolement, and she felt that behind that smile was something she wanted to share no matter what the cost either to herself or to anyone else. She moved towards him, watched by Gerta, who surveyed the entire scenario in terrified silence.

Karnstein stood beside the blonde girl, gently stroking her long hair, occasionally looking down at her with an expressionless gaze. The kind of look a butcher reserves for the next animal he's preparing to slaughter.

The Count beckoned Frieda to his side and slid one arm around her waist, drawing her nearer to him. She looked up at him, her eyes wide with desire, then she glanced at Gerta with something approaching contempt. Karnstein saw the look and let out a small grunt of approval, encircling Frieda's waist more strongly with his powerful arm. She turned her attention to him once again.

'For all our pleasures we must pay,' he said, quietly. 'Will you pay?'

Frieda held his gaze.

'Anything,' she breathed.

Gerta moaned and strained helplessly against the ropes that held her in place on the sofa. The Count glanced at her, then pulled Frieda gently towards the huge ornate mirror that hung on the wall of the main hall. She followed him willingly as he stepped in front of the glass. Frieda swallowed hard, her heart skipping a beat when she saw that he cast no reflection.

Her eyes widened in shock and fear for a second, especially as she now stood beside him, her own reflection clearly visible.

'What do you see?' Karnstein asked.

Frieda looked at her own face reflected before her and then at the blank space where the Count's image should have been.

'I don't understand,' she said, quietly. 'Why can't I see you?'

'We are the undead,' Karnstein told her, gently stroking her cheek. 'Immortal. No man can harm us, unless he drives a stake through our hearts or beheads us.' He ran his fingers through her long brown hair, feeling its silkiness. 'No one is protected from us, unless they hold the hated cross.'

Frieda tried to swallow, but it felt as if her throat had been filled with chalk.

'Do you understand now?' Karnstein asked.

'You're a vampire,' Frieda said, flatly.

'Yes. I can savour the most extreme of Satan's delights. I can feed on the blood of a human victim.'

Frieda took a step away from him.

'No, not me!' she gasped.

'It is a test,' Karnstein told her, gently. 'One who is dedicated to the Devil and his deeds will not die by a vampire's bite, but will become one of the undead. A vampire.'

Fear flooded through Frieda once again and she began to shake uncontrollably.

'You have nothing to fear,' the Count assured her. 'You came here tonight because you wanted to.'

'But I didn't know then what you were,' she protested.

'Would it have mattered?' Karnstein enquired. 'You would still have come. You seek more from your life than that offered by your uncle and his beliefs. Do you think he could ever understand what we have become? Could he ever comprehend the power? Could he ever match it? No. It is beyond his timid and feeble understanding. Join me now and share the power. Share eternity.'

Frieda stood motionless for a moment, then, very slowly, she began to undo her dress, finally pulling the top open, exposing her long slender throat. The Count smiled and, as his lips curled backwards, Frieda could see the two long canine fangs glistening in his upper jaw.

'The good and the innocent die,' he hissed, then he suddenly lunged forward like a snake striking at its prey.

Frieda moaned loudly as he buried the twin fangs in her neck, cutting through the veins he sought. He pressed his mouth to the torn vessel that had begun pumping blood.

Frieda groaned, but pulled him closer to her and his strong arms enveloped her, holding her upright as he fed on her life fluid, finally drawing his head away. Blood was running down his chin. Several droplets fell to the cold stone floor.

For a moment, Frieda thought she was going to pass out. Her head was spinning and she shot out a hand to support herself against the long wooden table, but Karnstein was close to her, ensuring that she didn't overbalance. She blinked hard, clearing her slightly blurred vision and, as quickly as it had come, the feeling of dizziness passed. Frieda sucked in a deep breath, aware now only of Karnstein's smiling face. Her own blood was still smeared over his lips and chin, but that didn't matter to her any more. She put one hand gently to her neck and felt the two large round wounds that the Count had inflicted. Both were as large as the tip of her index finger and blood was still running slowly from them both, but Frieda seemed oblivious to the damage he had inflicted and there was no pain now. She turned towards the large ornate mirror and inspected the fang marks, touching them again.

Then, as she stood there, she saw her own reflection begin to fade.

Like ripples of water on the surface of a still pond, it shimmered then seemed to recede into the glass itself, until there was nothing visible except the long table, the rest of the hall and whatever else was caught by the mirror's eye. Frieda and the Count were invisible before the glass, just as he had told her. She smiled and turned towards Karnstein, who held her tightly before him.

'What did I tell you?' he breathed.

Again Frieda smiled.

'Now,' the Count murmured, his long index finger pointing towards Gerta.

'No, please!' Gerta pleaded, straining violently against the rope and wincing when it cut into her soft flesh. 'Stay away from me!'

Frieda moved slowly and purposefully towards the bound girl, seating herself on the sofa beside her. She gently leaned forward and kissed Gerta delicately, almost lovingly, on the forehead, then on each cheek. The blonde girl stopped struggling when she felt Frieda's hand caress her face and, when Frieda bent towards her again and kissed her softly on the lips she accepted the kiss willingly.

Karnstein stood back, watching, his face still smeared with blood.

He saw Frieda slide her free hand along Gerta's extended right leg, pausing at the hem of her dress for a moment before exploring higher. She caressed the smooth flesh of Gerta's thigh with one hand as she stroked her hair with the other, planting more feather-light kisses on her lips and face. Gerta closed her eyes, relaxing under Frieda's attention. When Frieda finally pressed her lips more urgently to Gerta's she responded fiercely, her own excitement now overcoming the initial fear she had experienced. Frieda kissed her passionately, using both hands now to undo the front of Gerta's dress, pulling it open until she exposed her firm breasts.

Gerta gasped with pleasure as she felt Frieda's hands cup her breasts, her fingertips gliding across them lightly, teasing the nipples and coaxing them to stiffness.

Frieda drew back as Gerta slid further down the sofa, until she was almost completely horizontal. She was breathing softly, but her breath was ragged and the look that she gave Frieda was one of yearning now, not of loathing or fear. She pulled gently against her ropes, but not because she wished to be free of them to aid her flight. She wanted to pull Frieda to her, to encourage her to continue with the things she was doing, to increase the pleasure she felt. She wanted to slide her own hands up inside Frieda's yellow dress, wanted to feel the softness of the other girl's skin against her own. Wanted to taste that skin beneath her tongue and enjoy its warmth under her touch.

Gerta looked at Frieda and nodded gently, but the expression on Frieda's face now was not one of lust but of hunger and rage.

Frieda snarled at her, revealing the fangs that now grew from her upper jaw.

In that split second, the spell was broken. Gerta screamed in terror, the sound spiralling into one of pain as Frieda shot her head forward and bit deeply into Gerta's breast, just above the nipple. The fangs tore through the soft tissue easily and Frieda felt as if her body was on fire as she tasted the blonde girl's blood in her mouth. When she finally pulled herself away from the torn breast she was quivering, her face spattered with Gerta's blood. More of the crimson fluid had run down her chin and there were even several droplets on the material of her dress. Frieda looked down at them, her eyes blazing.

The Count smiled again, his own fangs glistening in the firelight.

Frieda looked around at him and they both laughed, the sound rising.

Gerta's body lay motionless on the sofa. Karnstein joined Frieda beside the blonde girl, his own hunger raging.

Another ten minutes and the body was completely drained of blood.

Nineteen

Gustav Weil sat astride his horse, his eyes fixed on the entrance to the small hut in the forest. He had watched as three of his companions had strode off towards the building only minutes ago, hammering on the door for a moment or two, before finally kicking the partition open and disappearing inside.

He had heard screams of fear and protest from inside, then silence, apart from the odd angry shout and what sounded like soft whimpering. Now he watched as one of the men who had entered the hut walked briskly back towards where Weil, Hermann and Franz still sat on their horses. The man, who sported a thick moustache and sideburns, walked up to Weil's horse, patting the animal's neck as he looked up at its rider. Weil looked down at him.

'She protests her innocence, Gustav,' the man said.

'What did you expect?' Weil told him. 'Don't they all?'

The moustachioed man nodded.

'It is hard to admit the truth,' Hermann added, also looking down at the man. 'Harder still when it means admitting heresy.'

Again the man with the moustache nodded.

'There is no need to hear a confession from her,' Franz added. 'We know she is guilty.'

'If she confesses her sins she might find easier passage into heaven,' the man said. 'Shall we persist with trying to exact one?'

'She will find passage into heaven once her body is purified,' Weil said, shaking his head. 'There is no need to hear the words, but if you feel you must . . .'

Weil allowed the sentence to trail off, then he glanced across at the huge pile of dry wood and kindling that had been built by other members of the Brotherhood in the clearing close to the hut. They had piled the wood around the base of a tree and Weil could also see thick rope wound around the trunk to secure the girl and prevent her escaping, once they brought her out for purification. Four of the Brotherhood members standing near the kindling held burning torches, which they turned gently in the air to ensure the flames remained bright and were not extinguished by the strong breeze that had begun to blow.

The moustachioed man hesitated a moment longer, then turned and walked back towards the hut, once more disappearing inside.

'I wonder what they're doing to her?' Hermann said.

'Why don't you go and look if it bothers you that much?' Weil offered.

'Whatever they are doing, they are performing God's will,' Franz echoed, patting the neck of his horse to calm it.

The three men sat in silence for a moment, then

Hermann looked at Weil, who was still gazing blankly ahead.

'Do you ever doubt yourself, Gustav?' he said, quietly.

'What do you mean?' Weil asked.

'I know that what we do is God's work and it is necessary,' Hermann went on. 'But do you ever find it difficult to do what we are called upon to do?'

'God tests us all in different ways, Hermann,' Weil told his companion. 'But if we ask him for strength it will be given.'

'Do you doubt our calling?' Franz wanted to know, looking at Hermann. 'Would you shrink from what must be done to rid this place of evil? If we do not act, who will?'

'I know that what we do is necessary,' Hermann snapped. 'I wouldn't have it any other way.'

'You sound as if you lack conviction, Hermann,' Franz told him. 'Perhaps you should have stayed in front of your hearth with your feet up and left true believers like us to carry out God's work.'

'Never doubt my conviction, Franz,' Hermann said, angrily. 'I know what these girls have done that we must burn them. I know their true nature.'

Franz smiled thinly.

'What we do keeps our families and this village safe from evil,' Weil announced. 'We were chosen by God for this work and we should be thankful that he saw fit to imbue us with the strength to carry it out.'

Hermann nodded.

'We are rewarded here on earth by the knowledge

that our loved ones sleep easier because we root out wickedness and evil,' Franz said. 'And we will be rewarded in heaven for the work we have done in God's name. Have no fear of that.'

'And yet we cannot touch the true evil that taints this valley,' Hermann intoned.

Weil looked at him.

'What do you mean?' he wanted to know.

'We all know the root of true evil lies in Karnstein Castle,' Hermann went on. 'Yet we must stand by idly, while the Count and those who share his vile pleasures go about their blasphemous business.'

'His time will come,' Weil said, quietly, his eyes still fixed straight ahead. 'No one can escape the wrath of God forever. Count Karnstein will know soon enough what it means to feel that fury.'

'For too long that accursed castle has spread its shadow over this village,' Franz added. 'Every member of that damned family has been similarly depraved and godless. We all know of the stories about his ancestors and their vile acts.'

'God has seen everything,' Weil told his companions. 'Judgement day will come for the Count and his followers, mark my words. When that time comes, none will escape.'

Franz pointed towards the wooden hut ahead and Weil nodded as he saw two members of the Brotherhood emerge carrying a young girl between them. She had long brown hair that cascaded over her bare shoulders, but her head was hanging limply as they dragged her over the rough ground, her bare feet trailing on the earth. Her simple peasant dress was torn in several places, and Weil could see vivid red marks on her arms and also on the inside of her legs as his companions hauled her towards the pile of kindling.

'She would not confess,' the moustachioed man told Weil, wiping his hands on a piece of material that he'd torn from the girls dress.

'Then she shall die unrepentant,' Franz pronounced.

Weil watched as the girl was pulled towards the tree trunk, the ropes fastened quickly about her. He could see her lips moving silently as she was bound and, at last, she seemed to be aware of her fate and raised her head. There were more marks on her face and blood was running from her bottom lip, its source a large cut.

'Does she wish to ask forgiveness of God now it is too late?' Franz asked, seeing that the girl was looking in their direction.

'Does it matter?' Hermann said, dismissively. 'Let us finish our business here and be gone.'

The girl barely struggled as she was tied to the tree, and even when the puritans carrying the torches advanced towards the pile of wood she merely raised her head and looked at Weil and his companions once again.

'She knows there is no need to beg for mercy, because she admits her own guilt by her silence,' Franz offered, a crooked smile on his face.

Weil snapped the reins of his horse and guided the animal to within a few feet of the girl.

She met his gaze, tears running down her cheeks, mingling with the blood that already stained her flesh.

'You will be purified in the flames,' Weil told her. 'Your sins burnt away.'

Still the girl did not speak. Weil nodded and the puritans holding the torches thrust them into the pile of wood. The kindling caught straight away and flames began to rise quickly, fanned by the breeze.

'You are not men of God!' the girl wailed at last. 'You are monsters!'

Weil watched her through the dancing flames.

'If you had remained true to God, you would not be suffering now!' one of the other Brotherhood members shouted. Angry calls of agreement greeted his remark.

'Burn!' another roared as the flames rose higher.

Weil sat motionless on his horse, his gaze fixed on the girl's face.

'God has seen what you have done and he will punish you!' she shouted.

Weil turned his horse away and guided it from the clearing, followed by the other members of the Brotherhood. Behind him the flames took hold, burning the girl as easily as they incinerated the wood around her.

Her screams of agony rose on the wind.

Twenty

Anton Hoffer pushed the poker into the fire, stirring the logs as they burned. Flames danced before him and the schoolmaster gazed distractedly at them as they flared in the grate, welcoming the warmth they exuded. It was a freezing cold night outside and he was glad to be seated here before such warmth, even if the look on his face currently failed to match his attitude. His brow was knitted, his jaw set in hard lines as he sat back in his seat, still watching the fire, as if fearing it might go out at any second.

'Another funeral pyre,' he said, quietly. 'Another sacrifice.'

He closed his eyes momentarily and sighed.

'They are frightened,' his sister told him. Ingrid Hoffer sat on the other side of the fireplace in a high-backed leather chair similar to the one occupied by her brother. She was cradling a small glass of wine in her hand as she regarded her sibling. It was, she told herself, one of her few weaknesses, and one she liked to indulge in during the peace and quiet of the evenings, when the day's work was finished. 'And from fear comes desperation.'

'Is that an excuse for wanton cruelty?' Anton retorted.

'Five people have been found dead,' Ingrid reminded him. 'Three others have disappeared.'

'And three young girls have been burned at the stake. Add those lives to the total. What is wrong with these people, Ingrid? Do they think we're still living in the Dark Ages?'

'You said yourself that superstition dies hard in these parts, Anton. We were raised with it, just as the other villagers were.'

'But we learned to distinguish superstition from reality.'

'We were lucky.'

'I sometimes wish we'd never returned here when we completed our time at university.'

'But Karnstein is our home. It always has been and it always will be. This house is our home. A reminder of everything good that we've lived through. A reminder of our parents.'

Anton continued gazing into the flames.

'Our father was a religious man,' Ingrid reminded him. 'Were his beliefs that different from some of the men in this village?'

'If you mean Gustav Weil, then yes, our father was nothing like him or any of his deluded followers.'

'Anton, I know how you feel,' Ingrid assured him, smiling.

'No,' Anton snapped. 'You don't.' He got to his feet and crossed the room, where he refilled both his glass and then Ingrid's. He returned to the fireside and handed his sister her drink, before settling himself once more in his chair. 'You think I'm just angry, but it's more than that.' He took a sip of his wine. 'I feel sick with fear and revulsion against myself.'

Ingrid looked at him aghast.

'Anton,' she began. 'Why should you feel like that? You aren't involved.'

'I live in this village,' he told her. 'That makes me involved. I'm a coward.'

'How can you say that?'

'If I wasn't I'd do something.' He shook his head. 'How much longer can decent people stand by and watch this reign of terror by Gustav Weil and his religious friends?'

'But what can we do? What can anyone do?'

Anton had no answer for her, and that only served to increase his anger.

'I know some of those poor girls were innocent,' Ingrid went on. 'I'm sure they were, but . . .'

'Anyone,' Anton interrupted. 'Anyone poor, living alone and not a devoted member of the church, anyone young and pretty, because then they question their morals.'

Ingrid looked on as he sat forward in his chair, his eyes still fixed on the flames of the fire.

'As if Weil and some of the members of his Brotherhood have any right to preach on the subject of morality,' he snapped. 'Their fanaticism is matched only by their hypocrisy. And who do they think they are protecting? Who do they think they are saving?'

'Gustav has two young and pretty nieces,' Ingrid reminded him.

'Just as well for them they are under his protection.

They are exactly the kind of girl Weil and his Brotherhood usually persecute.'

'He will protect them.'

'From what, Ingrid? From whom?'

'They have a great many admirers – Frieda in particular.'

'Pretty young women will always have admirers and no matter what Weil does he can't change that.'

'Some have more admirers than others, it seems.' Ingrid smiled, looking at her brother. 'Did you think I wouldn't notice, Anton?' she said, softly. 'I'm afraid it's rather obvious.'

Anton didn't look at her.

'Why Frieda, though?' Ingrid went on. 'Maria seems much nicer to me, though one can hardly tell the difference between them.'

'Oh, I can,' Anton breathed. 'Maria is very nice. Probably much nicer than Frieda, but Frieda has a kind of fire inside her. I can almost feel it burning when I'm near her. And she has a strange, mysterious quality.' He looked into the fire again, his expression almost wistful.

'She reminds you of Lisa, doesn't she?' Ingrid said, softly.

Anton looked at his sister, something akin to anger in his eyes.

'No,' he said, none too convincingly.

'Anton, I can understand why,' Ingrid went on.

'You think I find one of our new pupils attractive because she reminds me of the woman I used to love, is that it?' he said, wearily.

'I could understand it if that was how you felt.'

'The woman I loved, who killed herself because of me.' He looked challengingly at Ingrid.

'Lisa didn't kill herself because of you, Anton,' Ingrid protested. 'She was ill, very ill, you know that and there was no hope of her recovering. She killed herself because she wanted to save herself more pain, and she wanted to stop you from suffering while you watched her die.'

'Yes, watched her without being able to help her.'

'There was nothing you could have done. Even the doctors and surgeons couldn't help her. What did you think you could do for her that they couldn't? You can't blame yourself for the rest of your life. You nursed her as best you could. You did everything possible for her. You can't continue punishing yourself by thinking you could have done more, because you couldn't.'

'And when she killed herself they wouldn't allow her to be buried in consecrated ground because it was a sin,' Anton snapped. 'Do you remember that? I remember Weil and the others telling me that she had no right to lay with the other dead of the village, because she had taken her own life.' Anton got to his feet, his jaw set. 'I remember the looks on their faces when they told me that. They pretend to act in God's name, but God is supposed to embody love isn't He? They don't even understand the meaning of the word.'

Anton walked to the fire and stood there silently, warming himself before the flames. Images tumbled through his mind. He could still see Lisa clearly in his thoughts, even though it had been almost eighteen months since her death. He wanted to remember the sight of her smiling and laughing with him, but all his mind seemed willing to provide were images of her in pain as she lay in bed, helplessly waiting for death. A death that finally she welcomed, because it brought a release from the agony she was suffering. And when she died something inside Anton died, too. There had been an empty space inside him for so long, and he desperately wanted it to be filled.

'Is it too soon?' he murmured aloud. 'What would she think if she could see me now?'

'Lisa would be happy for you, Anton,' Ingrid told him. 'Happy that you have continued with your life, and also that you might have found someone else to share it with.'

'I wouldn't go that far,' he said, managing a smile.

'You find Frieda attractive,' Ingrid echoed. 'There's nothing to be ashamed of, Anton.'

'Maria is like an open book,' Anton observed. 'While with Frieda one feels you could go on learning about her forever.'

'I suppose it depends on what there is to learn,' Ingrid said. 'Still, it's a very romantic notion and you should embrace it, Anton. The only trouble is . . .' She allowed the sentence to trail off.

'What?'

'If you want to court Gustav Weil's niece you'd better not offend him.'

The smile slipped from Anton's face.

'Someone,' he said, sternly, 'has got to do something.'

'And that person must be you?'

Anton didn't speak. Once again he was staring into

the flames of the fire. He sat there, apparently mesmerised by it for what seemed like an eternity, then he rose suddenly to his feet, as if the spell upon him had abruptly been broken. Ingrid looked at him, seeing the dark expression that was still upon his face.

'I've got to get out of here, just for a while,' Anton told her. 'I need to walk, to clear my head.'

Ingrid nodded.

'I'll still be here when you come back if you want to talk,' she assured him.

Anton squeezed her shoulder gently as he passed.

'What would I do without you?' he said as he opened the door.

'I sometimes wonder, dear brother,' Ingrid smiled, watching him go. 'I sometimes wonder.'

Anton made his way out of the school and closed the large wooden door behind him, sucking in a deep breath in the process, allowing the cool night air to fill his lungs. It was a chilly night and he dug his hands in his pockets to ward off the cold as he walked. At such a late hour the village streets were deserted, and a thin film of frost had already begun to coat the walkways and narrow streets, signalling how bitter it would become as the night deepened. As he walked he could see lights burning in the windows of houses here and there, but many were in darkness, the inhabitants, he assumed, doing what he should be doing, and that was sleeping, but he knew sleep would not come easily to him tonight. There were too many thoughts tumbling through his mind and he had to try and clear them before he could think of settling down. If only he could have left those thoughts behind as he walked, Anton mused. Because ultimately, no matter how far he travelled, those thoughts were still with him, still inside his head, picking away at him like carrion feeders at a fresh kill. He blew out his cheeks, watching as his breath clouded in the air.

'Master Hoffer.'

The sound of his name startled him and he spun round, peering into the gloom.

Rolf Kessler stepped from the doorway where he'd been standing, his huge frame towering above the schoolmaster.

'You frightened me,' Anton admitted as he regarded the man before him.

'I apologise,' Kessler said. 'I saw you leave your house. I am Rolf Kessler.'

'You live out in the forest with your daughter, don't you?' Anton said.

'My daughter was killed. Burnt by Gustav Weil and his Brotherhood. I live alone now.'

'I'm sorry for your loss. Just as I'm sorry for all the other families that Weil and his friends have brought suffering to.'

'As you say, others have lost loved ones to Weil's fanatical beliefs, and yet he is allowed to continue with what he does. How can this be? He must be stopped.'

'I agree with you, and if there was anything I could do I would, but he and his Brotherhood seem to be above the law. No one can touch them.'

'They kill and yet they remain free. If you or I took a life we would be executed.'

'One of their number is a magistrate. They have protection. What do you propose should be done?'

'They should be made to suffer,' said Kessler. 'Made to feel the pain they have inflicted on others.'

'I agree, but that is easier said than done. While none oppose them they will continue with their quest. They think they are on some kind of mission from God and no one will persuade them otherwise.'

'There must be others in this village who would confront them. Others whose sons or daughters they have sacrificed. How many more must die before someone acts?'

'People are afraid of them, because they say they are doing God's work and people are afraid of God when you come down to it, Rolf. People in this village feel that to oppose Weil and the Brotherhood is to oppose God Himself. They are ruled by fear.'

'Then they're fools.'

'The world is full of fools, my friend. I wish it wasn't, but it is. Fools and simple men like us. Men who want to change things, but have no way to do it.'

'You're an educated man. You're more able to change things than someone like me.'

Anton shook his head wearily.

'Education is a poor weapon against fear,' he said, quietly.

Kessler lowered his head.

'Then there must be another way,' he said. 'Another way to fight back against them and what they have done. If they can do so much because of fear, then they must learn what fear feels like.'

'And how would you frighten them into stopping?'

'Hurt them or those close to them.'

Anton regarded the woodsman evenly for a moment, then reached out and touched his broad shoulder.

'If you do that you are no better than them,' he said, quietly.

'I don't care,' Kessler told him. 'I just want them to feel the pain I felt when they took my Sophie.' He let out a long almost painful breath. 'She was the light of my life. The only thing I had that made life worth living. When they took her they took away my reason to live.' He looked at Anton. 'How do you think you would feel if anything happened to your sister?'

'Grief does terrible things to a man, Master Hoffer,' Kessler told him. 'And all my grief was caused by Gustav Weil and his Brotherhood. And I will not rest until they pay for my pain.'

He turned and prepared to walk away.

'No one is safe,' Kessler added. 'Not while they are free to continue with their work. Imagine what would happen if it was your sister. If they came for her would you act? If you saw her tied to a stake and burnt, would that make you help me? Think about it, Anton.' Kessler wheeled away and stalked off into the enveloping night.

'Rolf, come back!' Anton called. 'If I can help you, I will!'

Kessler didn't turn.

Anton's words died on the wind.

Twenty-One

For a man with his strength, the corpse had been easy to carry.

Joachim had lifted the motionless form of the dead peasant girl effortlessly from the sofa in the main hall of Karnstein Castle and taken it through to the kitchens beyond, as the Count had instructed.

Never at any time had the black-skinned man questioned an order from his master, because he knew that was not the way. He existed to obey, and this latest task was just one of many he had already carried out unthinkingly, just as he would complete countless more in the course of his life.

He had transported Gerta's body through the kitchen and down the stone steps that led to the cellar below. The subterranean room was almost as large as the one above. A massive high-ceilinged cavern that smelled of damp, and where Joachim could hear water dripping slowly and relentlessly as he sat on the edge of the rough wooden bed jammed in one corner of the room. This was where he slept, when he was allowed to. When the day's toils were completed he came down here to the cellar and his little bed and he slept gratefully upon the rough straw-covered cot that he had been provided with. His clothes, what few he possessed, were kept folded in a large and battered old trunk; something else provided by the Count for his use, and for that Joachim had been grateful. He had a roof over his head, somewhere to sleep and a master to serve. What man could ask for more? Joachim thought.

Now he carried the body of the peasant girl to the far end of the cellar, where he dropped it unceremoniously on the cold floor. For a moment he looked down at the corpse, the limbs splayed like a discarded doll. He prodded the body with the toe of one boot, as if expecting it to move. When it didn't he turned and headed back across the cellar towards the steps that would lead him back up into the kitchen. From that room he crossed to the wall near the fire and gazed at the array of tools displayed there. Butchers saws, knives, cleavers and filleting blades all hung from a rack and Joachim studied each one for a moment before selecting a saw, a cleaver and one of the shorter knives. Nodding to himself he carried them all back with him down to the cellar.

He laid the tools on the bed and began to remove his clothes. The work he was about to perform was best done without garments. He had learned that on a number of occasions before.

Naked, he picked up the saw, cleaver and knife and headed back towards the waiting body, where he laid the butcher's implements on the cold stone floor.

Joachim knelt beside the corpse and reached for the hair, pulling the body almost upright, so that he could see into the face. The eyes were still open. He reached out and gently pushed the lids closed. He knew the girl was dead, but he didn't like it when their eyes were open. He had always hated that. It was as if they were watching him. He shook his head, as if answering some unspoken question, then he began to undo her dress, finally pulling it free to leave her naked. He tossed the dress aside and allowed his eyes to study the girl's now exposed body.

It was covered in raw bite marks. Deep, savage gashes that had ripped the skin and sliced through veins effortlessly. They were on the throat, the breasts, the stomach and arms. There were even some on the inside of the thighs. All were choked with congealed blood and there was also dried saliva slicked on some of these bite marks. Joachim knew what had been done to the girl, but it was not for him to question. He questioned nothing. It was not his way.

He reached for the knife, gripped it in one powerful hand and began his work.

Joachim cut across the joint of the shoulder, slicing through skin and muscle until he exposed bone. He did the same on the other shoulder and then at each hip.

With the bone exposed he reached for the butcher's saw, rested the serrated blade against the top of the femur and began to cut. The sound of metal against bone caused a high-pitched grating sound that reverberated inside the cellar, but the sound didn't bother Joachim and he kept up a steady motion, driving the saw blade downwards with tremendous strength as he cut. The leg came free easily and also with very little spillage of blood. After all, Joachim reasoned, there was very little blood left in the body anyway, so the meagre loss now was understandable. It was the same with the other leg and with both arms. By the time he had cut all four limbs from the torso there were only small puddles of crimson beneath the stumps of each.

He wondered if it would be any different when he removed the head.

Joachim used the cleaver for this task, driving the blade down three or four times with incredible power. The fourth stroke completed the task and the head came free. There were some desultory dribbles of blood from the stump and also from the head itself, but nothing like the jets of fluid he could have expected had the girl died any other way. He would have been drenched in her life fluid otherwise. As it was, his body was slicked with sweat from his exertions, but there was only a thin coating of blood on his hands.

Joachim looked down at the portions of body and nodded, pleased with his efforts. The Count would be pleased, too. Not that he would ever see what had been done to the girl down here, but she had been removed and that was all he had asked. He had told Joachim to get rid of her and that was what he had done. Later, Joachim would wrap the pieces of body in a sheet and carry it out of the castle to a hole in the hillside below the castle. He would put it in there with some of the others, then roll the large stone that he blocked the entrance with back into place. Some animals might be attracted by the smell of the flesh, but they couldn't get inside to feed on it. Joachim smiled to himself.

He reached for the head of the girl and lifted it by the hair, looking at the face. He stroked the cheek gently with one thick index finger and smiled once more.

Twenty-Two

Maria woke suddenly from the nightmare.

She sat bolt upright in her bed, perspiration clinging to her face. And as she sat shaking in the bed, she raised one hand to her throat and gently touched the left side of it, stroking the area gently with her fingertips, as if expecting to find a wound.

'Frieda?' she whispered softly, then she lay back against her pillows, allowing the nightmare images to fade.

She had dreamed of her sister and of the dark forest and the looming monolith that was Karnstein Castle. In the dream, Frieda had been running from something, pursued through the woods by whatever it was that wanted her. Maria hadn't been able to see what had been chasing her sister, all she could see was the terrified girl dashing headlong through the trees, occasionally tripping and falling, looking over her shoulder to see how close her pursuer was.

Maria put both hands to her face and sat shaking for a moment longer. For not only had she seen her sister's fear in that dream, she had felt it, too. Deep inside herself she had experienced a growing sense of dread that had grown more intense by the minute. She knew that dreams or nightmares only lasted seconds in reality, but this one felt as if it had been going on for hours, running over and over in her mind, until she, too, felt exhausted, as if she herself had been running wildly from something that wanted to harm her. For that was the overriding sensation that now enveloped Maria. She was convinced beyond all reason that someone or something wanted to hurt her sister. What it was she had no idea, and why anyone would wish to do this she couldn't begin to guess, but that was the conviction she felt, and no matter what she could not shake it.

She swung herself out of bed and padded across to the dressing table, where there was a bowl full of cold water. Maria dipped her hands into the cooling water and splashed her face with it, hoping the feel of the liquid would shock her from the way she felt, and perhaps wash away the last vestiges of the nightmare. She dried her face and gazed out of the bedroom window into the night. Once more, without even knowing why, she touched the left side of her throat and ran her fingers over the soft flesh there. Satisfied that she must have dreamed the imagined injury, she lowered her hand again and looked once more out of the window.

Where was Frieda, she wondered? She glanced up towards the gaunt silhouette of Karnstein Castle and wondered if she was still there. In fact, Maria wondered if her sister had made it to the castle at all, and if she had, what was she doing there? Maria turned and moved back to the bed.

She heard the floorboards outside her room creak and she froze.

Had someone heard her moving about? Was the bedroom door about to open? If either her aunt or uncle came in now they would see that Frieda was gone. All hell would break loose. Maria stood motionless, ears alert for the slightest sounds beyond the bedroom door.

Was it just the boards settling? Or was someone actually standing there? Still she waited.

Finally, unable to retain such stillness indefinitely, Maria moved very slowly towards the bedroom door and pressed her ear to it.

She was sure that if it had been Aunt Katy beyond the door, then she would have tapped lightly and walked quietly in to check on the two girls. If it had been her Uncle Gustav he would not have waited out on the landing for so long. He would simply have blundered in, demanding to know where Frieda was as soon as he realised she was missing.

Bolstered by this logic, Maria rested her hand gently on the doorknob and prepared to turn it.

There was still only silence from the other side of the partition.

Maria knew that, had her sister been present, she would have simply tugged the door open and confronted whoever was outside. There would have been none of this caution. Frieda would have investigated, regardless of the consequences for either of them. But Maria was not like her sister in that way, as in so many others. Identical in appearance, when it came to character the two girls could not have been more different. They were night and day. Sound and silence. Darkness and light. So opposite were they in the way they thought and acted. It had been that way ever since Maria could remember. If she had even a fraction of Frieda's nerve and confidence she would simply have pulled the door open and looked out. As it was, that simple act took every ounce of her courage.

She pulled the door open a fraction, peering through the tiny gap out on to the landing.

There was no one there. Maria let out a deep sigh of relief and stepped back into the bedroom, closing the door quietly once more, before turning to the bed.

From near the window, the figure moved towards her.

174

Twenty-Three

Maria just about managed to stifle a scream as she saw the apparition before her, looming from the shadows of the bedroom.

The realisation hit her immediately and she let out a deep sigh, one hand held to her chest, where her heart was hammering against her ribs.

'Frieda!' she gasped, looking at her sister, who had just finished climbing through the bedroom window and was now moving towards the bed.

'Who were you expecting?' Frieda asked, unbuttoning her dress.

Maria crossed to the window and looked out. Not too far away she could hear the sound of horse's hooves. She looked accusingly at her sister.

'That's Uncle Gustav returning,' she said. 'You only just got back in time.'

'I know it's him,' Frieda told her. 'I saw him and his little friends as I was coming back through the forest. They didn't see me, though. I was too clever for them. Besides, who cares if he sees me?'

'You'll care if he catches you sneaking out like you did tonight.'

Frieda shook her head.

'I may leave here altogether soon,' she announced. 'Although in a way I like having our uncle as our protector.' She sat down at the dressing table. 'It makes me laugh that he's so trusting of us. He really is a fool. If only he knew.' She turned towards the mirror, but where her reflection should have been there was nothing. Just empty air. Frieda bent forward and began unbuttoning the buckles on her boots. Both of them were spattered with mud, and Maria saw it and frowned.

'Have you been through the forest?' she enquired.

'You know I have,' Frieda told her. 'How else could I get to the castle?'

'Frieda you must stop it,' she said. 'Uncle Gustav is bound to find out soon. I can't keep covering for you. I don't want to.'

Frieda pulled her boots off and dropped them contemptuously on to the floor of the bedroom as she stood up, kicking them aside with one bare foot.

'Ssshhh, you'll wake Aunt Katy,' Maria warned her.

'Or disturb dear Uncle Gustav?' Frieda echoed. 'He'd like to walk in now, wouldn't he?' As she spoke she pulled off her dress, which she also dropped unconcernedly on to the floor next to her boots. She stood there naked, the cool breeze from the window caressing her body. 'What do you think he'd do if he walked in and saw me like this?' Frieda breathed.

'He would punish us both,' Maria said, looking away.

'Punish us for wearing no clothes,' Frieda smiled crookedly. 'No, he would punish us for what he felt if he saw me like this.'

'What do you mean, Frieda?'

'Men like him have thoughts they can't control. I've told you before. Thoughts about young girls like us. He would want to look at us naked, to touch us.'

'Shut up, Frieda!'

'They say that he and his Brotherhood go out at night and hunt down young, pretty girls, who they accuse of witchcraft, and then they burn them. But why do you think they always look for young, pretty girls, Maria? I'll tell you why. Because they want to look at them. They want to touch them. Then they burn those girls because they hate them for the feelings they've aroused in them.'

Maria shook her head and climbed on to the bed, while Frieda stood smiling at her, still defiantly naked in the now chilly room.

'He talks to me and he thinks I'm you,' Maria said. 'He can't tell us apart, and he treats me badly because he thinks I'm you. It was only luck that he didn't find out you were gone today.'

'What do you mean?' Frieda snapped, moving nearer to the bed.

'At supper he wanted to know where you were, and I had to tell him you were ill with a headache. Then, when he demanded to see you, I had to pretend to be you.'

'And he fell for it?'

Maria nodded.

'He's more of a fool than I thought,' Frieda laughed.

'You should be grateful that he can't tell us apart,' Maria countered.

Frieda sat on the bed beside her sister and held her arm gently.

'My poor Maria,' she said, without the slightest conviction in her voice.

'It isn't fair,' Maria said. 'I think tomorrow you should pretend to be me, and if he beats you for being disrespectful, then you'll know what I have to put up with.'

'If he ever touches me I'll kill him,' Frieda snarled. She got to her feet again and wandered back towards the bedroom window, gazing out wistfully into the night.

'Frieda, what's happened to you?' Maria wanted to know. 'Ever since you went to Karnstein Castle you seem like a different person. What happened there?'

Frieda smiled.

'Tell me,' Maria insisted.

'Do you really want to know, Maria?' Frieda asked, without looking around. 'Do you really want to know the delights Count Karnstein introduced me to? The pleasure we shared?' She smiled. 'He showed me things I could never even have imagined. He gave me pleasure the way no other man ever has before.' She shivered. 'There were others there, too, but I was the one he wanted to please.' As she spoke she slid one hand along her slim thigh. 'The Castle is magnificent, Maria, and the Count is an amazing man. So much knowledge and power.' She smiled wistfully and exhaled deeply. 'And the kind of knowledge worth having, not the kind of useless ideas and principles dear Uncle Gustav lives by.' She turned her gaze towards the outline of Karnstein Castle.

Maria turned her back to her sister, tears trickling down her cheeks.

'I dreamed you were in trouble,' she whimpered. 'In pain.' She touched her neck. 'I wanted to help you.'

'I don't need your help, Maria,' Frieda assured her. 'Not any more.' She let out a long sigh of pleasure. 'Now I know the Count I have nothing to fear from anyone,' she breathed. 'No one can hurt me now.'

She turned briefly towards the dressing table, sneering in the direction of the mirror that showed no reflection of her naked body.

'I feel sorry for you, Maria,' Frieda murmured. 'Because you can never feel what I feel now.'

'Don't feel sorry for me,' Maria said, sharply. 'I just wish you were the way you used to be.'

Frieda smiled broadly.

'I'll never be like that again,' she panted. 'That Frieda is gone forever. And she'll never be coming back.'

Twenty-Four

The sunlight that flooded through the windows of the schoolroom looked capable of eradicating every dark and unwanted thought that Anton Hoffer had entertained the previous night.

How he wished that were true. Seated before the harpsichord, his fingers resting lightly on the keys, Anton gazed at the sheet music before him and tried to force those thoughts from his mind. Thoughts of Frieda and her uncle, and the other men who shamed his home village, but more particularly, thoughts of Lisa. Of the woman he had loved so deeply and consumingly. The one he now played for.

Anton always felt that when he was playing music it was somehow for his lost love. She had rejoiced in every aspect of music, and his continued devotion to it cheered him a little, because he imagined that if she could see or hear him, then she would know that their shared passion continued. But was she watching and listening from some celestial resting place or were his thoughts of an afterlife just fanciful? His beliefs in heaven and anything to do with God had been so severely tested by the death of his former love that he sometimes wondered if he would ever fully regain the strength of faith he had enjoyed before. How could a God that was good inflict such pain and suffering on such a wonderful creature? It was a question he had asked himself many times since her death, and one to which he still struggled to find a satisfactory answer.

He played a few more notes, then reached for the quill pen and scribbled them onto the paper. Anton played more notes and wrote those on the sheet as well. He went back to the beginning and played the composition from the opening bars.

The girls who were seated around the large wooden table in the centre of the room watched approvingly as Anton played the tune, his fingers flashing across the keys with a speed and grace not normally associated with a man of his imposing build. He seemed lost in what he had created, his eyes blank as he played, as if they were fixed on something that Frieda, Maria and the other girls in the room could not see.

Frieda smiled to herself as she watched Anton, her hand in front of her face to mask the expression. She also afforded herself a glance at Ingrid Hoffer, who was watching her brother intently as he played, a look of pride on her face. When Anton finished playing, Ingrid clapped first, the action echoed by the girls.

Anton nodded in acknowledgement, glancing at the table in the centre of the room, where the girls sat looking at him. He caught Frieda's eye for a moment, then began to play once more, much more softly.

'Get ready to go out now, girls,' Ingrid urged, watching as the pupils gathered up their coats and cloaks somewhat reluctantly. They filed towards the schoolroom door as Ingrid moved nearer to her brother, touching his shoulder as she did.

'It's a lovely song, Anton,' she said. 'We'll leave you to finish it in peace.'

He nodded and wrote two or three more notes on the sheet in front of him.

'Right, come on girls,' Ingrid continued, and the girls began to file out of the room, followed by the school-mistress. Anton watched them go, then got to his feet and crossed to the desk on the far side of the room, where he pulled an old book from one of the drawers and flipped it open to the page he sought. He was about to scribble some notes onto a piece of paper when Ingrid's voice once again cut through the stillness.

'Anton,' she said. 'A visitor for you.' She stepped aside, allowing that newcomer into the room.

Gustav Weil stood silhouetted in the doorway. He nodded curtly to Ingrid as she left, closing the door behind her.

'Gustav,' Anton said, getting to his feet. 'Won't you sit down?'

Weil declined the offer, but he did remove his leather gloves, then moved briskly towards the desk where Anton was. It was now the younger man saw that Weil was carrying a large leather-bound Bible under one arm. He laid the book on the desk before Anton, like some kind of calling card.

'You sent a letter to the elders of our Church,' Weil began. 'Complaining of my ungodly behaviour.'

'Yes,' Anton told him. 'I think your devotion to your beliefs sometimes goes too far.'

'How dare you?'

'I did it for the good of everyone in the village, Gustav.'

'How so?'

'You and your brotherhood act as if you have the right to terrorise anyone you wish. It cannot go on.'

'If we have the right, then it was given to us by God. We carry out His work. Do you question that?'

'I question your methods.'

Weil regarded Anton evenly.

'The elders of my church have written to me asking that I investigate whether you are a servant of the Devil,' he said, his voice soft but full of menace.

He turned and walked across the schoolroom, stopping at one of the many bookcases that were crammed with volumes of all ages and descriptions. Watched by Anton, Weil pulled a number from their places on the shelves, noting each title before replacing it.

'You read a great deal!' Weil exclaimed.

'Yes.'

'Books of black magic,' Weil said, holding one of the older tomes up before him. It was leather-bound with a pentagram on the cover. 'Vampires.'

'I study history, and superstition is a part of history.'

'Superstition?' Weil snapped, the tone and volume of his voice changing markedly. 'Do you not believe in the existence of the Devil?'

'I believe that wickedness exists in every man,' Anton conceded, 'and that sometimes men cannot control that wickedness, even if they wish to.'

'What rubbish!' Weil snapped. 'Every man has

control over his own feelings and urges. If a man feels he is falling prey to evil then he seeks help from God.'

'Not every man can do that, Gustav. Some need help. Some lack the strength.'

'The only strength anyone needs is that given by God. If a man asks, then he will be redeemed.'

'Some men are beyond redemption.'

Anton held Weil's gaze.

'Then tell me now,' the older man said, slowly. 'Do you believe in the existence of God?'

'Not in the cruel and vengeful being that you believe in, which must always take a life for a life,' Anton snapped. 'Is that what is taught in this book you set so much store by, Gustav?' He motioned to the Bible lying before him.

'You doubt the word of God now?' Weil hissed, moving back towards Anton and laying his hand on the cover of the Bible. 'You question the blessed book itself? The very word of God?'

Anton looked at him.

'Where in the Bible does it say that you must burn innocent young women?' he challenged.

'Burning purifies!' Weil shouted.

'Does it even purify the innocent, Gustav? As they burn before you, screaming for mercy, do you feel you have allowed them passage into heaven? Is that your mission?'

'My mission is to do God's work and if that means burning, then so be it! I will say it again: burning purifies!'

'Not if you know anything about vampires,' Anton said, quietly.

Weil regarded him warily for a moment, then he touched the cover of the Bible again, almost unconsciously.

'By burning you char the body,' Anton went on. 'But the soul can recreate itself in another body and continue with its carnage.'

'And how would you suggest we destroy a vampire, schoolmaster?' Weil asked.

'Only a stake through the heart or decapitation will end their torment of evil,' Anton told him. 'If vampires exist.'

'You know they exist,' Weil snarled.

'There are many things even men of learning do not understand,' said Anton.

'This village and the land all around it is tainted by them and has been for hundreds of years, you know that. You pretend to study the history of this area, then you would accept that. Ever since that abomination on the hillside was built vampires and their kind have plagued these parts, and they will continue to do so as long as it still stands.'

'You mean Karnstein Castle?'

'Of course. How many of its residents have been practitioners of the black arts? How many have given their souls to Satan to follow this cult you will not even acknowledge?'

'I will admit that several members of the Karnstein family have been killed over the years for their belief in and practice of what you call vampirism, Gustav.'

'Killed by right-minded, good, God-fearing people. Men who had the courage to stand against them.'

'Like you?' Anton asked, almost tauntingly.

'Who else is there?' Weil said, sternly.

'Is that what you intend to do to Count Karnstein?'

Weil was silent, his eyes now fixed beyond Anton, as if he were considering the question.

'I did not come here today to talk about Count Karnstein and his evil practices,' he said, finally. 'I came to see you and to tell you that if you ever interfere with the ways of the Brotherhood you will suffer.' He pulled on one of his gloves. 'Take care, Anton. For your own sake.' He slid his hand into the other gauntlet. 'And your sister's.'

'Don't threaten me, Gustav!' Anton hissed. 'And don't ever bring my sister into this. I'm warning you.'

Weil touched the peak of his hat and headed for the door.

Anton watched him go. The older man walked down the short flight of stone steps from the schoolhouse door, then into the square beyond. As he crossed it, Anton saw another black-clad man approach Weil and speak to him. He recognised the other man as Franz, the magistrate and another member of the Brotherhood.

Weil didn't seem interested in what his companion had to say and merely strode off across the square without exchanging a word with Franz, who looked on in bewilderment.

Anton watched Weil until he was out of sight, the anger building up within him.

He sat down at his desk and, as he did, he brought one fist down hard on to the wood. The sound reverberated around the silent classroom, motes of dust turning slowly in the beams of sunlight still filling the room.

Anton slid open one of the bottom drawers of his desk and looked in.

The dagger hidden there was six inches long, double-edged and razor sharp. Anton looked at it for a moment longer, then shut the drawer once more.

Twenty-Five

Katy Weil brushed the hair from her face and made her way wearily up the stairs.

It had taken her two hours so far to clean the house, polishing every wooden and metal surface until it gleamed. The washing had been done and was hanging outside to dry. That had accounted for another two hours of her time. When she had finished upstairs she would have to begin preparing dinner in readiness for the girls returning from school, and also for Gustav returning from whatever business he was engaged in. Exactly what that was she couldn't be sure and to be honest, she wasn't sure she wanted to know.

She had washed his clothes today, as she did every time they needed cleaning, but had found herself a little more perturbed by the dried blood she found on the cuffs of two of his shirts, and the soot and ash stains she had discovered on one of his jackets. She would not ask him where the stains came from. It was not her way. It never had been. She trusted him and she did not question him. That was how it was for women of her age, especially in villages like Karnstein. The men and women practically led separate lives, coming together only to eat, attend church and procreate.

That particular aspect of the marriage covenant had never been part of Katy's experience, even at the beginning of their marriage. The Church and religion had always been more important to Gustav, and she had accepted that, never wondering in those early days if she would one day come to wish she had borne children. Occasionally, she felt the loneliness more acutely, but that pain had been assuaged slightly since the girls arrived from Venice.

Thoughts of the twins brought memories of her dead sister, too. If not for that untimely death, then she would not now be the surrogate mother to the two girls. They would still be with their parents in Venice. Katy had never been allowed by Gustav to visit her sister while she was living there. He had always insisted that the city – and indeed, the whole country – was far too decadent and corrupt, and Katy had not seen fit to argue with him on such a matter. She had corresponded with her sister on a regular basis – sometimes secretly, when Gustav had insisted on reading the letters before they were sent. Despite her respect for her husband, Katy had felt that some things should remain private. She didn't like the word 'secret', because it implied something improper. 'Private' was far more acceptable a word to describe the letters she had written to her sister, before the other woman's untimely death.

Now Katy reached the door of the girl's room and entered. She gathered up a dropped blouse and folded it carefully, before returning it to its rightful place in the chest of drawers next to the dressing table. Frieda's, she was sure. She was the more careless of the two girls in every way. Nonetheless, Katy didn't want her to get into trouble when Gustav inspected the room later on, something he made a point of doing every single day to ensure the girls were keeping it tidy.

As Katy walked around the room she felt something crunch beneath her feet and looked down to see what it was.

She was surprised to see dried mud in several places, especially near the bed. As she ducked down to inspect the debris she caught sight of something beneath the bed and reached under to retrieve it.

Katy looked at the boot and realised that this was where the dirt had come from. Mud was caked hard on the footwear as high as the ankle. And yet, to Katy's knowledge, neither of the girls had been on ground that was likely to soil their boots so badly. The mud was greyish in colour, too, not like that in the village square. Then Katy realised that some of the matter sticking to the leather was not dried mud but dust.

She frowned, even more puzzled by her discovery. Where could the girls have acquired this kind of detritus? The small rusty stain near the highest buckle of the boot was unmistakeable.

It was dried blood.

Katy swallowed hard.

There was more of it on the instep of the other boot.

Katy put a hand to her mouth, her fingers quivering. Why was there blood on the boots of one of the girls? As she turned she caught sight of her own reflection in the mirror and saw the look of concern on the haggard face that stared back at her. She hurried downstairs and cleaned the boots thoroughly, sponging mud, dust and dried blood from them, before returning them to the girls' room.

She would say nothing to either of them, she promised herself. And she would certainly say nothing to Gustav.

Twenty-Six

Ingrid Hoffer looked on with a combination of pride and sadness as she watched Anton playing the harpsichord. His voice, so mellow and so accomplished, filled the room, the words he sang delivered with perfect diction and passion.

'*Come unto my great heart,*
For my heart and the sea and the heaven . . .'

He sang, apparently lost in the music and melody.

'*Are melting away with love.*'

He held the final note, then completed the song with several bars of instrumental work that Ingrid listened to almost enviously. When he finished, she placed her hand warmly on his shoulder.

'I think you inherited your musical skills from mother,' she told him.

'Mother played the violin,' Anton reminded her.

'It's still a musical instrument, isn't it?' she smiled.

Anton grinned and nodded, closing the lid of the harpsichord and getting to his feet.

'I'm sure you must be sending me away for some other reason than the one you've given me,' Ingrid insisted. 'Why the sudden concern for Aunt Heidi?'

'I'm worried about her. She must be ill or she would have written to us by now.'

'She's probably just forgotten. You know how she is sometimes.'

'I'd like to be sure. Anyway, a few days away will do you good.'

'But I'm all right,' Ingrid assured him. 'It's you who seems nervous and upset. Why don't *you* go and visit Aunt Heidi?'

'And you'll look after the school?' he said, raising his eyebrows.

'Why not? You say that as if I'm not capable.'

'I didn't say that at all. Besides, I can take the girls.'

'For crochet work?' Ingrid chuckled.

'For extra choir practice,' Anton insisted. 'Or extra history or anything else I teach them that you, dear sister, do not.'

Ingrid hesitated for a moment, then nodded almost reluctantly.

'All right, I'll go,' she said. 'If you want to get rid of me that badly I won't disappoint you. As long as you're going to be all right here alone. That is, if you are going to be alone, of course.'

'What's that supposed to mean?'

'I'm not stupid, Anton. I know why you want me away from here. You want to spend time alone with someone, don't you? And I think I know who it is.'

'I don't know what you're talking about,' Anton protested.

'Don't you?' Ingrid said, unconvinced. 'I'm talking about Frieda, Anton. I know how you feel about her. It's obvious. I can read you like a book. I've always been able to.'

'That's true,' he conceded. 'But I am worried about Aunt Heidi.'

Ingrid smiled.

'I've already told you I'll go,' she went on. 'You don't have to push me out of the house, Anton. I'll leave as soon as I'm packed.'

'I might even join you in a few days,' he told her.

Ingrid touched him gently on the shoulder.

'I won't raise my hopes too much,' she said, smiling.

The coach was due to arrive in Karnstein Village square at four p.m., but as Anton checked his pocket watch he saw that it was now closer to five.

'Where the devil is that coach?' he muttered, peering from the window of the school building.

'Are you really so anxious to be rid of me?' Ingrid said, standing beside her luggage near the doorway.

'It isn't that and you know it,' Anton smiled. 'I just don't like it when things are late. If a person or thing is supposed to arrive at a certain time, then they should keep to that.'

'I'm teasing you, Anton,' Ingrid reminded him.

He nodded and peered out of the window once more.

'Be careful,' she said. 'That's all I ask.'

Anton turned to face her.

'What do you mean?' he wanted to know.

'I know how you feel about Frieda. I know you're attracted to her, but if it's going to cause trouble with Gustav Weil then just forget about her, Anton.'

'Weil lives in the Dark Ages and I don't see why Frieda should have to suffer just because she's living with him.'

'He thinks he's doing good.'

'Oh, I realise that. He made that more than clear when we spoke the other day. But Gustav's definition of "good" differs rather dramatically from mine, and from most other people's too, I'd say.'

'But he has power here in this village, Anton. Where there is superstition and fear, men like him will always find allies. Be careful they do not target you as an enemy.'

'I think they already have, but I can deal with them. They don't frighten me.'

'Perhaps they should.'

Anton shook his head and looked out of the window once more. He saw the coach pulling in, the driver bringing the four great grey horses to a halt.

'Come on,' Anton said, smiling. 'The coach is here.'

He picked up Ingrid's luggage and carried it effortlessly out of the building and into the square as she walked briskly along beside him, avoiding the deeper muddy ruts in the ground caused by the passage of so many wheeled vehicles. As they approached the coach the driver touched the brim of his hat deferentially.

'You're late, driver,' Anton reminded him, gently.

'Sorry, sir,' the man replied. 'Some of the roads leading from Carlsbad were water-logged. A stream had burst its banks and flooded them.'

He helped Anton place Ingrid's luggage on the top of the coach, then he scrambled up and secured it with several thick straps to prevent it falling during the journey.

'Looks like you're the only passenger, ma'am,' the driver called down from the roof of the coach. 'Unless I have to pick anyone up in Langsdorf. That's the next stop.'

'I have a book to pass the time, thank you, driver,' Ingrid told him.

'Give my love to Aunt Heidi,' Anton said as Ingrid climbed up into the coach and closed the door behind her. She pulled back the velvet curtain at the window and looked out, offering her hand to her brother, who squeezed it and kissed it warmly.

'Remember what I said, Anton,' Ingrid insisted.

He nodded and stepped back as the driver cracked the whip to stir the horses into action.

'Next stop Langsdorf!' he shouted, then he guided the coach slowly out of the square and through the narrow street towards the road that would take them away from Karnstein. Ingrid waved for a few moments, then ducked back inside the coach.

Anton watched it until it was out of sight, then he headed back towards the school building, glancing up towards the sky as he did so. Banks of cloud were moving in from the east, blown by an increasingly strong breeze, and already the sun was sinking, falling almost reluctantly from the sky.

Another hour and it would be dark.

Twenty-Seven

The air smelled of pipe smoke and ale and it was an altogether pleasing aroma, Dietrich thought, as he sat in one of the high-backed wooden chairs near the fire, warming his hands before he took a large sup from the stein of ale he held in one podgy hand.

On the small table before him there was a plate of stew and he put down his drink, so that he could devote his full attention to the food he so badly craved. His stomach had been rumbling for the last hour and he had decided that the only way to satisfy that craving was with a large plate of stew cooked by the innkeeper's wife. She served an excellent rabbit or mutton stew and Dietrich was happy to be enjoying it once more. He shovelled several mouthfuls down, then followed them with some deep sups of ale, belching appreciatively as he sat back in his seat, looking into the flames of the fire before him.

Horse brasses and various other ornaments decorated the walls of the inn, and hanging from several of the exposed roof beams there were also small sprigs of a plant that he realised was garlic. Superstition was still rife in this part of the world and Dietrich knew only too well that the garlic was there to ward off vampires. He smiled to himself, wondering how truly successful the sprigs would be, should they ever be called on to meet such a threat. He feared that they would be better off in the next stew the innkeeper's wife prepared. More useful as flavouring than as a weapon against creatures of the night. He gobbled down several more mouthfuls of stew and rubbed his belly.

The innkeeper wandered around from behind his counter, crossed to the fire and dropped two or three more pieces of wood on to the blaze, ensuring that it continued to burn brightly, warming the inside of the building and his customers. He shot Dietrich a disdainful look as he passed him on the way back to the counter. The chubby man was undeterred and raised his stein in the air, signalling that he wanted more ale.

The innkeeper's wife ambled over, took the empty stein from him, then returned a moment later with a refill. He pushed some coins into her hand and set about downing the fresh ale. Dietrich was using some bread to mop up his plate when he heard the inn door open and the sound of three or four loud voices filled the place.

He looked around and saw that there were some villagers heading towards the bar. They closed the door behind them, speaking good-naturedly as they spotted friends among the other denizens of the inn. The leading man, a woodsman with huge arms and a ruddy complexion, ordered drinks for himself and his companions. Dietrich moved his chair back slightly from the fire, retreating into an alcove beside the stone fireplace.

The four newcomers, carrying their drinks, wandered over to the fire, all of them spotting Dietrich, who was still soaking up the last of the stew gravy with a hunk of bread.

'What are you doing here?' the first man grunted, warming his backside before the fire.

'This inn is for the people of Karnstein,' a second added.

'I have as much right here as any of you,' Dietrich told them, chewing noisily.

'Why aren't you up at the castle, serving your master?' the woodsman snapped.

'That is none of your business,' Dietrich told the man.

'What goes on at that castle is our business when it involves deaths in the valley,' the woodsman snarled. 'Deaths caused by your master, the Count.'

Dietrich thought it best to try and ignore the men who were glaring at him now.

'He and his family have caused nothing but suffering in this valley for years,' the woodsman went on.

'What goes on up there?' one of the others demanded. 'You must see. What kind of things does he get up to?'

'What my master does in the privacy of his own home is none of your business,' Dietrich said. 'And even if I knew I wouldn't tell you. If you're that interested why don't you go up to the castle and ask him?'

'Very funny,' the woodsman grunted. 'I will go nowhere near that place. No God-fearing man would.'

'I am sure the Count will be happy to hear that,' Dietrich chided. 'He is most particular about the company he keeps.'

'He cannot be that concerned or he would not have you anywhere near him,' another man snorted.

A chorus of laughter met this remark. Dietrich took a sup of his ale and tried to ignore them.

'Why are you so happy to serve Karnstein, knowing what kind of man he is?' another of the men interjected.

'My family have been in the employ of his for many years now,' Dietrich explained. 'I am merely fulfilling the same role my father and his father before him fulfilled. It is a matter of duty and service. What the Count wants I try to provide.'

'Does that include girls from the village?' the woodsman wanted to know, his face flushed with anger now.

Dietrich didn't answer.

'Girls have gone missing from here and from other villages roundabout,' the woodsman went on. 'My bet is some have ended up at Karnstein Castle.'

Other voices echoed their agreement.

'If that is the case, it is nothing to do with me,' Dietrich offered.

'And you expect us to believe that?' the woodsman told him. 'God alone knows what your master does with them up there. He is an animal.'

'You had best not let the Count hear you speaking like that or he will have you thrown off your land,' Dietrich reminded the man.

'My land?' the woodsman snapped. 'It has never been my land and it never will be. Everything around here belongs to your master. That's how he and his stinking family keep their power, because we are all homeless if we dare to oppose them. They would see us homeless, evicted from houses we built with our own hands.'

'Then perhaps you should show a little more gratitude,' Dietrich offered.

'For what?' the second man demanded. 'It is the Karnsteins who should be grateful to us. We should have burned that stinking castle to the ground years ago – and your master inside it.'

'Aye!' another man added, loudly. 'Burn him and the evil he stands for!'

'You sound like Gustav Weil, my friend,' Dietrich said, grinning. 'Perhaps you should join his little group.'

'Weil is no better than your master,' the woodsman told Dietrich. 'They are both a menace to this village in their own way, but at least Weil and the Brotherhood have the safety of this village at heart. Unlike your master, who merely preys upon those who live here.'

'If you have nothing interesting to say you would be better advised to keep your opinions to yourself.'

The woodsman took a step towards him, fury in his eyes.

'My opinion is that you are not welcome in this place,' he snarled. 'Perhaps I should throw you out now.'

'Don't touch me,' Dietrich said. 'You lay one hand on me and I'll have you before the magistrate.'

'And what do you think he will do to me?' the woodsman hissed. 'He will probably reward me for hitting you. Any man would.'

'Aye,' one of the other men echoed.

'I think you are right,' Dietrich said, wearily. 'It is time I was going. The company in here is becoming decidedly tiresome.'

Dietrich got to his feet.

'Yes, go, run to your master,' the woodsman hissed. 'Leave us alone and do not return. You are not welcome here and you are not wanted. You've been warned before.'

Dietrich picked up his stein of ale and downed what was left in one mighty swallow, then he slammed the receptacle back on to the table and belched loudly before reeling towards the door.

'Peasants,' he snorted derisorily. He slammed the door behind him and wandered out into the village square, the cold wind whipping around him. He pulled up the collar of his jacket and set off, glancing back with disdain in the direction of the inn. As he crossed the square he stepped in some horse dung, a legacy of the coach that had left a while earlier. Dietrich sighed wearily and wiped the worst of the excrement off against the stone wall of the fountain that formed a centrepiece to the square. Muttering under his breath, he set off once again.

The walk to the castle should take him less than thirty minutes.

Twenty-Eight

'Langsdorf! This stop, Langsdorf!'

Inside the coach, Ingrid Hoffer heard the driver call out as he brought the vehicle smoothly to a halt. She thought about glancing out of the window to see if anyone was waiting for the coach in this village, but decided that she would find out soon enough anyway. She glanced down at her book and waited.

Sure enough, the coach door opened and she looked up to see a young woman climb in. Ingrid nodded gracefully and the woman smiled warmly at her as she seated herself on the opposite side of the carriage.

'Hello,' she said, smiling brightly. She had blonde hair, fastened in a bun on top of her head and topped with a blue hat that matched the expensive-looking dress she wore.

'Good evening,' Ingrid responded.

They were joined a moment later by a man, who almost stumbled as he clambered into the coach. The young woman shot out a hand to help him and he grinned at her and also at Ingrid as he settled himself on the seat, lurching backwards again as the coach pulled away sharply.

'Do all coach drivers in these parts drive like this?' the man said, smiling.

'I'm afraid they do,' Ingrid told him. 'The roads don't help, either. They are not the best, I have to admit.'

'Better than some we have seen,' the man told her, and he extended his right hand towards Ingrid. 'My name is Harcourt,' he said. 'Gerald Harcourt. This is my wife, Marianne.' He gestured towards the young woman, who smiled once again.

'I still can't get used to hearing you say that,' she giggled. 'Wife. It sounds so strange.'

'You'd better get used to it, my dear,' Harcourt told her. 'With any luck you'll be hearing it for many years to come.'

Ingrid introduced herself and found that the warmth exuded by the young couple opposite her was infectious.

'We've been married only a week,' the young woman explained. 'I can't get used to Gerald calling me his wife.'

'So you're on your honeymoon?' Ingrid exclaimed. 'How romantic.'

They both nodded.

'We thought we'd come to this part of the world, as we'd heard it was very beautiful,' Harcourt told her. 'We're English, as you might have noticed from our accents.'

'How wonderful,' Ingrid said. 'I've always heard that England is a beautiful country, too.'

'It is,' Harcourt told her. 'But travel broadens the mind, they say, so we thought we'd travel for our honeymoon. We've already been through France and Switzerland.'

'And Italy,' his wife reminded him.

'And we're heading for Vienna, ultimately,' Harcourt added. 'Then it's back to England and married life.'

'I'm sure you'll both be very happy,' Ingrid stated.

'Do you live around here?' Marianne enquired.

'In a village called Karnstein,' Ingrid told her. 'I'm on my way to visit an aunt who lives in Kleinenburg.'

'Ah, a much needed holiday, is it?' Harcourt asked.

'No, I'm afraid not,' Ingrid told him. 'She's ill.'

'I'm sorry to hear that,' the young woman said.

'It's probably nothing serious,' Ingrid smiled. 'But my brother insisted I go. I think he just wants me out of the way, so he can have the house to himself for a few days. He values his privacy.'

They all laughed.

'We live and work together, so I can understand him wanting some time alone,' Ingrid continued.

'What do you do?' Harcourt enquired. 'If you don't mind me asking.'

'I teach,' Ingrid announced. 'My brother and I run a school for girls in Karnstein.'

'My father used to teach,' Harcourt explained. 'So I can understand the need for you to get away for a few days.'

'They can be trying sometimes,' Ingrid confessed, smiling. 'What about you? What do you do?'

'I'm a solicitor,' Harcourt told her. 'Marianne is a nurse.'

Ingrid nodded approvingly.

'Solicitors are thought of as boring men in England,' Marianne noted. 'Is that true here?'

'Are you trying to say I'm boring, my dear?' Harcourt asked, feigning indignation.

'I said that others think of them as boring, Gerald,' Marianne said. 'Not me.'

More laughter filled the coach.

'How long have you been a nurse?' Ingrid asked.

'Only two years,' Marianne told her. 'I work at a hospital in London.'

'We live in London,' Harcourt added. 'The firm of solicitors I work for has offices there.'

'I've always wanted to see London,' Ingrid told them. 'In fact, I'd like to travel around the world if I got the chance, but I don't suppose I ever shall.'

'You never know,' Harcourt told her. 'After all, I never thought I'd meet a woman like Marianne, but I did.' He squeezed her hand.

'It's very nice to see two people as much in love as you obviously are,' Ingrid said. 'But then again, if you've only just got married I suppose you should be.'

'I think that if you love someone, then that love lasts forever,' Marianne offered. 'Don't you?'

Ingrid nodded.

'I've never been married,' she admitted. 'Perhaps I just never found the right man.'

'Not everyone does,' Marianne shrugged. 'He's probably out there somewhere waiting for you.'

'Do you think so?' Ingrid grinned. 'I wonder what my brother would say if I told him that?'

'Are you close, you and your brother?' Harcourt asked.

'We always have been,' Ingrid nodded. 'He's always

been my best friend as well as my brother. If I have anything to confide I always tell him first. He's the same. My mother used to say we were like peas in a pod. Not when it comes to looks, you understand, but in our characters.'

'That's very nice,' Marianne added. 'My brother and I were never very close, I'm afraid. When he joined the army we just lost touch. I haven't seen him for two years.'

'I'm sorry to hear that,' Ingrid offered. 'Family is very important.'

They rode in silence for a time, nothing but the steady rumble of the horses' hooves to break the solitude, then Marianne spoke.

'I hope you won't think me rude,' she began. 'But as you live here perhaps you could answer a question for me.'

Ingrid smiled graciously and nodded.

'If I can,' she announced.

'Are the people in this part of the world very religious?' Marianne enquired. 'It's just that when we told someone earlier today that we'd be passing through this part of the country they said I would do well to have my crucifix with me.'

'An old lady even tried to give us a cross,' Harcourt added, smiling. 'She said we might need it for protection. What did she mean by that?'

Ingrid frowned.

'Religion is very important to people here,' she began. 'But I fear that superstition is an even more potent force.'

'What could she have meant about the cross being for protection?' Marianne continued.

Ingrid drew in a deep breath.

'Many of the people who live in these parts are uneducated,' she began. 'They are not stupid, but they've lived their whole lives here and grown up with the traditions and beliefs passed down to them from generations before. Some of those beliefs are . . .' she hesitated. 'Fanciful, let us say, for want of a better word. There is much fear of the unknown in these parts.'

'What do you mean?' Harcourt insisted. 'What are they afraid of?'

'Superstition is a powerful thing here, as I said,' Ingrid told him. 'You would find it difficult to understand.'

'We'll do our best to try,' Harcourt told her, smiling. 'What is it they fear so much?'

'Have you ever heard of vampires?' Ingrid asked.

'Creatures that come out at night and drink the blood of the living,' Harcourt said, trying to suppress a smile. 'I've heard stories.'

'Well those stories are very real to the people in this part of the world,' Ingrid informed him. 'I know it sounds stupid to people like you but, as I said, the power of superstition should never be underestimated. That was why the old woman offered you the cross as protection. Vampires are afraid of the cross – of anything to do with the church.'

Marianne shuddered involuntarily.

'They sleep in coffins during the day,' Harcourt added. 'They kill by biting the neck of the victim and sucking their blood – that's right, isn't it?'

'That's what people believe,' Ingrid confirmed.

'That's horrible,' Marianne murmured.

'It's just a myth,' Harcourt told her.

'Every myth has a basis in fact, they say,' Ingrid offered.

'That's very true,' Harcourt conceded. 'But in this case, surely your common sense as a teacher stops you from believing in such stories?'

Ingrid shrugged.

'Do you believe in vampires?' he wanted to know.

'It's impossible to grow up in these parts without being affected in some way by what one hears from birth, Mr Harcourt,' Ingrid explained. 'I suppose there is a part of me that believes. And fears. Do you think I'm stupid?'

'No,' Harcourt said. 'I can understand how these legends have grown up over the centuries. Ignorance and lack of education are bound to lead to odd beliefs and customs.'

'Are there no odd beliefs and customs in England?' Ingrid wanted to know.

'Plenty,' Harcourt smiled. 'But none as strange as vampires.'

'Why are they frightened of the cross?' Marianne wanted to know.

'Because it symbolises good,' Ingrid told her. 'It is God's symbol. The opposite of everything they stand for. They are evil, they abhor good.'

'A basic law of all beliefs,' Harcourt interjected. 'For everything good there must be a balancing force of evil and vice versa. No God without the Devil. No angels without demons. That kind of thing.'

Ingrid nodded.

'My brother would be able to tell you more about this subject than I can,' she said. 'He has made a study of it over the years.'

'And does he believe in vampires?' Harcourt wanted to know.

'You'd have to ask *him*,' Ingrid said.

'If you'd told me these stories about vampires, I'd never have left England,' Marianne interrupted, squeezing her husband's arm.

'Don't worry, my dear,' Harcourt reassured her. 'If any creature rises from the grave trying to drink your blood I'll protect you.'

Ingrid regarded him evenly for a moment.

'Are you staying in Kleinenburg tonight?' she enquired.

'No, we're travelling on,' Harcourt told her. 'We're being met there by another coach that will take us to our destination for tonight. A friend of mine in England said that we could stay with a colleague of his who lives just outside Kleinenburg. They studied together at university. He's a doctor. His name is Ravna. He and his family have a large house and we have been invited to stay with them. Perhaps I should ask him what he knows about vampires, too.'

Harcourt grinned broadly.

Ingrid was about to reply when the coach suddenly lurched to a halt. She leaned across and pulled back the small curtain, glancing out of the window.

'What now?' Harcourt grunted, sliding across to the window on the other side. 'What's happening, driver? Why have we stopped?'

'There's something blocking the road, sir,' the driver called back. 'I'll have to clear it before we can continue. Shouldn't be more than five minutes.'

Harcourt rolled his eyes.

'It's a good job we're not in a hurry,' he said, wearily, glancing at his pocket watch.

'Why don't you go and help him, Gerald?' Marianne offered.

'Good idea,' Harcourt acknowledged. 'Otherwise we might be stuck here all night.'

Outside, the horses whinnied.

Twenty-Nine

'What else did he say?'

Maria crossed the bedroom quickly and joined Frieda on the bed. The shadows were deep within the room that was lit just by the light of two candles, one of which burned on the small bedside table. Outside, darkness had a firm grip on the land and with it had come a biting wind and also the first spots of rain. There had been talk that day of another storm, but so far, other than the gathering of some thick and portentous clouds, this had not happened.

Both the girls were wearing their nightdresses, but even as she lay on the bed Frieda was pulling agitatedly at the neck of hers, as if trying to loosen it. Even clothing in the Weil household, she told herself, had the ability to constrict and stifle. She raised her legs behind her and rocked gently and unconcernedly back and forth as Maria joined her, her own tone agitated.

'Frieda, what else did Uncle Gustav say?' Maria insisted.

'I don't know, I didn't hear it all,' Frieda told her, flatly. 'Aunt Katy shut the door.'

'But what did you hear?'

'Something about everyone going on trial from now

on for complicity with the Devil, so that the whole village can see how just and lawful they are, I suppose.' She shook her head and sneered. 'He makes me sick with his orders and his beliefs. Who is he? Who are any of them to tell people how to behave?'

'But he didn't threaten Anton?'

'I'm not sure. He has some kind of grudge against him, but I don't know why.'

Maria looked worried and the expression wasn't lost on her sister.

'What do you care?' Frieda asked, scornfully. 'Are you in love with him?'

'Of course not,' said Maria, dismissively.

'It's nothing to be ashamed of if you are, Maria. It's quite normal to be attracted to men, you know.'

'Be quiet, Frieda.'

'Does he excite you? Do you think about him at night? Think about what he could be doing to you? How he could be touching you?'

'You're disgusting,' Maria protested. 'I don't think about him like that. I'm not in love with him.'

'The rest of the girls seem to be. I think some of them imagine what it would be like to have him in their beds.'

'Stop it, Frieda!'

'I don't think about him like that,' Frieda announced.

'You're too concerned with Count Karnstein,' Maria said, watching as her sister slid off the bed and crossed to the bedroom window. She looked out into the night, a slight smile on her lips.

'Frieda!' Maria called and, when her sister didn't answer she, too, swung herself off the bed and joined the other girl at the window. 'Frieda. You won't go out tonight will you? Please. I get so frightened.'

Frieda looked out into the darkness, then back at her sister. She reached forward and gently touched Maria's neck, brushing her fingers over the smooth flesh.

'I have to go,' she said, her tone softening momentarily.

'But why?' Maria demanded.

'If I stayed, I might . . . ,' Frieda allowed the sentence to trail off as she pulled her hand away from Maria's neck. 'Just leave me alone,' she snapped, the harshness returning to her voice.

Maria retreated a couple of paces, watching as Frieda crossed to the wardrobe and selected a long dress for herself. She pulled off her nightdress, slipped on the dress, then pushed her feet into a pair of boots. Maria watched as she fastened them.

'Don't worry about me,' Frieda said, turning towards the window. 'You lay here and think about Anton.' She laughed, but the sound was devoid of warmth and humour, filled instead with spite and malice. It echoed around the room like a warning.

Frieda swung herself out of the window and onto the roof of the porch with an almost feline grace. She jumped down and, as Maria watched from the window, Frieda ran in the direction of the woods that soon enveloped her.

As Frieda moved through the trees it was with effortless ease, as if she belonged in the forest. There was a sureness to her step which she hadn't felt that first night she had ventured out, and the sounds she heard around her among the foliage and brush didn't bother her. Nothing did any more, except the gnawing cramps in her belly. She had been experiencing them ever since night fell and now they were almost intolerable. Her mouth was dry and she was constantly licking her lips. It was a thirst unlike anything she had ever experienced before and she knew that it must be quenched.

She headed through the forest along the pathway that led towards Karnstein Castle. As the ground began to slope upwards more steeply Frieda moved towards a rocky outcrop that looked as if it had been cut into the hillside by hand. There was a clearly defined entrance hidden behind some bushes, which anyone passing would have missed had they not known it was there. Beyond this entrance lay the passageway that would take her upwards into the bowels of the castle itself. Over the years the passageway had been hewn through earth and stone by the slaves of the Karnstein family. Part sewer outlet and also makeshift exit from the monolith above. Frieda wrinkled her nose slightly as she approached the rocks. There was a trickle of fluid coming from it and the stench that rose from it was foul. A rat scurried away from her as she stepped through the reeking liquid and moved on into the passageway beyond.

The walls inside were freezing cold, the stone like ice. Above her water dripped from the roughly hewn ceiling and she could see several bats hanging there in the darkest parts. Frieda felt no fear now, only the overwhelming thirst that tormented her so badly.

She peered out of the stone passageway and saw that

she had a clear view of the pathway leading through the trees outside. She also noticed that there was a figure moving somewhat unsteadily along that pathway.

It was a man and, as he drew closer, Frieda could make out first his rotund shape and then his features. She smiled to herself. It was Dietrich. He looked drunk and she guessed that he'd been into the village and spent too much time at the inn, as was his usual habit on nights when he wasn't at the Count's beck and call. More than once he leaned against a tree for support and Frieda watched him intently, wondering if he was actually going to overbalance and fall before he reached her. She drew in a shallow breath, her lips parted, her mouth still maddeningly dry.

Dietrich came closer and, as he did, she stepped from inside the passage entrance, silhouetted there.

He saw her at once. She knew he had, because he raised one index finger and pointed at her a little shakily.

Frieda smiled and remained where she was until she saw Dietrich take two or three faltering steps towards her. He stumbled and, for a second she thought he was going to fall, but he continued on his way, his eyes fixed on her, or at least as fixed as they could be for a man who had consumed so much ale and brandy. He even managed a thin smile as he continued to advance, surprising himself by how straight he could walk under the influence of so much alcohol.

Frieda stepped back inside the tunnel, swallowed by the darkness within. The smell of excrement from the sewer outlet filled her nostrils, but she blocked it out, the gnawing in her belly growing more intense by the second, the desperate and all consuming thirst she felt almost out of control.

Dietrich stopped for a moment, swaying uncertainly on his pudgy legs. He had seen her, he knew he had. Standing there in that same diaphanous yellow dress he'd seen her in the first night she was at Karnstein Castle. He knew that he'd seen her standing at the entrance to the tunnel. She hadn't been an alcohol-induced apparition. Had she? Dietrich sucked in several deep breaths, as if that simple act alone would be enough to clear his head. He blew out his cheeks and remained on the pathway for a moment longer, then he advanced once again towards where he knew he had seen the girl standing.

He thought about calling her name as he reached the entrance to the tunnel but, if he was honest, he couldn't even remember it. Even without the huge volumes of drink he'd consumed that night, he told himself, he'd probably have had trouble recalling it, but through the liquor-induced fog his brain was currently clouded by he had enough trouble remembering his own name let alone hers. What he had remembered about her, though, was her striking good looks. Her long brown hair framing a gorgeous face and with such full lips. Dietrich could think of so many uses for those lips, but he knew a girl like her would never look at him twice. She only had eyes for Count Karnstein.

Dietrich stood in the entrance to the tunnel, supporting himself against the cold stone for a moment longer. The stench of excrement filled his nostrils, but he ignored it as best he could, even when he glanced down at the deep trench full of rancid water that ran through the tunnel. If he followed it he knew he would come to some roughly shaped steps, cut into the hillside itself and that following these would take him up into the grounds of Karnstein Castle. He had used this tunnel before, but usually in a more clear-headed state. Thoughts of the girl returned and filled his mind. Her brown hair and full breasts pushing so invitingly against the flimsy material of her dress. He had watched her for as long as he could the other night, enjoying the gentle heaving of those pert globes, watching more intently when he saw the unfettered nipples beneath grow stiff and strain against the material.

It had been all he could do to hide the erection he had sustained, something that he now felt once more as he thought of her. Whatever her name was. He smiled at his inability to recall and proceeded deeper into the tunnel, using his right hand to guide him and steady him. It was pitch-black inside the culvert and he could barely see a yard in front of him.

Where had the girl gone? She couldn't have disappeared into thin air, and she couldn't have reached the steps up ahead that quickly.

Dietrich moved deeper into the tunnel, almost slipping into the sewage at one point.

He cursed under his breath, wondering why he was following this girl whose name he could not remember.

He was still wondering when she hurtled out of the darkness at him and flung her arms around his neck.

Before he could react he felt a sharp pain in his neck

as she bit deeply into the flesh and veins. Frieda held him firmly as she tore his flesh open, blood spurting from the wounds, most of it erupting into her open and thirsting mouth. She closed her lips over the jetting fountains of blood and drank.

Dietrich struggled for a moment, then his body shuddered in her grasp.

Frieda stepped back, her mouth coated and dripping with his life fluid. Her fangs were covered in the crimson liquid and she watched as Dietrich's eyes rolled upwards in the sockets. He pitched forward, his body falling into the stream of sewage, his head smashing into a rock as he fell. There was very little blood from the gash the rock opened. Most of his life fluid had been drained or had escaped through the gaping tears in his throat.

Frieda looked down at his body as it floated in the sewage. For now at least, that ravening thirst was quenched.

For now.

There was a short path leading to the front door of Gustav Weil's house.

That was where the severed head of the deer was left.

The person who left it dumped the hacked-off appendage as close to the front door as they could get, so that blood from the torn neck had spattered not just the path but also the door and the brickwork around it. The head had been propped up on its stump, held in place by two thick branches, so that the open eyes were staring directly at the front door, as if keeping watch.

The note had been stuck to the fur between the dead animal's eyes.

The writing upon the bloodied paper was barely legible, the letters large and crudely formed, but they were still clear enough for Weil to understand them when he found the grisly offering.

The message was simple. It read:

You die next

Thirty

Maria stood before the largest of the bookcases that dominated the schoolroom, her eyes moving back and forth over the titles. She ran one index finger over the spines of the books, occasionally stopping to pull one of the older tomes free.

'What are you looking for?'

The voice beside her startled her and she turned to see one of the other girls standing there.

'Anton was showing me a book about the history of Karnstein and I wanted to look at it again,' Maria said, smiling at the girl, who didn't return the gesture.

'Are you trying to impress him?' the girl wanted to know, eyeing Maria dismissively.

'No. I just find history interesting and I want to learn about the village and what's happened here,' Maria told her, running appraising eyes over the girl, who flicked at her own long brown hair as she spoke.

'It's your sister that he's interested in,' the girl said, spitefully. 'You must have seen the way he looks at her. Most of us can't tell the difference between you, but Anton seems able to. And it's your sister he's always staring at.'

Maria looked a little disconsolate and pushed the book back on to the shelf.

'That's your opinion,' she said, selecting a different volume.

Another girl joined them, a tall raven-haired girl dressed in a deep blue dress.

'Maria – or is it Frieda? – here is looking for a book of love spells, so she can enchant Anton,' the brown-haired girl said. Both of the girls laughed.

'Leave me alone,' Maria said, turning her back on them.

'You came here from Venice didn't you?' the raven-haired girl said. 'I suppose you think you're better than us. Better than the simple village girls, is that it?'

'I haven't thought about it,' Maria told her. 'Just because my sister and I were brought up in a city in another country it doesn't make me think I'm better than anyone else.'

'Were your family rich?' the brown-haired girl asked.

'No,' Maria said, defensively.

'But you lived in a big house, didn't you?' the girl went on. 'The one that burned down with your parents in it.' The girls laughed again.

'How do you know about me?' Maria asked.

'Word travels quickly in a small village like this,' the raven-haired girl told her. 'We know all about you and your sister.'

'You know nothing.'

The raven-haired girl turned to see Frieda standing beside her, her face set in firm lines. She glared at both girls in turn.

'Why are you bothering my sister?' Frieda snapped. 'Keep away from her! Keep away from both of us! I heard what you said to Maria. Yes, our parents' house burnt down.' Frieda took a step towards the girl. 'You'd better be careful what you say or your house might burn down, too.'

The girl backed off slightly.

'You make me sick!' Frieda hissed. 'You people understand nothing! Small villages make you small-minded. You two are proof of that. What other little stories have people been spreading about us?'

The two girls merely looked at her.

'Tell me,' Frieda insisted, angrily.

'Anton wants you,' the brown-haired girl said. 'Everyone can see it.'

'Do you blame him?' Frieda said, smiling. 'What is there in this stinking village for him to desire? Not you or any of your friends.'

'Did you learn your rudeness in Venice?' the raven-haired girl said.

'I learned it from stupid little girls like you,' Frieda said. 'And I learned how to deal with girls like you.' Again she moved menacingly towards them. 'And if you continue to bother me or my sister you'll find out what happens to girls like you.' She jabbed an index finger into the chest of the raven-haired girl. 'You've been warned.'

The schoolroom door swung open and the clapping of hands interrupted the exchange. Every head in the room turned in the direction of the sound.

Anton closed the door behind him and nodded a greeting to his pupils.

'All of you take your seats,' he said, moving to the head of the table.

The girls did as they were asked, and when all of them were in position around the table, Anton smiled.

'I regret my sister cannot be present this morning,' he began. 'An aunt of ours in the next village has been taken ill. However, I hope she will be back this afternoon. In the meantime I shall be taking her classes.'

Some of the girls laughed quietly.

Anton nodded and held up his hands for silence once again.

'I realise I am not really competent to instruct you in the art of needlecraft,' he admitted, and again the girls laughed. 'So, we shall be having extra choir work instead.'

'Sir, can we have your song?' one of the girls asked.

'Well,' Anton said, hesitantly. 'I don't know about that.'

'Please,' another girl insisted.

'All right,' said Anton.

'Is it a hymn, sir?' another girl enquired. 'My father only allows us to sing hymns.'

'Why?' Frieda asked, looking contemptuously at her. 'Does he think it will take you nearer to God?' She smiled, mockingly.

'He says that music should be used to praise the Lord,' the girl explained. 'Not for trivial reasons.'

'Well, my song is a kind of hymn,' Anton offered.

'Perhaps you'd better get your father to come and

listen,' Frieda said to the girl. 'He might not approve of the song and try to punish us all.'

'Like your uncle?' the raven-haired girl hissed. 'At least our fathers don't go around torturing young girls.'

'How do you know what your fathers do when they leave your houses?' Frieda challenged.

Anton held up his hands.

'Now, now, girls,' he said. 'We'll have less of this please. You're here to learn, not to bicker and argue. If your parents could see this they'd demand that I was replaced with a new schoolmaster.'

'I don't think some of the girls here would like that, sir,' Frieda told him. 'If that happened, they'd have to find someone else to think about when they were alone in their beds at night.'

Frieda's words hung in the air like a bad smell and a number of the other girls around the table lowered their gazes, unable to look at their teacher for a moment.

Anton sucked in a deep breath and turned towards the harpsichord behind him.

'Come now, girls,' he said, hoping to change the subject as rapidly as possible. 'Gather round and we'll try to get something done, otherwise we'll all be in trouble. You'll be in trouble with your parents and I'll be in trouble with my sister for not teaching you properly while she's away. She'll think me incompetent and she won't let me teach any of you again.'

The girls laughed and moved from the table to form a semi-circle around the harpsichord where Anton was now seated. He lifted the lid on the keys and began playing, the sound filling the room.

'What's the song called, sir?' one of the girls wanted to know.

'It's called "True Love",' Anton informed her.

Maria looked on admiringly, watching his fingers move so expertly across the keys.

'I'll play the song through once or twice, so you can all get used to the melody,' Anton told them. 'Then we'll try the words.' All around him the girls nodded their agreement as he began playing once again. The sound filled the room and Anton was momentarily lost in the sheer pleasure of playing the music that he had created. He finished with a flourish and smiled broadly when the girls applauded his efforts.

'You're very clever, sir,' one of the girls said. 'Very talented.'

Anton smiled and shook his head.

'Let's see how talented you are now,' he began. 'Mary and Caroline, would you sing the two leading parts of the song please?'

The two girls he had indicated nodded and both cleared their throats as Anton began to play the song's introduction once more, again lost in the mellifluous sound. When it came time for the girls' vocal participation he pointed and they sang, their voices filling the room.

'If there is somewhere in this world,
Somewhere dreams can be fulfilled.'

Maria smiled happily as she listened to the song, glancing at the girls who were singing back to Anton.

'Where the sky's full of golden light,
And there is no fear of endless night.'

Frieda looked at her sister and then at the faces of the other girls gathered around the harpsichord, each one of them seemingly mesmerised by the sight of Anton and the sound of the song. She rolled her eyes, disdainful of their slavish interest.

'*Only in the arms of true love,*
Only in the warmth of your love,
Stay here by my side and somewhere
We will find true love.'

Anton brought the song to an end and smiled appreciatively as the girls applauded.

'Well done, Mary and Caroline,' he said. 'That was beautifully sung.'

The two girls he had picked out blushed as he smiled at them. Anton had forgotten how much pleasure it gave him to share his music with others and he was gladdened by the girls' reaction to his latest composition.

However, his mood was shattered seconds later as the schoolroom door was flung open. The heavy partition crashed back against the wall and all eyes turned to see who had entered.

Gustav Weil strode into the room.

Maria looked warily at Frieda, who merely squeezed her sister's hand reassuringly.

'So, schoolmaster!' Weil snapped, pointing an accusatory finger at Anton. 'You do not believe in the Devil?'

Anton leapt to his feet angrily to confront the intruder.

'What is the meaning of this?' he rasped. 'I demand an explanation!'

Weil stood in the centre of the room and everyone else saw him snap his fingers, beckoning others in from the hallway. Anton was horrified to see that four black-clad members of the Brotherhood were now pushing their way into the room, carrying a stretcher. There was a blanket draped over whatever lay upon it, but its shape and outline instantly marked it out as a body.

'Gustav, what kind of charade is this?' Anton demanded, his rage now growing almost uncontrollable.

'No charade,' Weil told him. 'A victim of the vampires you scorn. Found this morning.'

The four members of the Brotherhood moved into the centre of the room and gently placed the stretcher on the floor, before stepping back.

'This is a schoolroom, not a burial chamber,' Anton went on. 'You are disgusting! Barbaric, all of you!' He took a step towards Weil and the other men. 'Now get out!'

Weil stood his ground.

'These girls are all our kin,' he said, pointing at the young women gathered nervously around the harpsichord. 'We leave to you the training of their voices, but we teach them the path to God and the byways of the Devil.'

'You teach them fear and superstition,' Anton snapped. 'Now take that thing,' he gestured towards the body beneath the blanket. 'And get out of here, all of you!'

'Not before these girls have seen the work of the Devil, schoolmaster,' Weil snapped. 'They must know the kind of evil that pollutes this land. They must see it.'

Weil knelt down beside the body and gripped the corner of the blanket, preparing to pull it free.

'No! I forbid it!' Anton said angrily, grabbing Weil's wrist to restrain him.

'Let them all see!' the older man insisted. 'Learn your lesson, choirmaster!' Weil pulled the blanket away, exposing the body beneath.

Several of the girls in the room, including Maria, screamed. Frieda merely smiled faintly, concealing the action with one hand.

Anton gaped at the body, his mouth open wide and his breath coming in gasps. He shook his head as he stared down at the corpse.

There were two large wounds on the neck, still clogged with congealed blood, more of which was smeared over the cold white flesh of the face and throat. The expression on the stiff features was one of terror and pain, but it was not that which transfixed Anton.

Lying on the stretcher was the body of his sister, Ingrid.

Thirty-One

Gustav Weil stood behind the long wooden table in the high-ceilinged room and crossed his arms over his chest.

Beside him Franz also stood, both men looking out into the mass of other Brotherhood members who were standing on the tiered benches inside the room, their fists raised.

Weil glanced at Franz and nodded, a signal of approval as the other men in the room chanted in unison, their voices merging together into a deafening chorus.

'And prophets and then wise men and then scribes!' they called vehemently. 'And some of them he shall kill!'

The chanting went on, the words well known to all the members of the Brotherhood, they spoke them so often. Weil looked at the faces of those before him and was pleased to see such fervour mirrored there. Franz, too, nodded as his companions continued their litany.

'Where is Hermann tonight?' he asked, leaning closer to Weil.

'He said he had business to attend to,' Weil replied, his gaze still on the other puritans. 'He will join us soon.'

Franz nodded in acknowledgement.

The chanting went on.

Whether the horse was lame or not Hermann couldn't tell. In the darkness of the night and on such a narrow and unlit path he could not be sure why the creature had pulled up so suddenly. He had examined its forelegs as best he could and found no damage. It hadn't thrown a shoe and there didn't appear to be any damage to the limbs, yet the animal was still limping. He wondered if there was a stone stuck in one of its hooves, but due to the gloom it was impossible to carry out a satisfactory examination now. Besides, he reasoned, he was only a few hundred yards from his destination. The horse could be walked the remainder of the distance and one of the other members of the Brotherhood could inspect it after the meeting. There were at least two men he knew of among their ranks who worked with horses during the day. One a farrier, the other a farmer. Either of them should be able to help both him and his mount.

When he squinted through the blackness he could see the Brotherhood's meeting house up ahead through the gaps in the trees. Even from this distance he could hear the horses of the other members neighing or snorting from where they were tethered outside the building. Hermann patted his own mount's neck and pulled gently on the reins to coax it along the pathway.

It was cold and Hermann shivered, anxious to be inside the meeting house and out of the chill. He walked on, holding the reins more tightly, when the horse began to toss its head agitatedly.

'What's the matter?' Hermann said, patting the animal once again.

The horse neighed and twisted its head once more, its nostrils flaring.

'Smelled a fox or something have you?' Hermann went on.

The horse stopped momentarily and began pawing the ground, seemingly reluctant to go any further along the pathway. Hermann tugged on the reins, but still the animal stubbornly refused to advance.

'Come on, damn you!' Hermann snapped. 'What's frightening you?'

The horse suddenly reared violently, both its front legs flailing, and Hermann had to move quickly to avoid contact with the hooves. The animal bucked wildly and shook its head, its mane flying. Hermann held its reins and glanced around into the night, wondering if something bigger than a fox might have frightened his mount. It wasn't unknown for wolves and even bears to come down from the hills and mountains at certain times of the year in search of food, and he felt a twinge of fear as he considered the prospect of being confronted by such a predator. The horse had scented something – that seemed certain. Hermann decided his best option was to reach the meeting house as quickly as possible. He jerked the horse's reins again and slipped one hand through its bridle as well, tugging hard enough to persuade the animal to advance, even though it did so reluctantly and it whickered loudly as it moved along the pathway.

Hermann glanced to his left and right, glad he was

within a hundred yards or so of his destination. He patted the horse's neck once more in an effort to calm it and slid one hand to his saddle to touch the saddlebag that hung there. He had a loaded pistol inside and he was beginning to wonder whether or not he might have to use it. Whether the one-ounce lead ball the pistol fired would be enough to stop a wolf or a bear was open to question, but just knowing he had the firearm with him emboldened Hermann a little more. He made the horse move on, reluctantly.

Something flashed by on his right.

Hermann shot out a hand to grab the pistol from his saddlebag, but the horse reared again and he missed the leather flap, stepping back and almost overbalancing. The horse whinnied loudly and, despite its apparent lameness, it turned and bolted back down the pathway, disappearing into the darkness, swallowed by the dense trees.

For a second Hermann thought about going after it, but then he narrowed his eyes, squinting through the gloom, and he was able to make out the shape in the trees more clearly.

It wasn't an animal. He could see that now. The look of fear on his face slipped away to be replaced by one of puzzlement. He moved off the pathway slightly, one hand extended towards the figure he now recognised.

It was one of Gustav Weil's nieces – of that much he was certain of. Which one? He couldn't tell, but it was unmistakeably one of the twins. Hermann moved nearer.

'Child, you should not be out so late,' he said. 'Your uncle will be very angry.'

Frieda saw him approaching and hesitated for a moment, her eyes darting around in the gloom to ensure he was alone. When she saw that he was she advanced towards him.

'Maria?' he said. 'Or is it Frieda?'

Frieda didn't answer, she merely put her hands up to his shoulders, then snaked them around his neck and pulled him to her. Hermann was surprised by the action, but he embraced her almost despite himself. Frieda pressed herself closer and Hermann looked down at her, his gaze coming to rest on her cleavage.

'I will protect you, child,' he said, quietly, still holding her. 'But you should not be out here in the forest at night. There are dangers.'

'I know,' Frieda told him. 'Just hold me.'

Hermann did as she asked, feeling her breath against his neck as he stroked her long brown hair.

Even above the tumultuous sound of their own chanting, every member of the Brotherhood in the meeting house heard the scream.

As one they froze, voices dying away quickly. The scream seemed to reverberate not just inside the building, but also within the forest itself. A keening yell of fear and pain that tore through the night.

Franz shot Weil a glance and they were already heading for the door of the building, hurrying after several other Brotherhood members who had burst out into the darkness, having snatched burning torches from the walls to light their way. They dashed out into the enveloping night, looking in all directions for the source of the scream and the poor soul who might have uttered it.

'There!' shouted one of the black-clad men, and he and a companion dashed off towards the pathway that snaked through the forest, running past the tethered horses that were tossing their heads in distress.

'Oh my God!' another of the Brotherhood gasped as he saw the scene before him.

Hermann was slumped on the ground with his back to a tree, the trunk the only thing holding him up. The figure that crouched beside him had a hand gripping his jacket and as the first of the puritans drew nearer he saw that the crouching figure was a young woman. As she turned he saw the blood that was splattered across her mouth and chin. There was more of the crimson fluid spouting from two savage wounds in Hermann's throat. His eyes were bulging wide in their sockets, but it was obvious even from a distance that he was dead. Muscular spasms caused his hands and legs to twitch periodically, but the movements were involuntary. Such was the savagery of the gashes to his throat it looked as if his head had almost been severed. It flopped uselessly to one side, the gaping wounds opening and closing like the gills of a fish as more blood poured from them and splashed down the front of Hermann's tunic.

'No!' the leading puritan gasped and he dug a hand inside his jacket, pulling free a silver cross, which he held before him.

Frieda raised a hand to shield herself as she saw the cross, snarling and showing her bloodied fangs when another Brotherhood member also held a cross before her, the silver shining in the light of the glowing torches.

Like a cornered animal she hissed and rasped at the men, trying not to look at the crosses they brandished, but seemingly helpless to avoid gazing at them. As she roared her defiance, droplets of blood sprayed in all directions, some of it spattering the face of the leading puritan, who backed off in disgust and rage, but held the cross before him knowing the debilitating effect it was having on Frieda.

Franz had joined his two companions by now and he, too, held his own crucifix before him, looking down at the snarling figure in front of them. Frieda opened her mouth wide like a snake preparing to strike, but she could get no closer to the men while they held the crosses.

Behind Franz, Gustav Weil strode forward and Frieda covered her eyes with one arm and ran towards him, sprawling at his feet.

'Uncle!' she wailed. 'Save me! It was terrible! We were attacked by vampires! I only just escaped!'

As she lifted up her head to look at him Weil saw the blood on her mouth and chin.

He grabbed her hair and yanked her upright, disgust on his face as he glared down at her.

'There is blood on your lips!' he told her.

Frieda put a hand to her face and gently ran her fingers through the thick crimson fluid that was there. She held her shaking hand before her as she looked at Hermann's blood.

'It came from a vampire!' she insisted. 'He tried to kiss me! Uncle, please! You've got to believe me!'

Still gripping Frieda's hair in one gloved hand, Weil reached inside his jacket and pulled out his own silver cross. He thrust it towards Frieda, his face contorted with rage.

She snarled and tried to pull her head away when she saw the cross, but Weil held her by the hair, forcing her to look upon the holy symbol.

'Look at it, you spawn of Hell!' he snarled. 'Look at the symbol of your enemy! The mark of your destroyer!'

The other members of the Brotherhood advanced around her, each of them brandishing crosses in her direction.

Frieda whimpered helplessly, blood still covering her mouth and face. Weil dragged her to her feet by her hair, then flung her to the ground, standing over her, as if preparing to drive his boot into her face. He looked up at the black heavens, his head tipped back and his voice tinged with despair.

'The Devil has sent me twins of evil!' he roared. Then he turned to the men nearest him. 'Take her to the gaol! Get this filth out of my sight!'

They dragged her towards their horses and two of them strapped her to the saddle of one, ensuring that she could not move. Frieda looked furiously at each of them, but there was only disgust in the expressions that met her probing stares. Led by half a dozen of the Brotherhood and flanked by more, the little procession set off towards the village.

Had they known they were being watched, there was little any of them could have done about it.

He stood in the shadows and became a part of the umbra. Invisible and secreted by it. Joachim stood behind a tree, watching as Frieda was captured, but he made no move to help. There were too many of the black-clad men. He could do nothing alone. Not now. Not yet.

Comfortable in the blackness, he moved away swiftly.

There were things he must do.

Thirty-Two

Anton Hoffer stood beside the coffin, his eyes fixed on the body of his sister.

He reached out slowly and with great tenderness and delicacy he touched her left cheek.

'I'm sorry,' he murmured under his breath. 'If I'd believed. If I'd have recognised that some superstitions are more than just the workings of ignorant minds, then perhaps you'd be alive now.'

Despite himself, Anton moved his hand from Ingrid's cheek to the high lace ruff of her dress. It finished just below her chin, but it was what lay beneath the material that Anton needed to look at. He gently moved the lace, pulling it down carefully until he exposed the two wounds on his sister's neck. They still looked red and angry against the paleness of her skin, and Anton stared at them for interminable moments, his mind spinning.

Had she felt pain when she'd been attacked? Had it taken her long to die? The questions tumbled through his mind uncontrollably. He felt tears forming in his eyes and let out a deep, almost painful breath.

Vampires. Even the word seemed to belong to another age and time, a less enlightened era. But then, Anton told himself, what was so different about Karnstein and most of its residents? Enlightenment of a spiritual, religious or artistic nature seemed to have bypassed most of the inhabitants of this small corner of the world. They knew only superstition and fear. It governed their lives and was alleviated only by their beliefs in a forgiving God and the promise of a reward beyond the grave in heaven. Anton knew that Ingrid had held stronger religious beliefs than he and, for her sake and the sake of her soul (if such a thing existed), he prayed that she was now at peace somewhere beyond. It would be words of that kind that the priest would intone over her grave when they buried her. He would speak of God and Satan and good and evil, and Anton would listen with the same grinding contempt he always reserved for men of the cloth and their bigoted beliefs.

But perhaps they were better than him, he reasoned. Perhaps even men like Gustav Weil were better than he was, because they had something to look forward to. Death held no fear for them, because they were convinced they were going to a better place. Anton couldn't help but think that anything was better than the life many were forced to live while on earth. Perhaps when he thought about it in those terms it wasn't difficult to see why so many sought solace in religion.

He knew Ingrid had prayed every night before she retired to bed, and he knew that some of those prayers were for their dead parents. If there was a God and he did rule a place called heaven, then Anton tried to find comfort in the fact that Ingrid would be with him now. In a better place, perhaps with their parents. Perhaps with Lisa, too.

The only two women he had ever needed in his life had both been taken from him, and now, for the second time, he stood looking down at a coffin that contained the body of someone he loved. Both he and Ingrid had been too young to perform a vigil such as this at the side of their parents, and for that he was grateful. He had enough memories of death and loss already to last him a lifetime.

There would be many at Ingrid's funeral, of that he had no doubt. She was well liked and respected within the village and its neighbouring hamlets. She had always been a very easy woman to like. Quick to smile and always ready with a kind word or deed.

Why had she died this way? Would a God who was good inflict this kind of death upon one so faultless and undeserving of such an end? But if a man like Gustav Weil was to be believed, then God had nothing to do with what had happened to Ingrid. Not God, but his sworn enemy the Devil and those who served him.

Anton shook his head. Even now, looking down at his dead sister, staring at the wounds on her throat that could only have been inflicted by a vampire, he still found it hard to accept. Creatures who hunted the living by night to feed on their blood and who could only be destroyed by decapitation or the act of driving a stake through their hearts. No wonder they had been the stuff of nightmares for so many years. And one of these vile creatures had killed his sister. Torn open her veins and sucked the blood from them, drained her body until she had died.

Anton clenched his fists and turned away.

He walked to the door of the bedroom and paused there for a moment, his back to the coffin. Tears trickled down both his cheeks, but he made no attempt to brush them away.

'I'm sorry, Ingrid,' he whispered. 'Forgive me.'

He stepped out of the room, paused a moment, then locked it behind him.

Thirty-Three

For what seemed like an eternity, Gustav Weil stared at the flickering flame of the candle as it burned before him.

He slowly rolled up both sleeves of his shirt, glancing down at his forearms as he did so. For a man of his age he still had fairly well defined muscles in that area. There was power in those arms and he thanked God for that much. Strength would be needed in the days to come, he thought, both physical and mental strength, and he felt that he would have to be the one to exhibit that psychological readiness. Others looked to him for how to behave and he revelled in that role. He didn't find leadership a burden but a blessing that God had given him. One among many.

Weil reached towards the back of the chair nearest to him and picked up his belt, hefting the thick leather strap before him. He pulled it through his hand and nodded, satisfied with its weight and strength. Sucking in a deep breath he got to his feet. As he reached the bottom of the stairs he heard a familiar voice.

'No!'

Weil looked up to see his wife standing before him, three or four steps above.

'I won't let you go near that child!' Katy said, a note of desperation in her voice.

'You know what must be done,' Weil said, evenly.

'Frieda, yes,' Katy went on. 'I can believe anything of her. A lot has happened that you don't know about.'

'It might have been better if I had known. Why did you keep things from me?'

'I know what you're like, Gustav. I know you mean well, but there are limits.'

'After all these years of marriage you choose now to judge me?'

'I am not judging you. I am trying to make you understand.'

'I understand only too well what is happening in this village, even in this house. That is why I must take the action I now take. Had you told me everything from the beginning I may well have been able to change things.' He flexed the belt in his hands once more and put his foot on the first step.

'And now what?' Katy said, angrily.

'I will deal with the situation,' Weil said, evenly.

'Violence isn't always the answer, Gustav. Why do you need your belt? So you can beat the Devil out of her?' Katy protested.

Weil climbed another couple of steps, but Katy stepped in front of him. He looked her in the eye, holding her gaze.

'Yes,' he said, softly.

'Have you ever thought that you might have helped to beat the Devil *into* her?' Katy countered.

Weil continued to hold his wife in that penetrating

gaze, but this time she did not flinch or retreat from it.

'The young must be chastised,' he said.

'I will not let you touch Maria!' Katy told him, tears welling up in her eyes. 'Please, Gustav, consider what you are doing. What you are about to do.'

'What I am about to do is necessary.'

'You say that everyone is entitled to a fair hearing and yet you condemn Maria without giving her a chance. You would punish her before you even know if she deserves that punishment.'

Weil hesitated a moment.

'The Brotherhood will want to see her,' he said, quietly.

'Then let them see her now, asleep,' Katy told him.

He looked puzzled for a moment.

'Asleep?' he murmured.

'Yes, and clasping the holy cross to her breast. And you'd call her a daughter of the Devil.'

The words hung in the air.

'Asleep,' Weil said again under his breath.

'I asked the apothecary to give her a potion to calm her,' Katy continued. 'The way you appeared, ranting and raving, I was fearful for her state of mind.'

'Woman, in what state of mind do you think *I* was?' Weil snapped.

'Truly, I cannot imagine,' Katy told him. Still she stood her ground, surprised when Weil turned slowly and headed back into the room. He ran a hand through his hair, his head bowed.

'I have always tried to be a good man,' he said, quietly, his tone almost apologetic.

'Yes, you've tried and I have always respected you for that,' Katy told him, descending the steps and standing on the other side of the table from him.

'Respected, not loved?' Weil asked, a slight smile on his face.

Katy didn't answer.

'You have to understand what is happening in this village,' he told her. 'The evil grows stronger every day and steps must be taken to stop it. I act not just for my own sake, but for everyone who would live a peaceful and godly life.'

'And Frieda? What will become of her?'

Weil exhaled wearily.

'There is no denying what she has become,' he said, quietly.

'A vampire?'

Weil nodded.

'I saw her with my own eyes,' he said. 'Her mouth still stained with the blood she now needs to survive. I saw her recoil from the sight of the blessed cross. I saw what she had done to Hermann. His throat had been ripped open as if by some wild beast. She is not the girl who arrived here. What we see now is but a shell that houses the most obscene evil and it is an evil that will spread even further if something isn't done.' He glanced at the belt he still held, then suddenly hurled it to one side.

'Can nothing be done for her?' Katy asked. 'The spirit exorcised?'

Weil pulled his cloak from the back of another chair and wrapped it around himself, then he reached for his hat and fitted it carefully on his head.

252

'The Brotherhood will decide,' he said, flatly.

'Gustav!' Katy called as he headed towards the door. 'This isn't just some peasant girl whose fate you and your friends are deciding. This is my niece. My flesh and blood!'

'Not any more. I told you that. She is not the girl who arrived here in Karnstein. The girl locked up in the gaol is a creature of the Devil, no matter what her outward appearance. There is nothing human inside her to save.'

'So you will burn her?'

Weil hesitated beside the open door, his back to Katy.

'Gustav?' she insisted.

'God's will must be done,' he said, then he stepped through the door and closed it behind him.

For long moments Katy glared at the door, rage filling her until it threatened to overflow. She looked towards the belt he had thrown aside and the feeling seemed to grow even more acute. Katy crossed herself, then turned and headed up the stairs, slowing her pace as she reached the door to the girls' bedroom. She paused, her ear to the partition, and from inside she heard softly spoken words. Katy eased the door open and stepped across the threshold. She closed the door behind her, then moved towards the bed where Maria lay sleeping. It was very dark inside the bedroom, the curtains at the window having been pulled across and the candles that lit the small room long since having been extinguished. In that deep and enveloping darkness Katy heard those softly spoken words once again.

It was a second or two before she realised they were coming from Maria. The girl tossed agitatedly, her eyes still firmly closed. Katy moved closer, bending nearer to the sleeping girl.

'No, Frieda, don't go,' Maria murmured in her sleep. 'Please, not to that man. He's wicked.'

Katy swallowed hard and reached out a hand towards the sleeping girl as if to wake her from her slumber, but she remained still, listening as Maria continued to murmur softly in her sleep.

'Frieda, don't go to the castle,' she breathed, turning her head back and forth on the pillow. 'Not tonight.'

Katy caught her breath, her eyes widening in shocked surprise. She reached out and gently squeezed Maria's arm in an attempt to wake her.

'Maria,' she whispered. 'Wake up.'

Maria sat up with a start and looked at her aunt. She sucked in a breath, then embraced the older woman, fighting back her tears.

'Oh, Aunt Katy!' Maria cried. 'It's Frieda! I'm so worried about her!'

Katy was about to tell her niece the whereabouts of her sister when Maria spoke again.

'She went to Karnstein Castle to see the Count.'

'Why would she go there?'

'She's been before. I know I should have told you, but I was so afraid of what you'd do to her – of what Uncle Gustav would do to her. But I can't keep this to myself any longer. I'm afraid for her. She's been obsessed with him ever since we got here. She thinks he can give her a better life, a more exciting one.' Maria looked at her aunt imploringly. 'Please don't tell Uncle Gustav, I beg you. He will condemn her. He will punish her. He will punish both of us. I don't want that. She can't help herself. The Count is the one to blame. He has some kind of hold over her.'

'And you think she's at the castle now?'

Maria nodded.

'Many times I've thought about going there myself to help her,' she said. 'To save her.'

'You must never go near that place, Maria,' Katy said, shaking her head.

'But I could help her,' Maria protested.

'No. Never.'

Katy smiled at her niece and brushed the hair from her forehead.

'You lay down,' she purred. 'Go back to sleep. I won't tell your uncle what's going on, I promise you.'

Maria nodded and lay down, pulling the sheets up around her neck.

'You poor child,' Katy whispered, then she leaned down and kissed Maria very gently on the forehead. Katy sighed and moved away towards the bedroom door. 'Now you sleep,' she intoned.

'Thank you, Aunt Katy,' Maria said, as she rolled on to her side and prepared to slip back into the welcome oblivion of sleep.

Katy stood there for a moment longer, peering at the girl through the gloom, then she gently and carefully closed the bedroom door behind her once more and headed downstairs.

Maria had expected sleep to elude her but, helped by the sleeping draft she'd taken earlier, she found she drifted off easily, perhaps because she had cleared her mind, too, she thought. She hadn't enjoyed the burden of guilt concerning Frieda and with that burden now discharged she felt more relaxed. She stretched once or twice beneath the sheets, then let out a long breath as sleep enveloped her once more. Within a minute or two she was oblivious to everything. And with slumber came dreams. Some of them unwanted.

Inside the bedroom there was movement from close to the window.

A large shape, as black as the shadows themselves, emerged and moved slowly towards Maria.

Count Karnstein loomed over her, looking down at the motionless girl.

He smiled, lips sliding back to reveal his long canine fangs. Maria did not stir. Even when he gripped the edge of the sheet and pulled it gently back to reveal her sleeping form she didn't stir.

He stepped back angrily when he saw that she held a silver crucifix in her hand.

The Count looked away from the holy object, enraged by the sight of it. While she held the hated icon he could not touch her and that knowledge only served to infuriate him more. He stood beside the bed helplessly. He could see Maria's lips moving slightly and he heard the words she uttered in her sleep.

'No, no,' she murmured, her head moving from side to side.

When she moved slightly, the hand gripping the cross flopped limply to one side, but the holy symbol still remained in her hand and Karnstein gritted his teeth with continued anger as he glanced at it.

'I . . . no . . . let me out.' Further words from Maria as she moved more urgently in her sleep, tormented by images that Karnstein could only guess at.

Her fingers opened and closed, both hands clenching momentarily and Karnstein noticed something and smiled. The hand that gripped the cross had loosened its grip. The holy icon was slipping from her fingers.

He moved closer, still unable to get too near the hated symbol, but at least now there was a chance.

'I can't stand it,' Maria gasped in her slumber. 'I can't . . .'

She opened her right hand wide and the cross slipped from it and hit the wooden floor below.

Karnstein smiled triumphantly. With one sweeping motion of his strong arms he lifted Maria from the bed, gazing at her face for a moment before he made for the window. Below him the imposing figure of Joachim waited, staring up at his master, who nodded, still holding the figure of Maria.

Karnstein looked at her once again, struck by her resemblance to Frieda. There wasn't so much as a blemish to distinguish them. No one would ever be able to tell the difference between them. No one.

He smiled. It was just as he had planned.

Thirty-Four

The gravedigger leant on his shovel and gazed down into the grave of Ingrid Hoffer.

The coffin was a plain one, as were most of the boxes he provided graves for during the course of his work. The people of Karnstein could afford nothing too expensive and wanted nothing too ornate or ostentatious. What need for displays of wealth or opulence in the grave? Only the rich sought to decorate their final resting places with statues, crypts and mausoleums. Monuments to their standing and the only lasting reminder of their being. Once death claimed you, as far as the gravedigger was concerned, nothing else mattered. All you left behind were memories of yourself. Of what you had done and what kind of person you'd been. The only concrete reminder that a person had even walked the earth were the grave markers that stuck up out of the earth and bore the name of the corpse six feet under.

Ingrid Hoffer had a simple wooden cross at the head of her grave. It bore her birth date and death dates, and a small inscription that read:

Beloved sister.
God has welcomed home one of his angels.

The gravedigger nodded appreciatively at the sentiments of the inscription as he continued to stare into the deep hole where her coffin had been placed earlier that day. He himself had stood in the trees watching the ceremony, unsurprised by how many people had turned up to pay their respects to this good and decent woman. And there lay the irony of it for the gravedigger. Ingrid Hoffer, a good and decent woman, a woman of compassion and gentility, lay in a grave, while others continued to walk the earth and live lives they scarcely deserved. If God watched all of his children as everyone was taught, then his choice of who to call to his side was sometimes suspect, thought the gravedigger.

He often entertained such thoughts, and had done for the whole of his working life. He spent a great deal of time alone, even when he was working. He was always an outsider, a spectator to the misery that each new death brought. He tried to stay on the periphery of the tragic events. His only job was to cover the departed with earth in a hole that he had dug for them. It was not his duty to provide solace and comfort for them. And for that he was grateful, because he had often wondered what kind of words would truly bring comfort to someone who had lost somebody dear. Should the thought that the departed was now in heaven be enough to offer succour? The gravedigger doubted it and, he reasoned, what good was having a loved one in heaven? They were wanted here, now, in this life, not in the afterlife. They might be with God, but the person who had lost them needed them more on earth.

He had felt like that when his brother had been taken from him.

They had been inseparable. None of the usual sibling rivalry had affected their relationship, and they had enjoyed a friendship and closeness that many brothers and sisters could only dream about. Not for them the petty squabbling and arguments so many relations endured. They had barely spoken a cross word throughout their entire lives, even as children. Their parents had even remarked on it as they were growing up. They had cared for and protected each other from their earliest days, and when the accident had happened and his brother had been killed, the gravedigger felt as if a part of him had died, too. There was an empty space inside him now that could be filled by nothing other than the return of his brother, and he knew that was never going to happen.

They were promised an eternity together in heaven. That was what the priest had intoned over the grave, but the gravedigger didn't want that. He wanted his brother back with him now. He wanted him alive, not in some distant celestial paradise that they could only share when both were dead.

His brother had died four years earlier and the pain of his loss was still acute now for the gravedigger. It had been wintertime. A terrible deep winter unlike any had seen for many years in the area. Snow had fallen regularly and several metres thick, making travel almost impossible and virtually cutting off Karnstein from the rest of the countryside. From a personal point of view the gravedigger remembered how appallingly difficult his job had been during those long freezing months. Excavating earth from the ground to place a coffin in was hard and backbreaking work at the best of times, but trying to dig soil that was frozen harder than stone was impossible. The only way he'd been able to perform his duties was by lighting a huge fire on top of the ground he would have to dig, and waiting for the heat to warm through at least a couple of feet of the frozen earth. Of the dozen or so people who died in Karnstein during that appalling winter, the gravedigger had managed to bury them all but no deeper than two or three feet below the surface. It was just deep enough to protect them from the wolves and bears that also roamed the forests desperate for food. The scent of a body was not detectable, even to the most determined scavenger through three feet of soil.

It had been the searing cold that had caused the death of his brother and the recollection brought a lump to his throat. One of the many small rivers that ran around the area had frozen over and the local children had taken the opportunity to play on the refrigerated surface, but one had fallen through a thinner patch of ice, dropping into water that was so cold it virtually stopped the heart on first contact.

The gravedigger's brother had seen the child fall and scrambled across the slippery surface, pulling the boy free, pushing him to safety on the bank, but the remaining ice had given way beneath his increased weight and he had been sucked below, frozen before he could help himself, shocked into unconsciousness before he could drag himself from the icy depths. They had found him frozen almost solid, half in and half out of the water.

The gravedigger had dug his brother's grave himself, weeping fresh tears with every spadeful of earth he'd turned.

And now he stood looking into Ingrid Hoffer's grave and he imagined the grief her brother must be feeling. Anton was a good man and he would suffer her loss acutely. But that was the way of it, as far as the grave-digger was concerned; there was no guarantee of long life for the good, any more than for the bad. Death's choices were arbitrary and no one could do anything about their fate. That was one of the few things the gravedigger had come to accept during his life.

He glanced at the pile of earth beside the grave, thinking that it would take him about an hour to fill in the hole. He always waited until nightfall as a mark of respect. The last thing relatives and loved ones wanted to see as they filed away from a funeral was the first shovelfuls of earth being flung on to their dear departed. The gravedigger always waited until no one could see him and the darkness covered his work perfectly. He drove the spade into the mound of earth. Yes, he thought, he should be finished inside an hour. It took far less time to fill in a grave than it did to excavate one in the first place. Once he was finished he should have time to walk into the village and enjoy some ale before the inn closed for the night. It would be some reward for his labours.

He threw the first of the dark earth on to the coffin of Ingrid Hoffer.

'A sad loss.'

The gravedigger turned as he heard the words.

Rolf Kessler stepped into the clearing, his gaze fixed on the grave.

'All death is sad,' the gravedigger intoned. 'Worse still when it comes to one so young. You should know, Rolf.'

Kessler nodded.

'Did Gustav Weil come to the funeral?' he wanted to know, watching as the gravedigger once more set about filling the hole.

'No. Why should he? I don't think he and the Hoffers saw eye to eye about some matters, if you know what I mean.'

Again Kessler nodded.

'No one agrees with Weil, except for those other fools in the Brotherhood,' he snarled.

'There is much wrong in this village, Rolf, and yet most are too blind to see it,' the gravedigger went on. 'If it doesn't affect them they don't care.'

Kessler stood silently beside the grave, watching the earth falling on the coffin lid.

'I remember when my Sophie was buried,' he said, finally.

'A sad day,' the gravedigger intoned. 'I wept with you.'

'She didn't deserve what they did to her,' Kessler said through clenched teeth. 'None of those killed by the Brotherhood deserved it. They think they can see evil where no one else can, and yet they are the most evil of all.'

The gravedigger looked at him for a moment, then continued shovelling the dark earth.

'Evil found a home long ago in this valley,' he said, softly.

Kessler nodded. 'You mean the castle?'

'That is true evil, my friend,' the gravedigger added.

'Perhaps, but Weil is as guilty as anyone,' Kessler offered. 'I look forward to the day when you are burying him.'

The gravedigger laughed.

'That might not be for a long time,' he said.

Kessler didn't answer.

Thirty-Five

Smoke rose in mournful plumes from the torches that lit the inside of the Brotherhood's meeting house.

Franz glanced absently at them, watching the yellow flames, knowing that he would soon be staring at much larger and more ferocious ones. The time was drawing near and no one could prevent what was going to happen. Indeed, no one wanted to. If evil was to be banished forever from the land that he loved, then certain measures had to be taken and he would help. He got to his feet, trailing one hand almost unconsciously over the back of Gustav Weil's empty chair as he walked to the front of the large table that stood on the plinth at the front of the meeting house.

From the tiered benches before him dozens of black-clad members of the Brotherhood watched as he raised a hand to silence their rumbling chatter.

'The hour grows late,' Franz said. 'Why delay any longer? Let us burn her now!'

Another rumble of conversation began to build as the other puritans in the room gave voice to their thoughts.

'We know what must be done,' Franz insisted. 'There is no other way. Who among us would let this evil remain for a minute longer than necessary? We know our duty to our families and to God. She must burn!'

'But we agreed only two days ago that we would hold a trial,' one of the men near the back of the room called. More mutterings greeted his words.

'What is there to hear?' Franz challenged. 'Weren't we all there? Didn't we see her with Hermann's blood on her lips?'

'Aye!' a tall man at the front of the room called.

His exclamation set off more rumblings and a chorus of voices began to build.

'I agree,' another intoned. 'She is a daughter of Satan! She must be burnt! Just because she's Gustav's niece . . .'

'Brother, pray that your family may not be stricken,' the man next to him said, sharply.

'If it were my daughter or any of my kin I would be of the same mind,' the other puritan went on. 'Those who serve the Devil must burn. There is no other way.'

'And if it was your daughter, would you stand and watch as we purified her in the flames?' the second man challenged.

'I would light the fire myself,' the other retorted.

'None of us can say what we would do,' a tall thin man further back offered. 'This situation must be intolerable for Gustav. To know that one of his own kin is stricken, possessed by evil, and to know there is only one way to deal with it. He must be deeply troubled.'

'And where is Gustav?' Franz demanded. 'Has he forgotten his duties to us, his brethren, to this village and to God?'

There were more words spoken, more shouts, some of them tinged with anger.

The door of the building opened and Gustav Weil entered quietly, unseen by Franz. The others were well aware of his entrance and instantly quelled their conversations.

'He must speak to us,' Franz went on, unaware of the arrival of his companion. 'We must know the balance of his mind.'

Weil pulled off his gloves and dropped them on to the table, the sound causing Franz to turn.

'Gustav,' Franz said almost apologetically. 'We were waiting for you. There are things we must discuss.'

Weil nodded.

The cell smelled of urine and damp straw.

Frieda walked back and forth across the room, glancing helplessly at the thick stone walls. The cell – and the eleven others like it – was roughly twelve feet square, the walls dripping wet, the floor covered with filthy straw. There were holes in the floor and the base of the walls, and Frieda knew only too well that rats had made them over the course of hundreds of years. Even as she looked, one of the vile creatures scurried across the cell, then disappeared into another hole. She watched as the tail flicked, before being swallowed by the fetid darkness. But rats were not her concern at present. She crossed to the single barred window and looked out.

Her only concern was escape.

Exactly how she was going to accomplish that feat she had no idea, but she knew what fate awaited her if she was still inside this place when they came for her. A funeral pyre would be built for her. They would tie her to a stake and they would stand around watching as the fire destroyed her. The thought of such an agonising death caused her to shudder and she crossed to the barred window once again, tugging at the iron struts as if she could actually pull them free of the stonework that held them. She snarled something under her breath, then turned and crossed to the thick wooden door that marked the only way in and out of the cell. It was at least four inches thick and braced with metal struts. A small barred window enabled the gaoler to see in and the prisoner to see out. Frieda put her face to the small opening and peered out into the gloom of the corridor beyond.

The passageway was stone like the cells and barely wide enough for a man to spread his arms. From the stench that now reached Frieda's nostrils, and from what she had remembered when they first brought her here, the entire walkway beyond the cell was like an open sewer, filthy through years of neglect and lack of cleaning. Even as she looked out into the corridor she could see two rats scuttling along unhurriedly.

The corridor led towards the main entrance of the gaol and was guarded by the man responsible for caring for both the prisoners and also for their environment. He seemed to have little regard for either. Frieda could remember the look of contempt on his face when she had been dragged in. He had even laughed as he had slammed the cell door behind her, using the large rusted keys he carried to lock it, before peering into the cell at her, as if she had been an animal on display in a circus.

How she would have loved to have driven her fangs into his throat, to have bitten and torn at the tender flesh until she could feast on his blood. She wondered if he would still have sported that vile, crooked-toothed grin of his had she been able to reach him. She wondered if she would ever get the chance to make him pay for locking her in the cell. First him, and then so many others. She would avenge herself on all of them. Them and their families. She wouldn't stop until she had destroyed all those who now sought to destroy her.

How long she had before they came for her she had no idea. But it didn't matter if it was an hour or a week from now, Frieda knew that the next time the men of the Brotherhood took her from this place it would be to burn her alive. She remembered what Count Karnstein had told her about eternal life, about how only decapitation or a stake through the heart could destroy beings like them, but she did not want to endure the agonies of burning. To feel the flames licking around her legs and feet and then her stomach and back, peeling away the flesh before they took a hold properly and incinerated her like paper in a candle flame. She shuddered even at the thought and the unspeakable suffering she would have to go through if she did not free herself.

Again she looked around at the interior of the cell. But how was she to do that? One window. One door. There was no other way out. Frieda slumped back against one wall and slid slowly to the floor of the cell, her mind racing.

A rat appeared from one of the tunnels close to her,

only this one showed no fear at all. It sniffed the air, then advanced a foot or so towards her, its beady black eyes fixed on her. Frieda watched it with disdain, amazed by its lack of fear as it approached. It even sniffed her hand and she drew back her teeth as she felt its long whiskers brush against her flesh. Frieda looked at the hole from which the bloated rodent had emerged and wished she were small enough to escape through it. The rat sniffed at her dress, then seemed to tire of her and turned away.

She shot out a hand and grabbed the rat, ignoring its squeals of protest. She raised it up and with one bite she tore off its head. Blood from the decapitated rodent jetted on to her face and neck, but she seemed untroubled by the warm spurts. She spat the head out and threw the twitching body across the cell, watching it as it laid there, the last muscular spasms racking its form.

Frieda wiped the blood from her face with the back of her hand, her eyes once again flickering around the cell. The same thought forced its way into her mind again.

There had to be a way out.

Thirty-Six

'Guilty!'
The word rang around the inside of the Brotherhood's meeting house.

Gustav Weil sat motionless in his seat behind the great wooden table at one end of the room, aware of the eyes of his brethren fixed on him. He saw another of them stand.

'Guilty!' the next puritan intoned.

Three more voiced the same word, delivered with equal solemnity, their eyes meeting Weil's each time as they spoke.

Franz finally got to his feet and looked first at the assembled throng of puritans and then at Weil.

'Guilty!' Franz proclaimed.

Weil rose slowly to his feet, his gaze unblinking and unwavering.

'Then she must burn,' he said, flatly.

Weil surprised even himself that he felt a tremor of emotion as he spoke the words. He knew the creature they would be destroying was evil, yet still he felt that twinge of something indefinable deep down inside him, as the image of her filled his mind. He could see her tied to a stake, wood piled high around her. Perhaps she would scream her defiance at them as they lit the pyre. Or would she beg for mercy? Whatever she did, Weil knew there was only one possible ending to the scenario. The girl would be burned alive, as others had been before her. He had watched, unmoved, as other girls had perished in the purifying flames of the Brotherhood's fires, but now he was to destroy a girl who had lived in his house for a time. Who he had once called a niece. He closed his eyes tightly for a moment and told himself again that this creature they were to incinerate was no kin of his. She wasn't even one of God's own any longer. She was pure and undiluted evil. A servant of the Devil with no more right to life than any other who dared to oppose God.

When the time came he would take strength from the Almighty, Weil was confident of that much. God would give him the strength to ensure the evil was wiped out. The knot of muscles at the side of his jaw throbbed and pulsed.

'Speak the words again, Gustav,' Franz insisted. 'It is you we look to for leadership.'

'She must burn!' said Weil again, his voice full of its customary power. 'It is God's will!'

Frieda heard the sound of knocking from what seemed like far away.

She sat up in the cell, the loud bangs echoing along the stone corridor. She got to her feet and crossed to the window in the door, aware now that the pounding was coming from the main door of the gaol. Even standing on tiptoe she couldn't see along the corridor, because of the angle of the cell to the walkway, but the sound seemed to grow in intensity for a moment before stopping abruptly.

Who was outside, she wondered? Had her uncle and his brethren found someone else to punish? Another lost soul? Again she craned her neck to see out of the barred grille in the door. There was more banging, then silence.

She heard a voice and recognised it as the gaoler.

'I'm coming!' he called, irritated by the hammering on the main door. It had woken him from fitful slumber. He selected the key to the main door from the ring hanging on his belt and made his way towards the gaol entrance.

There was more banging.

'I'm coming! I'm coming!' he shouted. 'What are you trying to do, wake the dead?'

Who in God's holy name, the gaoler thought, was disturbing him at this hour of the night? Any right-minded person would be tucked up in bed by now, not hammering on the door of his gaol, creating enough noise to deafen a man. He muttered agitatedly to himself as he wandered along the corridor from the small room that he called his, set back from the main entry-way of the gaol. It contained a wooden bed, a table and two chairs, a washbasin and some of the gaoler's personal items. He had a home on the outskirts of the village, but spent most of his time here at his place of work, and he had seen fit to try and make the place at least resemble something of a haven for him while he was here. He ambled along until he reached the main door, fumbling for the key. He found it and pushed it into the lock.

'Just take your time,' he called as he heard the heavy metallic click of the mechanism. 'I've got things to do around here. Banging on the door like that isn't going to make me get here any quicker.'

He shook his head and pulled open the door, wincing as a cold breeze blew in.

The gaoler's jaw dropped as he saw the figure of Count Karnstein standing on the other side of the door.

The Count took a step towards him, his eyes fixed on those of the gaoler.

Karnstein extended a hand towards the gaoler, who backed away, his breath coming in gasps now. He felt as if his body was turning to stone, as if he were staring at some kind of gorgon instead of a man. He tried to swallow, but couldn't. The vision of the Count before him became blurred and he thought he was going to pass out. There was a growing pressure at the base of his skull that seemed to be spreading through his bloodstream as quickly as a virus.

The Count remained where he was, the hypnotic glare in his eyes doing its work with surprising speed, but then, as Karnstein had always found, the weak-minded were far easier to control. He smiled thinly to himself as he saw that the gaoler was completely entranced. The Count reached out one finger and jabbed it into the man's cheek, but the gaoler did not react. His mouth was still open, a globule of spittle hanging from his bottom lip. The Count looked at him with disgust, then pulled the keys from the man's hand. Karnstein gestured to somebody behind him.

Joachim emerged from the shadows carrying Maria as easily as a child carries a doll. Karnstein strode off down the corridor towards the first of the cells. He peered through the small barred window in the door and saw it was empty. The second cell was the one he sought and as he saw Frieda inside he smiled, slipping the key into the lock and turning it.

Frieda ran to him as he entered, her lips sliding back in a smile of pleasure and triumph.

'I knew you'd come!' she said.

Joachim moved into the cell and, as Frieda watched, the huge black man gently laid Maria on the bed. She remained fast asleep, oblivious to her own peril.

'You will be Maria now,' Karnstein said, touching Frieda's cheek with one long index finger. 'Unsuspected, good and kind and virginal.' He smiled. 'Think of the havoc you can cause.'

The Count turned to Joachim and jabbed a finger in Maria's direction.

'Quickly!' he snapped. 'We must change them.'

The black man nodded, his large fingers moving with surprising dexterity as he began to unbutton the front of Maria's long white nightdress. He opened it, seemingly oblivious to the sight of her breasts, lifting her carefully, pulling the garment free. She murmured in her sleep but did not wake.

'Take off your dress, my dear,' Karnstein said, smiling at Frieda, his own hands already deftly unbuttoning the low-cut blue garment.

Frieda smiled and allowed him to pull it open,

exposing her breasts, the nipples grown to stiffness because of the chill in the room. Karnstein bent his head and kissed each one in turn, then he straightened up and watched as she hastily undid the other buttons, pulling off the dress and standing naked before him, enjoying his gaze upon her, wanting him to look at her.

Behind them, Joachim was tugging the nightdress from Maria's motionless body, until she, too, was naked.

Karnstein looked at her, the same lascivious smile still etched across his face.

'So alike in every way,' he murmured, his gaze travelling over Maria's pale skin.

Frieda also smiled, reaching for the nightdress the Count handed her, while Joachim dressed Maria.

'We must hurry,' Karnstein insisted. 'Your uncle and his puritans are on their way here.'

All three of them slipped out of the cell and Karnstein locked the door behind them, looking back through the opening in the partition to where Maria still slept on the rough bed, now clothed in Frieda's blue dress. Then he looked at Frieda, who sported Maria's white nightdress. The Count smiled, happy with the deception. He led the way back down the corridor and up towards the main door of the gaol, glancing contemptuously at the gaoler as they passed. The man was still in a deep trance and Karnstein had no idea how long it would last, but that was not his concern now.

The Count led the way out into the night.

Thirty-Seven

Gustav Weil sat motionless in the high-backed chair he always occupied at Brotherhood meetings and surveyed his black-clad companions evenly. Inside the meeting house the other puritans were talking among themselves, restless and eager to set about the business they knew must be concluded as quickly as possible. Some viewed the impending purification as necessary, while others looked forward to it with unnatural and repellent relish. Perhaps it was some kind of twisted relief that the subject of their puritanical zeal was to be the kin of their leader, rather than one of their own flesh and blood. Whatever the case, they talked and gesticulated as Weil sat and listened; some raised their voices here and there, and although he couldn't pick out individual conversations he knew the gist and intent of their words.

Some pointed towards him as they spoke and finally, unable to stand it any longer, Weil got to his feet and raised his hands to silence his companions.

'Brothers,' he called, 'we have seen death enough this night! Let it be at dawn!'

Louder words greeted his pronouncement.

'The evil must be destroyed!' one of them called.

'The longer she lives the greater the danger to all of us and our families!' echoed another.

'She is a captive in the gaol,' Weil reminded them. 'She can do none any harm. She is helpless there. Let us wait and purify her in the rays of the morning sun.'

'No!'

The word was barked from next to him. Franz shook his head.

'Why give the Devil time to come to the aid of his servants?' he went on. 'Burn her now!'

Weil met his steely gaze, unflinchingly.

'You would act swiftly enough if we were to burn anyone other than your own kin, Gustav,' Franz said, accusingly. 'Is that why you hesitate?'

'I told you, she is no kin of mine. She is a daughter of Satan now,' Weil countered. 'I know what must be done.'

'And yet you shrink from doing it,' Franz insisted.

'She must burn now!' one of the other puritans shouted.

'Every minute she lives she is an affront to God!' another added. There were more shouts of agreement and Weil nodded almost imperceptibly.

'It is God's will, Gustav. You said that yourself,' Franz added.

'So be it,' Weil said, flatly, but he remained in his seat despite the fact that Franz and the others had risen from theirs. Movement to his left caught his attention and he turned his head to see that the meeting house door had opened.

Anton Hoffer stood silhouetted there, a look of fury on his face.

'Gustav!' he called, moving into the meeting house and ignoring the angry stares of the other Brotherhood members. He made his way towards Weil and Franz.

'You have no right to be here, schoolmaster!' one of the others shouted.

'What happens among us is our business!' added another. 'It is not for your ears or eyes!'

Anton ignored their shouts and stood glaring at Weil.

'I've only just heard,' Anton snapped. 'It's not true about Frieda?'

'Yes,' said Weil, without looking at him.

'But its madness!' Anton told him. 'What proof have you?' He glanced at Franz and then at some of the other puritans gathered nearby. 'What proof have any of you?'

'The proof of our own eyes,' Weil told him.

'Oh, no,' Anton murmured, shaking his head.

'It was clear enough,' Weil continued.

'What did you see?' Anton insisted.

'She killed Hermann!' one of the other puritans shouted.

Anton looked at Weil for confirmation.

'We saw her with his blood on her lips,' the older man said. 'There is no doubting it, Anton. The evil is among us. It has been from the beginning. You of all people should welcome its destruction. Your sister died because of it.'

'Are you saying that Frieda killed Ingrid too?'

'Do you deny the possibility? You saw her. The marks on her neck. Your sister was killed by a creature of the Devil, and Frieda is Satan's slave now and has been for God alone knows how long.'

'But Maria,' Anton breathed. 'Don't you see if you kill Frieda you will kill Maria, too?'

'Nonsense,' Weil said dismissively. 'You can do nothing for Frieda. Maria is at the house.'

'Then I will go to her,' Anton said.

'Be careful, Anton,' Weil warned him. 'This evil is powerful, take care that it has not tainted Maria too.'

'Maria is pure. Dear God, is no one safe from your suspicion and persecution?' Anton hissed. He turned and barged angrily through the throng of puritans gathered at the door of the meeting house.

'Why do you show so much concern for one who serves the Devil, schoolmaster?' Franz demanded.

'My concern is for the innocent,' Anton rasped. 'And so should yours be. You are not servants of God, you are fanatics!'

'We do the will of God,' a tall puritan with a thick beard said.

'You do no will but your own,' Anton snapped, pushing free of the black-clad men.

'Let him go,' Franz sneered. 'We have the Lord's work to do. Bring fire!'

Thirty-Eight

The hammering on the door seemed to be coming from miles away. The gaoler could hear the thumping, but he could not work out where it was coming from.

He felt cold from head to foot, as if iced water was coursing through his veins instead of blood. His eyes were open, but everything before him was blurred. When he tried to move his muscles were frozen. And still that infernal hammering continued, that far off banging that was growing louder and more insistent.

The gaoler closed his eyes and it felt like a monumental effort to force the lids shut, then open them again. His head still felt as if it was made of wood, his entire body still paralysed as surely as if he'd broken his spine. He attempted to flex his fingers, but the digits moved only with the greatest of will power; he had to concentrate all his attention on getting them to move, and even then the motion was slight and almost imperceptible.

And the hammering continued.

For a moment he wondered if it was actually inside his clouded brain. Was he imagining the sound? He managed to screw his eyes shut once more and his head cleared a little. He was even able to move his fingers. Could he hear voices, too, now? They seemed to be as distant as the banging, but he was sure he could detect them somewhere. Unless they were as much a figment of his imagination as the hammering which began again almost immediately. Like a man emerging from a thick and impenetrable mist, the gaoler felt the warmth returning slowly to his body. His muscles loosened and his vision gradually cleared. The process only took a minute or so, but to him it felt like an eternity as he stood there waiting for the terrible feeling of inertia and paralysis to pass.

And all the time, as he slowly regained his senses, the banging continued.

He felt a jolt that seemed to shake his entire body and suddenly his senses, his wits and his faculties flooded back all at once like a breaking damn releasing the water behind it. The gaoler swayed and almost overbalanced. He put a hand to his head, his mind spinning. For fleeting seconds he had no idea where or even who he was. He felt his heart pounding against his ribs, but at least the accursed feeling of numbness and senselessness was gone. He rubbed his face like a man waking from a deep sleep, and he looked around at the dank walls of the gaol and recognised them.

The banging was even more insistent now, but he realised where it was coming from and reached for the key he needed to unlock the main door of the gaol. He found it and pulled the door, almost bundled over by the black-clad men who tried to push past him. He recognised them as members of the Brotherhood and he knew their leader instantly. Gustav Weil regarded him evenly, but it was another man, the man he knew as Franz, who spoke.

'What the hell are you doing, man?' he snarled. 'Why didn't you open the door?'

The gaoler merely shook his head.

'Where's the girl?' Franz snapped.

The gaoler was about to speak when Franz and some of the others pushed past him, snatching his keys as they did.

'You can't take her out of here!' the gaoler shouted.

'Are you going to stop us?' one of the puritans snapped, glaring at him. The gaoler merely held up his hands in supplication and allowed the men to blunder along the corridor towards the cell they sought. Gustav Weil followed, stepping into the cell as one of the other men unlocked it.

Weil looked at the sleeping form of Maria and swallowed hard. He knew what must be done, he knew what had to be done, but that did not make things any easier for him, nor did it prevent him feeling a twinge of regret. Something deep within him felt sorry for the girl. Not for what she had become, but for her soul and what she had lost. She had not asked to be transformed into this creature from Hell and now, lying motionless on the bed before him, she looked strangely peaceful. Had she known how close her death was, then perhaps, he reasoned, that would not have been the case.

'If proof be needed,' snarled Franz pointing at the sleeping girl. 'Look how the Devil's own sleep, careless of their sins.' He moved to enter the cell, wanting to wake the girl. Weil was beginning to think that Franz was actually enjoying the situation.

Weil looked at his companion and put a hand across him to block his advance, then he himself moved into the cell and bent over her.

'Frieda,' he said, quietly.

He saw the girl before him open her eyes and blink myopically.

Maria saw his face, then immediately was aware of more men in the room, men wearing black who looked down at her with hatred in their eyes.

'Get her out of here!' Franz snapped. 'Let us not delay any longer!'

Maria gasped as rough hands pulled her to her feet. The stone floor of the cell felt cold beneath her bare soles and she shivered as she was half-dragged, half-carried from the fetid room. Weil merely looked on as his companions took her out into the corridor.

'Let me go!' she pleaded. 'I shouldn't be here!'

Her cries went unanswered.

'Where are you taking her?' the gaoler demanded as they reached the end of the corridor. 'I need a written order from the magistrate before I can release any prisoners.'

'I am not a prisoner!' Maria said, imploringly. 'I was brought here by Count Karnstein! He is trying to trick you!'

Franz sneered dismissively in her direction.

'You know what she is?' one of the Brotherhood snapped.

The gaoler looked vague.

'She is evil! She must be burnt!' another black-clad man added.

'No!' Maria protested.

The gaoler looked at the stricken girl, then at Franz.

'God's law supersedes any magistrate,' Franz snapped. 'If you try to stop us, then you are siding with the Devil and you will pay, as will this creature.' He stabbed an accusatory finger towards Maria, who was dragged out of the main door of the building and ushered towards a waiting horse.

'Let me go!' she protested. 'Why are you doing this?'

'You know why,' one of the Brotherhood hissed.

'You think I'm Frieda,' Maria said, the realisation hitting her hard. 'You think I am my own sister. You are wrong.'

'Hear how she tries to save herself,' Franz rasped.

'I am Maria! I have done nothing to hurt anyone!' Again she tried to shake free of the hands that held her so tightly. 'I swear to God! You've got the wrong person!'

Weil followed, watching as Maria was lifted on to the horse, secured firmly in the saddle by two of the Brotherhood.

'Let us rid the world of this hell spawn!' Franz shouted.

'Burn her!' another bellowed.

Others roared their approval.

'Listen to me!' Maria called. 'I am Maria! You've got the wrong girl! You've been tricked!'

Weil looked at Maria as she was led away, her eyes

brimming with tears. He hesitated a moment, then followed.

'I hope she dies in agony.'

The words caused him to turn.

'Do you hear me, Weil?' Rolf Kessler went on, a slight smile on his lips. 'I hope your niece suffers the torments of the damned as she burns, the way my Sophie did. This is judgement on you. To have to watch while one close to you dies in so much pain. Now you will feel what I felt.'

'Get away from me!' Weil hissed.

Kessler smiled.

'Go and watch her,' he offered. 'See how the flames strip the flesh from her bones. Watch as the blisters form on her face, how her eyes burst in their sockets as the fire devours her. It will take a good ten minutes for her to die – longer if the wood is damp. Make sure the wood around her is dry, Weil. Make sure the blaze does its job.'

Weil allowed his hand to slip to the inside of his jacket.

'I'll be watching,' Kessler called after him. 'I'll always be watching.'

'I've had enough of your threats!' Weil snapped. He pulled the pistol from his belt and aimed it at Kessler, the barrel levelled at his face. 'I will not tolerate this any longer.'

Kessler sneered, apparently unperturbed by the sight of the weapon.

'You haven't got the guts to use that,' he rasped. 'Killing innocent girls and shooting a man are different things. Killing a man requires courage that you don't have.' He pulled his knife free and brandished it before him, the point glinting wickedly.

Weil took a step back as he saw the blade.

'I warned you!' he hissed.

'Kill me if you dare,' Kessler challenged. 'You killed part of me when you murdered my Sophie, why not complete the job now? If you have the guts. Because I tell you, Weil, I will think nothing of gutting you like a fish when the time comes. You and your whole stinking family!'

Weil shook his head, then pulled the trigger.

There was a loud bang as the pistol went off, a cloud of smoke billowing from the barrel as the weapon spat the heavy lead ball. It slammed into Kessler's face, just below the left eye, shattered his cheek bone and ploughed on into his brain. He was dead before he hit the ground.

Weil looked down at him and the huge puddle of blood that was spreading rapidly around his head. He prodded the body with the toe of his boot, then knelt and turned it over onto its back, looking into the glassy, lifeless eyes.

'I warned you,' Weil whispered, then he jammed the pistol back into his belt, hauled himself to his feet and dashed off up the street.

Rolf Kessler's body lay prone, his eyes open and staring blindly at the sky.

Thirty-Nine

Anton Hoffer slowed his pace slightly as he approached the front door of Gustav Weil's house.

He looked up at the building, wondering why there was no light either upstairs or downstairs. Weil was not present, that much he knew, but the older man had told him that Maria was in the house and, Anton assumed, Frau Weil was there, too. Why, then, the darkness? Or was it simply that sensible, God-fearing people like those inside the building were sleeping at this hour of the night? Nevertheless, for reasons he could not be sure of, Anton felt a growing sense of unease as he moved closer to the door.

He knocked twice and waited.

There was no answer. No sounds of movement from inside. So he knocked again.

Again he was greeted only by silence.

Anton turned the handle and was a little surprised to discover the door was unlocked. He pushed it open a fraction, knocking on the stout wood as he did so.

'Frau Weil?' he called.

There was no reply, so he moved inside the house, pausing at the threshold.

'Frau Weil?' he said a little more loudly, now stepping inside and closing the door behind him.

The only illumination in the house came from the watery moonlight seeping through the windows. The candles that had been burning at various points in the house, Anton noticed, were burned as low as they would go, so that they resembled little more than wicks floating in puddles of melted wax. He frowned again and moved further inside, narrowing his eyes to see better in the gloom. Frau Weil had left some of her embroidery on the table before him and, as Anton passed the piece of material, he brushed it with his fingertips, his gaze now fixed on the bottom of the stairs.

He paused at the bottom step, looking up towards the upper storey of the house.

'Frau Weil?' he called again, and his voice seemed to echo within the gloomy structure. When there was no answer, he called a different name.

'Maria?'

Still only silence greeted him. Anton began to slowly climb the stairs, the wooden steps creaking beneath him. As he climbed he looked up towards the firmly closed doors ahead of him, squinting to see even the tiniest band of light beneath. Something that would tell him there was someone inside one of those rooms. As it was all he saw was darkness. And yet Anton knew that someone should be here. Weil had told him that Maria was present; sleeping in her bed and that should have meant that Frau Weil was in the house, too. Where was everyone? he wondered, as he finally reached the landing. He turned to his right, to the nearest door and tapped lightly on it.

'Maria?' he said.

As ever, there was only silence to greet his voice, so Anton turned the door handle slowly and edged into the room.

'Maria?' he murmured again.

The figure that lay on the bed before him was sleeping, seemingly oblivious to his presence, and Anton smiled as he saw her. He crossed to the bed and sat down gently on the edge of it, bending over the sleeping figure.

'Maria,' Anton said.

Frieda opened her eyes and saw him smiling down at her. She, too, smiled. She had never doubted the ruse would work, that she would be mistaken for her angelic sister, while Maria would be mistaken for her, but now, hearing Anton speak Maria's name while he looked at her proved beyond all reason to her that she had triumphed. She sat up, propping herself against the wooden headboard of the bed.

'I didn't mean to startle you,' Anton said as she looked at him, tears in her eyes.

'I wasn't sleeping soundly,' Frieda told him. 'I couldn't sleep for thinking about my poor sister, Frieda. Oh, Anton, what will they do to her?'

Anton pulled her to him and held her comfortingly.

'Maria, Maria,' he said. 'I am so sorry, but there is nothing that can be done to help her now.' He held her more tightly.

'What will they do to her?' Frieda insisted.

Anton held her, reluctant to speak the words.

'They will burn her,' he said, finally.

Frieda held him more intensely, enjoying the strength in his arms and the warmth in his grip.

'And my uncle will let them do it?' Frieda said, sniffing back more fake tears.

'He has no choice.'

Hidden from his view, Frieda smiled.

Anton finally opened his arms and allowed Frieda to pull back from him. She remained against the headboard dabbing at her eyes and doing her best to look distraught.

'Where is your aunt?' Anton asked.

'I don't know,' Frieda told him. 'Is she not here?'

'No.'

'Then we're alone.'

Anton nodded. Frieda put our her hand and tenderly touched his cheek, stroking softly. Anton shifted closer to her, gazing into her eyes. He felt light-headed, as if her beauty and the situation somehow intoxicated him. She licked her lips, then parted them slightly and he could hear her breathing. He bent closer, wanting to taste those lips, but she put one finger to his, smiling as she did.

'No, not yet,' she breathed. 'There's plenty of time, Anton. Plenty of time for us.'

She touched his neck with her fingers, her eyes focussing on the pulsing vein there and, inside her mouth she gently ran her tongue over the tips of her fangs.

Forty

Anton looked on, watching as she slowly unfastened the front of her white nightdress. He could see her nipples pushing against the almost transparent material and he felt his own excitement growing steadily. She ran a hand through her hair, then pulled the nightdress open a little further, so he could see the full swell of her breasts. Anton moved closer to her, one hand straying to her thigh. He felt the softness of her skin and the sensation excited him even more. Frieda parted her legs a little, allowing his hand to slide higher as she pulled the nightdress open at last to fully reveal her breasts.

Anton let out a sigh and again moved his head closer to her, wanting to kiss her, but, as before, Frieda moved backwards slightly. However, this time she did slide her hands around his neck, stroking fingers through his hair and gazing deeply into his eyes. Anton was about to speak her name when she leaned towards him, her lips finally touching his, her tongue probing urgently inside his mouth. He responded fiercely, his hands closing over her breasts, massaging the firm globes and outlining the nipples with his thumbs. It was Frieda's turn to gasp and she arched her back, pushing herself closer to him, taking one of his hands and guiding it between her legs. He felt the moisture there and the discovery of her excitement and arousal only served to inflame him more.

They broke the kiss and looked at each other, both of them gasping for breath.

'Anton, you don't know how much I've always wanted you,' Frieda breathed, pulling him close once more, her right hand gliding across his groin, squeezing the stiffness she felt there. She smiled and slipped from his grasp, standing up and backing away from him playfully, her tongue flicking out to lick her lips. She moved a few paces across the bedroom, watching as Anton got to his feet to follow her, enjoying this game now.

'Maria,' he whispered, advancing towards her expectantly.

She was standing next to the mirror now, the nightdress open to reveal her body. Anton looked at the perfection before him, his gaze travelling upwards from her bare feet and shapely legs, past the tiny triangle of light hair between her legs upwards to her flat belly and pert breasts to her face with those wide and eager eyes and full moist lips that were still curved upwards into a smile. He wanted her badly and he knew that she felt the same about him, and that knowledge spurred him on.

'Is this right?' he whispered, moving towards her.

'Everything about it is right,' Frieda told him.

'But your uncle . . . ,' he began.

'Will never know,' she interrupted.

'And your sister?'

'What of her? She deserves to die. She is evil. She always has been. That's why I've always hated her. I hope she dies in agony.'

Anton frowned, surprised by the words.

'You can't mean that,' he murmured.

'Why does it matter to you?' Frieda went on, taking a step towards him and shrugging off the nightdress completely. 'You're with me now, not with her. I will show you pleasure you never dreamed of.'

'I didn't expect you to speak like this, Maria,' Anton admitted.

'Why not?'

'You are pure and good.'

'Unlike my sister? Unlike that Devil's bitch who will burn tonight? And while she burns we will make love and you will be mine!'

Frieda smiled, the softness suddenly leaving her features, her fangs now clearly visible as her lips slid back.

Anton felt as if someone had thrown cold water in his face. He shook his head and the haze that had previously enveloped his mind cleared rapidly. He turned his head from her, glancing at the mirror and his own reflection, but he could not see the reflection of Frieda there. Where she was standing was only blank space.

Anton looked back at her with an expression that combined shock and fear, and in that split second she understood that he knew. Frieda opened her mouth, her fangs now gleaming in full view. She lunged towards him and Anton put up both hands to block the attack.

She slammed into him with a strength that took him

by surprise, knocking him backwards on to the bed. As she launched herself at him he managed to grab her wrists, holding her back as she ducked her head savagely at him, her fangs missing him by inches as she hissed maniacally. He could feel saliva dripping from her fangs on to his face and her breath was hot on his skin as she leered down at him, still intent on biting him. Anton used all of his strength to push her away, shoving her backwards with such force that he sent her crashing into the chest of drawers. But the impact did nothing to slow her down and Frieda sprang up immediately, hurling herself at him once more.

Anton rolled off the other side of the bed as she grabbed at him, raking her nails across his left cheek and ripping the flesh. He slipped as he backed away, but something caught his eye. Something that lay just beneath the bed. Something that gleamed.

It was a silver crucifix.

Where it had come from he had no idea, but it offered salvation. Anton snatched it up with one hand, driving the other hand into Frieda's solar plexus as she leapt at him once more, hissing furiously, her fangs bared. She fell on to the bed and rolled over, ready to spring up and grab for him once again, but Anton stepped backwards, swinging the silver cross up into view. He held it before him, brandishing it at her

As if someone had placed an invisible wall between them, Frieda could get no closer. She looked at the hated crucifix, her eyes blazing, both repelled by it and seemingly helpless to look away from the object that was paralysing her. She waved at it, hoping to knock it from Anton's hand, but he drew back, keeping the cross before him as he backed towards the door, away from the spitting, hissing creature.

The proof was there now, in the same room with him. The embodiment of evil that he had always prayed was just a figment of superstitious minds, but he now saw only too clearly to be monstrously real. Anton shook his head in stunned disbelief as the thing that had once been Frieda writhed before him, eyes still fixed on the crucifix. He wondered if the very sight of the holy object was causing her pain and a part of him hoped it was. He glanced at her long fangs and wondered if they had been the ones that had torn into his sister's neck.

Frieda was on her knees now, one second trying to crawl towards him, but the next retreating, until she was against the headboard, her shoulders pushing against the wood as she sought to escape from the gleaming glare of the cross Anton held. He reached back with one hand and felt for the door handle, tugging it open, the cross still held before him.

Frieda hissed at him as he slipped through the door, preparing to drag herself off the bed and pursue him. Once the hated cross was out of her sight she could follow him, possibly catch him on the stairs where he was defenceless. There she would kill him, plunge her fangs into his throat and feast on the blood that jetted from his ruptured veins. The thought galvanised her and she managed to slide off the bed and take a couple of steps towards him, but Anton hurled the crucifix at her as if it were a missile. As he did he slammed the bedroom door behind him and ran for his life.

Frieda shrieked as the silver struck her, the cross forcing her back. She fell onto the bed, the cross landing on her body just below her left breast. She grabbed instinctively for the crucifix, pulling it off her flesh, but as she did and her hand closed over it she felt excruciating pain. It was as if someone had forced a branding iron into the palm of her left hand, searing the flesh there. Frieda opened her hand, shaking it as her skin rose and blistered under the touch of the cross. She managed to fling it aside, but as she looked, the imprint and shape of the holy object was burnt into the skin. The flesh there was raw and angry, weeping where the blisters had risen and burst almost immediately, so powerful had been the touch of the crucifix against her tainted flesh. She whimpered like a beaten dog as she looked at the mark, the pain that now enveloped her hand spreading as far as her elbow. She opened her mouth and shrieked with rage and pain.

As Anton hurtled down the stairs of the house he heard the sound, but didn't look back. Instead he crashed through the door and sprinted for his waiting horse, expecting that at any second Frieda would come out of the house, chasing after him, still determined to taste his blood.

He swung himself into the saddle and snapped the reins, urging his horse on with a shout.

'Go on!' he roared. 'Get up! Get up!'

Speed was needed now like never before and, as he ducked low over the neck of the galloping animal, Anton prayed to God that he wasn't too late.

Forty-One

Maria sat astride the horse, secured to the saddle by ropes. The cold breeze blew into her face, drying the tears that had run down her cheeks. She made no attempt to escape from the ropes that held her. She knew there was no point. Even if she managed to get free, there was nowhere for her to run. She could not escape these men. Maria looked around at them and saw the same expression on all their faces. It was a combination of triumph and hatred. Triumph because they felt they had finally conquered evil, and hatred for that same pestilence they had fought against all their lives. She also knew that telling them they had the wrong girl was useless. They would not listen. They were convinced that what they intended to do was right. No amount of pleading would dissuade them. She was helpless. The knowledge of her fate only served to make her more desperate.

At the head of the small procession moving through the forest was her uncle, sitting upright on his horse. She had called to him a number of times since they left the gaol, but he had either ignored her or greeted her entreaties with a look of disdain. She glanced skyward, as if hoping that God himself would intervene, and, she reasoned, who else was going to save her? No man could help her now. Only divine intervention could prevent them from lashing her to a stake and burning her alive.

The very thought of such a death caused her to shiver and, as if the animal itself sensed her fear, the horse she was secured to whinnied and tossed its head. The puritan leading it jerked its bridle hard to steady the animal and it continued plodding on along the track leading through the trees. There were mounted puritans ahead of her and behind, too, just to reinforce the hopelessness of her situation.

Maria began to pray softly, her lips moving soundlessly as she bowed her head. She prayed for help, but she also prayed for forgiveness for these men who were about to burn her. She asked God to give her strength, and also that she not feel pain for too long once the fire was blazing around her. She prayed for a swift death. It seemed like the only thing she could do.

The puritan leading her horse saw her whispering and looked angrily at her.

'Asking the Devil to help you?' he sneered.

Maria merely shook her head.

'No one can help you now,' the puritan went on. 'Not even that fiend up there in his castle.' He jabbed a finger towards the hills, where the outline of Karnstein Castle was clearly visible against the night sky. 'It will be his turn next. Him and all those like him. He will burn just like you.'

Maria felt more tears run warmly down her cheeks.

'You weep for your fate?' the puritan rasped. 'Does

the thought of the fire frighten you? Did your master tell you that flames could not harm you? Well, you will see how he lied when you are roasting. When the flesh is peeling from your bones and you are screaming for death, begging for the end to come to end your suffering once and for all.' He spat on the ground.

Maria sniffed back more tears and bowed her head.

Time seemed to have slowed to a crawl for Anton Hoffer. Every movement that he and his horse made felt as if it was in slow motion. He snapped the reins and drove the animal on, and it thundered along the roads leading through the woods around Karnstein like a cavalry mount hurtling into battle, but still, to Anton, it was not fast enough. He knew where he had to get to and the longer he remained in the saddle the more he convinced himself that he would not complete his mission. As the countryside flashed past him he guessed he still had another mile or so to ride before he found the place he sought.

By that time he was almost positive he would be too late. Too late to save the innocent twin from the fate that should have been so rightly reserved for her sibling. The one who had tried to take his life that very night. Even as he rode, Anton could still see the image of Frieda in his mind. That fanged creature that had tried to first seduce him and then kill him, and there was still a tiny piece of his mind that refused to accept what he had seen.

A vampire had attacked him. The phrase stuck in his mind like a splinter in soft flesh. A vampire! A creature of superstition and nightmare. Something he had read about but never in a lifetime ever dreamed he would have to confront. He could still see her in his mind's eye, full of hunger, rage and desire. And now he wondered where she had gone when he left the house. Had she pursued him somehow? Weren't these foul monsters able to take on the form of bats, rats or wolves? Was she even now racing through the forest as he was, eager to reach him or to watch as her sister died in the flames meant for her?

That thought wrung yet more anguish from Anton as he thought about Maria and her fate. If only there were some way of telling her captors they had the wrong girl, that they were about to incinerate a good and God-fearing young woman in the flames of their fanaticism. The image of Maria dying in agony as the fire engulfed her was almost too much to take. Anton dug his heels into his horse, forcing it over a bridge and onward. It was already badly lathered and he wondered how much longer the animal could continue at this pace, but he could not stop or slow down. He knew only too well what would happen if he did.

A portion of a tree trunk lay across the track just ahead, but Anton merely urged the horse on, gripping the reins tightly as the animal soared upwards and over the obstacle. He patted its sweating neck as a sign of encouragement and gratitude, the wind blowing strongly in his face as he rode on.

Three quarters of a mile to go.

A part of him felt as if he might as well be a million miles from his destination. He was increasingly sure that he had no chance of saving Maria. A heavy, cold feeling began to grow in his chest and no matter how hard he tried, he could not shake it. He spoke her name silently as he rode, fearing he would soon be intoning it again in front of her blazing pyre.

She had expected to find them at the Brotherhood's meeting house, but had found only an empty building. Katy Weil had entered and stood silently for a second, her eyes taking in the details of the interior. The tiered benches, the huge wooden table, the torches on the wall and, on the lectern in the centre of the room, the huge leather-bound Bible. She had never seen the inside of the building before, although she had often wondered what it looked like. It was not, her husband had told her, a place for anyone not initiated into the Brotherhood. For the first time in her life she had felt a twinge of hatred for the name of those men her husband was so proud to be a part of. He had given more to them during the course of their marriage than he ever had to her. They had seen more of him and he had shown more devotion to them. She felt entitled to hate both the Brotherhood and her husband for that.

Now, as she made her way through the forest, she found strength she never realised she had. Evil was abroad this night, that much she knew, and yet she still found herself in the blackest depths of the forest with thoughts not of her own safety, but the life of her niece.

She knew where they would take Maria, and she knew she had to find that place before it was too late. The appalling irony of the situation was not lost on her as she hurried through the trees. Her own sister had died in a fire and now her niece was to meet the same fate.

Katy shuddered as she advanced, occasionally touching the crucifix she wore around her neck as if she expected this show of faith to be rewarded by some action from on high. What kind of action she didn't know, but she still absently touched the crucifix as she made her way through the woods, almost stumbling on more than one occasion. Up ahead, beyond a clearing, there was a road that led all the way to where she needed to go and Katy quickened her pace, sure that her footing would be better on the road and that she could move faster. Speed was of the essence, she knew that. Time was running out for Maria now and Katy felt tears welling up in her eyes as she thought about her niece.

But it was grief for both girls if she was honest. Despite what Frieda had become, Katy liked to think that there was still some shred of humanity alive within the cloak of evil that now enfolded her. Perhaps there was a way to save both girls. Some way to ensure the purity of both their souls before it was too late. Frieda might be lost, but Katy had to save Maria. She had to prove to her husband and his brethren that they were mistaken. She prayed she would be able to do that. She owed it not just to her nieces but also to her dead sister. Katy could not bear to think that she had betrayed her kin by letting her nieces die. The thought nagged at her like a terrier shaking a rabbit.

The two girls had come to live with her in the hopes of being able to resurrect their lives, to start again.

Instead they had found only suffering, violence and evil. And in some way even she didn't fully understand, Katy blamed herself for that, and she knew the only way to expunge that guilt was by saving Maria's life. Poor, sweet, innocent Maria! She glanced heavenward, as if that gesture would somehow goad God into aiding one of his true followers. Maria didn't deserve to die and certainly not in the manner she was going to. Katy shuddered as she imagined the girl suffering so ghastly a fate.

She reached the road and slowed her pace momentarily, her breath coming in gasps. But she couldn't stop for long; she had to force herself on.

Somewhere up ahead she heard shouts, carried to her on the night wind. Then there was silence and she wondered if she had imagined it, but then they came again and she realised she was closer to the place she was looking for than she thought. That knowledge gave her renewed strength and she hurried on.

Forty-Two

The rope had been pulled so tightly around her wrists that it had grazed the soft flesh.

Maria didn't struggle as two Brotherhood members tied her to the stake at the centre of the clearing, she merely kept her eyes closed, as if hoping that her inability to see what they were doing to her might negate the seriousness of her situation.

She had seen the huge piles of wood spread around the stake as they had led her into the clearing, and her blood had run cold at the sight. She had cried softly when they dragged her from the horse and to the stake where she was now secured, and she had remained silent as they pulled the bundles of wood around her, some of them cursing her as they built the pyre that would finally incinerate her once it was lit. As she stood there helplessly, the ropes holding her in place, Maria could smell the aroma of the cut wood and it made her feel sick.

Several of the puritans gathered around the pyre held lighted torches; the flames flickering like portents of what was to come. That final conflagration was moments away, and Maria felt fresh tears running down her cheeks at the thought of what she would have to endure.

She could see their expectant faces all turned in her direction, some of them coloured yellow by the light of the torches they held. Her Uncle Gustav and the man she knew was called Franz stood next to each other among the other members of the Brotherhood. Maria searched her uncle's face for any flicker of emotion, but there was none. It was as if his features had been carved from granite. If he was feeling anything at all then it did not show on his gaunt face.

One of the other black-clad puritans approached Weil and nodded deferentially in his direction.

'Everything is ready, brother,' he said.

Weil remained motionless.

'Let us act now!' Franz urged. 'Let us destroy this evil!'

Weil swallowed hard and glanced at Maria briefly, but he could not hold his gaze upon her. Deep inside him it felt as if someone had knotted his intestines, screwed them into a tight ball. He sucked in a deep breath.

'Gustav,' Franz muttered.

Weil continued staring straight ahead, seemingly oblivious to what was going on around him.

'Gustav!' Franz insisted. 'We must act now! The time has come! If you cannot do it, then . . .'

'I know what must be done, Franz!' Weil snapped, looking at his companion. He held out his hand.

Franz gave him the lighted torch and Weil took a step towards the pile of wood that surrounded his niece. He looked at the girl, the breath catching in his throat.

'Please, uncle,' Maria said, mournfully.

Weil clenched his teeth, his hand wavering slightly. Franz moved closer to him.

'A Devil's trick to weaken your resolve!' he hissed. 'You know what you must do. She is not your niece any more, but a shell filled with evil. That evil must be destroyed! The soul must be cleansed! If you have not the strength, then let me rid the world of this creature!' He jabbed an accusatory finger at Maria.

'I will do it,' Weil said, his voice low. Franz saw the fury in his eyes. 'Do not doubt me, Franz. When have you ever seen me shrink from my duties as a servant of God?'

'But this is different.'

'No it isn't. Evil is before us. Evil must die. There is nothing different here.'

Weil took a step towards the bundles of wood and thrust the burning torch forward.

'Gustav, wait!'

The shout made him turn and he was surprised when he recognised the voice, too. A woman's voice. Several of the watching puritans were pushed aside as Katy Weil shoved her way through to reach her husband. She almost stumbled in her haste, waving her hands before her to stop him.

'Please, Gustav!' she called. 'Put down the torch! Listen to what I have to say!'

'There is nothing to say,' Weil told her. 'There is nothing we can do for her.'

'She couldn't help it!' Katy blurted. 'It was Count Karnstein! He seduced her! Gustav listen, I beg you!'

'Not now, woman!' Weil snapped.

'She was under his spell!'

'Not now!'

He looked at his wife, then at two of the puritans standing nearby.

'Take her away,' Weil said, calmly. 'There is no need for her to see this.'

Two of the puritans gently gripped Katy's arms and began to pull her back, away from the appalling scene before her.

'Oh, for God's sake have mercy!' Katy called as they dragged her back, but only as far as the edge of the clearing, by turning her head Katy could still see what was happening.

'No!'

The shout came from Maria this time.

Weil looked dispassionately at her, the torch wavering in his grip.

'Please!' Maria called.

Franz grabbed for the torch.

'I will do it!' he snarled.

'No!' rasped Weil. 'How many times must I tell you? I know what must be done, and it is right that I be the one to do it. Now step aside!'

Franz hesitated a moment longer, then backed off.

'Prove yourself, Gustav,' he said, quietly. 'Prove to us all that you have the strength.'

'I have no need to prove anything to you, Franz,' Weil challenged, looking around at his companions. 'You or anyone else here.' He stepped forward and held the burning torch close to Maria, gazing at her through the flickering flames. She struggled helplessly against the rope that secured her to the stake. Weil began intoning prayers silently as he lowered the torch towards the wood, his lips moving soundlessly. He prayed for strength and he prayed for God to guide his hand. He pushed the torch into the nearest pile of wood, waiting for the flames to take hold.

Maria closed her eyes, her body shaking with fear now. Tears rolled warmly down her cheeks. She knew it was too late. Nothing could save her now.

Forty-Three

Something came flying at Weil. It whirled through the air and struck his arm, knocking the torch from his grasp. He spun round, clutching his arm in pain, seeing that another torch had been hurled at him and temporarily disarmed him.

'You've got the wrong girl!'

Weil saw that the words came from Anton Hoffer.

'You're burning Maria!' Anton shouted, advancing towards Weil. 'Stop, in the name of God!'

He strode into the clearing and stood only feet from Weil.

'It is in God's name that we act,' Weil told him. 'This is none of your concern, schoolmaster.'

'My sister was killed by a vampire,' Anton reminded him. 'Perhaps the vampire you now wish to burn, but she,' – he pointed at Maria – 'is no vampire!'

Weil shook his head.

'You cannot know this,' he said.

'You are bewitched by her!' Franz added.

Weil glanced at two of his companions. 'Seize him!' he snapped, pointing at Anton.

The two men nearest grabbed Anton, restraining him, one of them bending his right arm roughly.

'No, no, you fools!' Anton shouted, squirming against his captors. 'You've got the wrong girl! The Devil has outwitted you!'

Weil bent slowly and retrieved the torch that had been knocked from his hand. He held it before him, again gazing at the flames, then once more he moved nearer to the piles of wood.

'It's Maria you're burning!' Anton insisted. 'You must believe me!'

Weil turned his back on the schoolmaster.

'Why won't you listen to him?' Katy Weil called, her voice echoing across the clearing.

'Frieda's the evil one!' Anton continued, still struggling against the two men who held him. 'And while you're burning this innocent girl, Frieda is claiming more victims!'

'Don't listen to him, Gustav!' Franz insisted.

'The Devil has taken your mind!' bellowed Anton.

'You are as filled with evil as the one you seek to protect!' Franz told him.

'Am I?' Anton challenged. 'Hold up the Holy Cross and see if either of us flinches.'

Weil looked at Maria, then turned slowly and glared at Anton.

'Do it!' Anton insisted. 'Hold up the cross before us both.'

'It is a trick,' Franz insisted, looking at Weil. 'Don't listen to him.'

Anton managed to pull free of his captors. He fell to the ground, but hauled himself upright immediately and stood before Weil.

'Show us the cross!' he said, angrily, pushing one of the puritans away with one powerful hand when they made to grab him again. 'Do it!'

Weil met his gaze, then nudged Franz, who immediately slipped his hand inside his tunic and pulled out a gleaming silver cross. He took a few steps towards the stake, then pushed the holy symbol towards Maria.'Oh God! Oh God!' Maria gasped gratefully at the sight of the cross.

As Franz moved it closer, she leant forward and kissed the crucifix.

'You see!' Katy Weil called, shaking loose of the men who held her. She ran across towards the bundles of wood, tears running down her cheeks. She crossed herself, dropping to her knees thankfully. 'Oh Maria! Maria!'

Weil swallowed hard, his expression lifeless, his face as white as milk.

'Set her free!' one of the other puritans shouted.

'Wait!' Franz insisted.

'For what?' Weil snapped. 'We have seen the truth with our own eyes. She is innocent.'

'Yes, she is innocent, but what of her sister?' Franz continued. 'Where is she?' He turned and looked at Katy, who was still on her knees, her hands clasped in prayer.

'She is with Count Karnstein,' Katy told him, flatly. 'He transformed her. She seeks his protection now.'

'Do you believe now?' Anton snapped, glaring at the other puritans. 'You would have killed another innocent girl for the sake of your beliefs and your ignorance.'

'How were we to know?' Franz asked. 'The girls are identical.'

'You fool!' sneered Anton.

Weil dropped to his knees beside his wife as several of the other puritans hurried to free Maria, cutting through the ropes with knives in their haste to release her.

'Oh Lord!' Weil wailed, his head turned heavenward. 'Lord, forgive me!'

Anton looked down at the older man and, despite his anger, he could not prevent himself from feeling a twinge of sympathy.

'Your devotion almost cost the life of your own niece, Gustav,' he reminded him.

'I know that,' Weil breathed. 'Thank God she was spared.'

'Now what do we do?' one of the other pilgrims called.

'Seek the evil where you know it to truly be,' Anton answered, gazing around at the black-clad men. 'You know of who and what I speak. That is the evil that must be destroyed, the wickedness that must be cleansed!'

Franz nodded.

'It must be scourged from this land forever!' Anton intoned.

Katy moved towards her husband and touched him gently on the shoulder.

'Frieda is with Count Karnstein, Gustav,' she said, softly. 'Will you dare burn him?'

Forty-Four

'The Emperor would send soldiers to burn our homes, our churches!'

The voice echoed around the building for a moment, before being engulfed by the sound of raised voices, which reverberated around the inside of the Brotherhood's meeting house.

'We would all be executed for treason!' another roared.

Men shouted to make themselves heard above one another, each call louder than the next. On the tiered benches some were standing, others remained seated, attempting to either listen to the viewpoints being put forward or desperate to add their own thoughts. Some were arguing with their companions, and it seemed that the verbal free for all would go on for some time unless quelled.

'With the Emperor supporting him, the Count is untouchable,' another man offered.

Anton Hoffer stood close to the large wooden table in the centre of the room, then walked towards the lectern where the large leather-bound Bible lay.

'Oh, yes!' he called, his voice cutting through the babble of conversation. 'You're very quick to ride out into the forest to seek a young girl or a mad old man! Anyone you can use as a convenient sacrifice to your conscience!'

Fingers were pointed angrily at Anton, but he continued, unbowed by the furious reactions of the Brotherhood.

'But when it comes to the great lord at the castle, though you know he works with evil, you hesitate,' he grunted, dismissively.

'We cannot touch him!' one of the men called.

'How can we defy the Emperor?' another added.

'Count Karnstein defies God Himself – is that not reason enough to confront him?' Anton barked at them.

Several shouts of agreement greeted his comment.

Behind the great wooden table, Weil sat motionless, his eyes barely leaving Anton as the schoolmaster spoke. The older man still seemed shaken by what had happened earlier, the knowledge of what he had come so close to doing had chilled him to the very core. Beside him, Franz also listened, banging the table with his hand on more than one occasion to demand silence, so that each voice could be heard and each viewpoint considered, but it was useless. The men of the Brotherhood were in no mood to be silenced this particular night.

'Are you afraid of the Emperor or of the Count himself?' Anton continued defiantly.

'We are not afraid,' Franz told him, getting to his feet. 'We serve the Lord. He is our protection.'

'Then let him be your protection and seek out the evil you fear where it really is!' snarled Anton. 'In the castle on the hill!' He jabbed a finger through the air, as if to point out the edifice of which he spoke.

'Aye!' roared several of the Brotherhood. Some stamped their feet on the wooden floor as a sign of agreement, the sound mingling with the voices to form a cacophony.

Anton stood before the table now, his eyes darting back and forth at the faces of the men who watched him.

'For centuries the Karnsteins have practised every evil known to man with their master the Devil,' he shouted, 'and no one has seen fit to stop them!'

There were more shouts of agreement.

'That time has come, and we must not let it pass!' continued Anton vehemently.

'He's right!' another of the Brotherhood shouted, and another chorus of shouts and floor-beating greeted his words. 'We cannot allow this to continue!'

'We all know what Karnstein does!' another of the men called. 'We know of the vile goings-on up at the castle, so others must have knowledge of it, too. The Emperor must be aware of the heresies the Count performs. Why doesn't he act?'

'Because every man, king or peasant is afraid of the Devil,' Anton proclaimed. 'But there comes a time when courage must outweigh fear, when a belief in the Lord must be not a pious belief, but a reality in the face of death and damnation!'

'Aye!' chorused several of the Brotherhood.

'We know what we must do!' another shouted, raising his fist in the air.

Again Franz held up his hands for silence and gradually the noise in the room died down. He lowered his hands slowly, aware now that he had the attention of all the brethren.

'If Count Karnstein is a vampire, then no ruler on earth will save him,' he said, flatly.

'Let him burn as others before him have burned!' bellowed one of the puritans at the back of the room. He was a huge man with fists like ham hocks and several of those near him patted his broad back as he shouted his words.

'No!' Anton called, waiting until the throng had quieted once again. 'Burning is useless.'

The Brotherhood looked at him, all eyes on the schoolmaster now as he spoke. They listened to each word with something approaching deference.

'Fire will not vanquish vampires,' Anton told them. 'You must stake them through the heart or cut off their heads.'

'But they will burn, too,' Franz offered.

'Their bodies will burn, but their spirits will survive and they will possess others,' Anton went on. 'They have powers unlike anything we have ever encountered before.'

'Is it true they can change their form?' one of the other men called.

'Some of the more powerful vampires can supposedly transform themselves into wolves or bats,' Anton informed the watching group. 'They are creatures of the night, so they have an affinity with others that thrive in the darkness. They can also control animals such as rats if necessary. And certain scholars believe they can also control the elements, the rain or the storm, and that they can summon fog or mist if that is their wish.'

'How can we fight power like that?' one of the Brotherhood enquired warily.

'Because the powers we have against them are just as strong,' Anton insisted.

'Can they cast spells like witches?' another man asked.

'They have the power of hypnosis,' said Anton. 'The ability to induce trance-like states in those they seek to victimise.' He shuddered involuntarily as he thought of his encounter with Frieda in the bedroom only hours earlier. How easy it had been for her to use those powers on him, he thought. If her powers were so strong, then Count Karnstein's must be even more formidable. He leaned back against the wooden table for a moment, swallowing hard at the recollection.

'And their bite?' Franz interjected.

Anton sucked in a deep breath before continuing.

'The bite kills,' he said flatly. 'Unless the victim actually desires it. If that is the case, then the victim will also become a vampire.' He turned and glanced at Weil. 'That is what must have happened in Frieda's case. She must have been bitten by Count Karnstein and he infected her with his evil.'

Weil did not move, but merely sat in his immobile position, the noise and conversation washing around him like water rushing past a broken dam.

'And what of Karnstein himself?' one of the Brotherhood asked. 'Who turned him into a vampire?'

Anton could only shake his head.

'Some other creature of the night,' he offered. 'We will never know. He may have been infected with this pestilence for a year or a hundred years.'

'And the black man in his employ?' Franz demanded. 'Is he a vampire too?'

'No,' Anton told the other man. 'He is human. A servant and a protector. It would be his duty to guard Karnstein when he rests in his coffin. Something he must do every day between sunrise and sunset. He cannot emerge from his hiding place during the daylight. The rays of the sun will destroy him.'

'But I've seen Karnstein in the village during the day,' Franz protested. 'Why didn't he die if what you say is true? How could he have walked around in the daylight?'

'The daylight itself is not fatal to a vampire,' Anton informed him. 'Only the direct rays of the sun. On a cloudy or foggy day the vampire is still free to move about, even between sunrise and sunset, but his powers are more limited. When the night comes his true strength returns.'

'So now he is at his most powerful,' Franz intoned.

'Powerful, but still vulnerable if we use the right weapons,' Anton insisted. 'Remember, decapitation or a stake through the heart will destroy him and his kind. Sharpen the end of your wooden stakes, use lances, axes.'

'Aye!' the assembled throng boomed in chorus.

'Let us rid ourselves of this evil forever!' another man shouted and, as one, the Brotherhood rose and surged forward from the tiered benches, pouring towards the doors of the meeting house imbued with a strength and determination that seemed to carry them on like a tide. Anton nodded as he watched them. Only as the last of the men hurried out of the building did Gustav Weil finally get to his feet. He walked slowly around to join Anton, his face ashen.

'Anton,' he said, quietly. 'Is it true that the stake through the heart or decapitation returns the victim's innocence – sends their soul to God?'

Anton nodded gently and placed one hand on the shoulder of the older man, who suddenly looked very frail and unsteady.

'So there is some hope for Frieda?' Weil enquired. 'That the innocence will return when she is freed from this evil?'

'If one spark of God's spirit remains in her, then yes, Gustav, she will be free again.'

Weil nodded and turned away from the schoolmaster.

'Thank you,' he murmured under his breath. 'I pray that you are right.'

Forty-Five

The cutting edge of the machete gleamed as the black-smith raised it into the air. He turned the weapon, hefting it before him, then handing it to Gustav Weil, who inspected the blade.

'Sharper,' Weil insisted, handing the machete back to the huge man wearing the leather apron.

The blacksmith nodded and took the blade back, grinding its already razor edge on the stone, causing a loud hissing noise each time he drew the metal back and forth.

He had been woken from a fitful sleep less than an hour earlier by a furious banging on his door, and also by dozens of voices in the narrow street. Tumbling out of bed, the blacksmith had seen not just members of the Brotherhood milling around outside his shop, but also lots of villagers whom he recognised, and every one of them, it seemed, carried a weapon of one kind or another. Even from his bedroom window a quick scan of the crowd had revealed men brandishing pitchforks, scythes, sickles, swords, spears, lances and knives of every length. His wife, also woken by the fracas outside, had asked him what was happening, but the blacksmith had been unable to furnish her with an adequate answer as he'd struggled to pull on his clothes and find the keys to unlock the door of his business before it was battered down.

What the hell could so many men want of him at such an ungodly hour of the night? he had wondered as he made his way to the main doors. The presence of the Brotherhood members had made him feel uneasy from the beginning, but he had also seen faces that he recognised among the other villagers. The baker, the apothecary, the innkeeper and several other men he knew well had been down in the street, talking agitatedly among themselves and occasionally waving whichever weapon they held in the air before them. But he had seen women in among them, too. Katy Weil, for one, he had seen talking to the schoolmaster Anton Hoffer, and also one of Gustav Weil's young nieces. Which one he couldn't tell, but he had certainly seen the girl. He could hear a cacophony of sounds filling the street and rising into the night air, and his only thought was that there was trouble in store for someone. This crowd could not have looked more bloodthirsty and filled with hate had it been going off to war, and the blacksmith wondered who was to be the recipient of so much obvious fury.

He had opened the door of his house to be met by Gustav Weil, who had ordered him to open his stable so that the men could all be attended to as quickly as possible. The blacksmith had asked why, but had been told only that they were on God's business, and that if he did not help them, then he would have a higher power to answer to. One of the men had mentioned the name of Count Karnstein and the blacksmith had shuddered at the name, hurrying back into the house to call on his son for help. The boy was seventeen and learning the trade of smithing from his father. He hurried down to help, still dressed in a long nightgown, his eyes bleary from sleep.

The blacksmith and his son, under instructions from Weil, had swiftly and expertly sharpened every single implement pushed their way, including a bundle of long tree branches. More than once the blacksmith had thought about asking what the purpose of this was, but he had been kept so busy that the words had not come. Now he passed the machete back to Weil and watched as the Brotherhood man swung it through the air, where it caused a loud whoosh as it cut through the night. Weil nodded as he pressed his thumb to its edge.

No sooner had he stepped aside than one of the villagers moved into his place, handing the blacksmith a large double-edged axe. He took it and set about honing the edges, while his son did the same with a wickedly curved sickle that another Brotherhood member passed him. The blacksmith was sweating now, despite the chill of the night; the perspiration dripped from his face and chin, some of it landing on the razor-sharp blade of the axe. He wiped it with a cloth and handed it back to the villager, who nodded his gratitude before following Weil, who was now standing before the assembled throng of men in the street. Beyond them there were horses, the animals pawing the ground and neighing expectantly. They seemed as tense as their masters, the blacksmith thought.

Weil looked once more at the men gathered around him, then walked to his horse and swung himself into the saddle, raising the machete above his head like a cavalry officer about to lead a charge into battle. Katy and Maria looked up at him expectantly, and he even managed a brief grim smile in their direction as he sat there proudly on his horse.

'God is with our cause!' he shouted. 'To the castle!'

'Aye!' the others roared back, the sound filling the narrow streets of Karnstein like a tidal wave. A sea of weapons were raised into the air and the men watched as Weil snapped the reins of his mount and turned the animal, urging it along at a walk, while other puritans mounted their own horses and the villagers hurried along in pursuit.

The blacksmith looked on in bewilderment, his son also gazing at the horde of men and women who moved off as one in pursuit of Gustav Weil.

The boy looked at his father, as if seeking an answer, but the blacksmith could only shrug. As the two of them stood there the blacksmith's wife also appeared at their sides. She crossed herself and then pulled at the arms of her husband and son, wanting them back inside the house. They were only too happy to oblige and retreated, the blacksmith locking the door once again.

High above, in the night sky, the moon cast a cold white light over the entire landscape and, not even knowing why, despite the fact there was still sweat dripping from his body due to his recent exertions, the blacksmith shivered and felt the hairs at the back of his neck rise.

Forty-Six

From the battlements of Karnstein Castle the advancing throng of villagers was clearly visible. The moon illuminated them, but the fact that many also carried flaming torches also made them less than anonymous, even within the dark confines of the forest that led up to the approaches of the building.

The castle had been built to withstand attacking armies, constructed to protect its inhabitants from assault over the centuries and it had succeeded in that task admirably. As he stood at the mullioned window of one of the highest turrets, Count Karnstein saw the villagers approaching and smiled to himself. What chance had they when the castle had been a haven for centuries against aggressors? What did a group of peasants hope to do when armies had failed? He sneered at their presumptuousness. But a part of him also felt rage that these peasants would dare to challenge his authority. How dare they defile the land that had been his family's for centuries? What right had they to put their dirty feet on ground he considered inviolate? His sneer turned to a scowl as he regarded the flickering flames of their torches.

Beside him, Frieda also saw the hordes of people as

they made their way towards the castle, but she was not so confident and moved closer to the Count, as if for comfort.

'You are shivering,' Karnstein observed, feeling her close to him. 'Is it the night air? Or fear of your Uncle Gustav?'

She didn't answer, but continued to gaze at the torches held by the advancing villagers.

'I often wondered if this would happen, and it has,' the Count mused. 'They have finally found enough courage in their weak and feeble hearts to confront me. Well, let them come.' He turned and headed down the stairs of the turret.

Frieda hesitated for a moment then followed him.

'B-but . . . ,' she stammered.

'But what?' the Count challenged. 'Are you frightened?'

Frieda shook her head, none too convincingly.

'No,' she murmured.

'They will never get in,' he told her. 'This castle has stood for centuries against far greater forces than theirs. I do not intend to concern myself with the antics of a handful of peasants and those fools led by your uncle.'

'They have torches. What if they set fire to the castle?'

'Is that what you are afraid of? Of that lovely white flesh burning in the fire of purification?'

'I don't want to die.'

'You have nothing to fear from those fools. You have nothing to fear from anyone any longer. No man can harm us, I have told you that before. Let them bring their fire.'

Frieda ran to him and gripped his arm.

'Let us go, quickly!' she insisted.

'Why? Fire will not burn us. Even if they do manage to set light to the castle we will be unharmed. The flames will melt our bodies, but without pain. We will just laugh at them and find new bodies and new victims. We are beyond them. They fear *us*, we should not fear them.'

'If they fear us why are they coming here now?'

'They have been encouraged by your uncle, most likely. Perhaps he has found some new courage from somewhere. What do you think he did when your sister was burnt?' The Count nodded. 'Oh, yes, they will have purified her by now. Thinking that she is you they will have cast her into the flames. Does that thought not make you hate him even more?'

'Maria didn't deserve to die,' Frieda offered.

'Then she should have done as you did and come to me,' the Count proclaimed. 'Had she done so she would be here now, and she would be able to laugh at those fools as we do.'

Karnstein made his way briskly down the remainder of the curving stone staircase, emerging in the great hall of the castle. Frieda hurried after him, and as she made her way into the hall she saw a large figure enter from the other side of the cavernous room. A black-skinned figure that she recognised. Joachim ran towards his master, his ebony skin greasy with perspiration and his eyes wide with fear. He was grunting unintelligibly, motioning with his huge hands.

'Yes, Joachim,' the Count said, evenly. 'We know they are coming. We are waiting for them.'

The black man opened his mouth again, but once more only babbled sounds came forth, no words that Frieda could understand, but he crossed his hands before him, holding them up to show the Count.

'They have crosses?' Karnstein said, evenly.

Joachim nodded and pointed furiously over his shoulder in the general direction of the main entrance to the castle and the approaching villagers.

He extended one long index finger and scraped the other against it in an unmistakeable gesture. Then he slammed a fist against his heart and shook his head.

'And stakes?' Karnstein intoned, his expression growing darker.

Joachim nodded and hastily mimed the swinging of an axe several times, then pulled one index finger across his throat.

'And axes?' the Count hissed.

Once more the black man nodded, still babbling.

'Your uncle thought that the only way to destroy us was by fire,' Karnstein snapped, looking at Frieda. 'If they now have axes, crosses and stakes, then he has spoken to someone with more knowledge than he.'

The Count turned away for a moment, then suddenly spun back towards Frieda, swinging one powerful hand at her. The blow caught her across the cheek and sent her sprawling.

'Anton Hoffer!' he snarled. 'That schoolmaster has been talking to them. The man you lusted after has given them the tools to destroy us.'

Frieda knelt before him, rubbing her cheek and gazing up at Karnstein.

'We have to get out of here,' he told her as she scrambled to her feet, turning towards the archway that led to the main entrance to the castle.

'No!' Karnstein shouted. 'We will take the old tunnel.' He shot out a hand and pulled her to him. 'Come.'

'What tunnel?' Frieda asked.

'Over the years many tunnels were built beneath the castle offering escape routes for those inside, in case attackers managed to breech the walls,' the Count explained. 'They run deep underground and no one but myself has knowledge of them.'

'And can we get out using one of them?' Frieda asked.

Karnstein nodded and pulled her towards a huge metal-braced wooden door set into the wall of the great hall. The lock and hinges looked rusty from years of neglect, but when the Count pulled the door it opened easily, despite the whine of the rusted hinges.

'This way,' he urged.

Frieda stepped through the opening and Joachim made to follow her, but the Count held up a hand to block his movement.

'No, Joachim,' he said, firmly. 'Someone must hold them off. You must go that way.' He jabbed a finger in the other direction

The black man hesitated a moment, then nodded almost imperceptibly, watching as the door Karnstein had opened was closed behind him and Frieda. Joachim heard their footsteps echoing away on the other side of the door and he turned, snatching a mace and a machete from a display on the wall nearby. The machete he slid into his belt, the mace he swung before him. The heavy

335

metal ball, welded to a chain, was tipped with iron spikes and it made a loud whoosh as he swung it. Satisfied with the weapons, Joachim made his way back through the great hall towards the main entrance of the castle.

Outside he could hear the shouts and triumphant howls of the villagers, and then a series of loud impacts against wood. He realised they were trying to batter open the castle gate. He hurried off to meet their attack.

He knew what he must do.

Forty-Seven

It took ten men to carry the fallen tree trunk, but the villagers found strength they didn't know they had as they slammed it against the large wooden gate, the last obstacle between them and the courtyard of Karnstein Castle.

Urged on by the others, they swung the battering ram back and forth, the impact jarring them each time it struck the door, but with each blow the wood of the gate seemed to bow. They shouted encouragement to each other as well, sweat pouring from their faces as they strove to breach the gate. They knew that beyond it lay the object of their attack, the figurehead of the evil they sought so vehemently to wipe out once and for all, and the knowledge drove them to greater efforts.

Another man ran across the drawbridge and swung his axe at the recalcitrant wood of the gate. Others joined him and it seemed that if the battering ram couldn't gain entry for them, then they would simply chop their way right through the barrier to get to the Count. Those watching brandished their torches in the air and bellowed encouragement. Even the group of women, who had made the journey from the village with them, screamed and howled like mad things as their men continued to hammer at the gate.

Seated on his horse towards the rear of the throng, Gustav Weil watched, as did Anton Hoffer, both men gazing fixedly at the castle, occasionally glancing up towards the battlements.

Another thunderous impact against the gate from the battering ram and the sound of splintering wood suddenly filled the night air. A large split appeared in the gate around the lock and, encouraged by their efforts, the villagers slammed the battering ram against the weakening gate with ever-greater ferocity. The next impact caused the entire gate to shake uncertainly on its massive hinges. A piece of wood the size of a man's arm came free. More men rushed in to help lift the tree trunk, and the increased power meant it could be wielded more efficiently. Back and forth, back and forth in a rhythmic motion. Each impact now was causing more damage. The gate wobbled uncertainly each time it was struck. The villagers saw this and shouted expectantly.

With one last superhuman effort they sent the tree trunk smashing into the gate with such power that the heavy partition simply burst open. Portions of the gate splintered, but it opened far enough to allow the leading men through. Shouts of triumph echoed through the night as the villagers and the Brotherhood poured through the open gate into the courtyard of the castle, weapons brandished above their heads, their desire for revenge now filling them like some kind of raging fever. They called Karnstein's name in tones brimming with hatred, their eyes darting around the courtyard towards the many archways and embrasures, each one of which would have to be explored as they searched for the man they sought.

Anton and Weil urged their horses across the draw-bridge into the courtyard, followed by other mounted members of the Brotherhood.

'Franz!' Anton called, jabbing a finger around him. 'See that the women stay back near the gate! We must search every tunnel! Karnstein must be found!'

Franz swung himself from the saddle and moved towards the group of women who had entered the courtyard, led by Katy Weil and Maria. He stood before them to block their advance.

'Stop!' he said. 'Wait! We must find Karnstein first!'

'Let us help!' Katy protested.

'No, it's too dangerous!' Franz insisted.

'The entrance to the great hall is there!' Anton roared, pointing towards a set of stone steps that led up to a large wooden door to their right. 'Come on! Karnstein must be inside somewhere!' He ran towards the steps, but several of the villagers got there before him and pounded up the stairs towards the door, brandishing their weapons.

They were halfway up when Joachim emerged from the doorway and stood in front of them, swinging the mace. With his free hand he reached for the blazing torch that was jammed into a bracket on the wall close to the door. He moved it back and forth before him, watching as the villagers hesitated.

'Kill the black savage!' one of them shouted, and two men advanced towards Joachim.

He swung the mace and caught the first man in the face with it. The heavy spiked ball smashed into the man's cheek, shattered the bone and almost ripped the bottom jaw free. Blood erupted from the wound and the man fell backwards down the stairs. Another man ran forward and swung his axe at Joachim, but the black man avoided the stroke and jammed the burning torch forward into the man's face. The villager shrieked in agony as the fire burned his skin, blackening the flesh there and bursting the eyeball as it made contact with the sensitive orb. He fell backwards, too, those behind stepping over him in their eagerness to get to Joachim, who swung the mace once more, catching another man across the shoulder, splintering his collar bone and causing him to drop to his knees in agony. Another quick swing of the metal ball pulverised his skull. However, the spikes remained jammed in what was left of the skull and as the body fell forward, the mace was pulled from Joachim's grip.

Snarling, he pulled the machete from his belt and blocked the downward swipe of a sickle with the blade. He struck out in defence and caught the attacker across the throat with a blow so powerful it practically severed his head. Blood burst from the massive wound, some of it spattering Joachim, who pushed the man away and turned his attention to two more villagers jabbing at him with knives.

He struck ferociously at the first of them, severing the man's hand just above the wrist.

The other he cut downwards through the shoulder and then the head, driving the sharp blade so deep it practically cleft the man's head in two. As Joachim tore at the blade and tried to pull it free, portions of brain matter sprayed those nearby.

One of the other villagers struck out with a pitch-fork, driving one of the prongs into Joachim's left thigh. The long metal spike punctured muscle and scraped the bone as it was driven home. Blood erupted from the wound and Joachim roared madly, grabbing a man and twisting his head sharply to one side to break his neck, but sheer weight of numbers was too much for him and the villagers attacked from all sides with their weapons and fists.

An axe caught him across the face, laying it open to the bone. Then a heavy stick smashed him repeatedly across the top of the head and he felt himself losing balance. Hands dragged him down, spread-eagling him on the stone steps, holding him helpless there.

'Stake him!' someone roared.

Franz stepped forward, gripping in both hands a length of wickedly sharpened wood. He looked at Joachim and smiled crookedly as the black man struggled helplessly against the hands that pinned him down.

'Through his heart!' a voice bellowed.

'Destroy the beast!' called another man, his face contorted with hatred and rage.

Joachim tried to scream, but no sound came.

Franz drew back the stake, then, with tremendous power, he drove it forward, ramming the pointed wood through Joachim's chest and into his heart. There was an eruption of blood, the crimson fountain arcing into the night air drenching several of those holding him. Franz put all his weight on the stake, pushing it deeper until it burst from Joachim's back and scraped the stone steps beneath him.

Cheers greeted the act and the villagers backed away from the body, some spitting on it as they passed.

'Find Karnstein!' someone shouted. 'Find the master! He's the one we want!'

The furious horde swept on into the great hall of Karnstein Castle.

Forty-Eight

The tunnel was narrow.

As Frieda hurried along the subterranean passageway behind Count Karnstein she had to duck her head occasionally, the roof of the tunnel was so low. The walls seemed to press in from both sides, bare rock that appeared to be held together solely by the thick spider webs that covered it and hung from the roof like gossamer streamers. The size of the creatures that spun webs as large as this was best not considered. But for the most part the webs were covered in a thick film of dust, showing how long it had been since anyone had frequented these underground walkways.

There was an overpowering stench of damp and neglect throughout the whole length of the tunnel. The ground was bare earth in many places, and worms writhed in this dark and fetid soil. There were metal brackets on the walls on both sides, where torches would once have been placed to give light to those who used them, but not this night. The only light was from the torch carried by Count Karnstein as he led the way along the tunnel, as sure-footed as a mountain goat on a rocky ledge. It was as if he didn't need the light of the torch. He could move perfectly well in the enveloping blackness, at home within its embrace.

Frieda could feel the cold stone beneath her feet and the chill felt as if it was seeping through her entire body, coursing through her veins like iced water, but she hurried on, anxious not to become separated from the Count in this underground labyrinth. Because as she moved on she could see that there were other archways leading off from this main tunnel. Some were barred shut by heavy, metal-braced wooden doors, but others were open to reveal the black maws of fresh tunnels beyond. Where these other walkways led Frieda had no idea. For all she knew they went to the very centre of the earth, right down into hell itself.

Karnstein strode on almost disinterestedly, and he certainly looked sure of his destination. Not once did he glance over his shoulder to check that Frieda was still close. Escape was his only concern and if he should attain his goal with her then that was fine, but if he was the only one to extricate himself from the situation, then he seemed equally satisfied with that eventuality, too.

'Where do these other tunnels lead?' Frieda wanted to know.

'Does it matter?' Karnstein said, without looking around. 'If we carry on this way we will find our way out.'

'Are you sure?'

'Of course I'm sure! I know every inch of this castle.'

'What of my uncle? What if he and the others find us?'

'Those fools couldn't find a silver coin in a heap of horse droppings. We will be away from here before they even know we are gone. Joachim will hold them off until we escape.'

'But he is one, they are many.'

'If he has to die to protect me, then he will.'

'You expect him to die for you?'

'It is his duty. He has always known that.'

They moved on, the tunnel floor sloping downwards slightly. Frieda could hear the sound of dripping water and glanced upwards. The smell inside the tunnel also seemed to be getting stronger, a heavy rancid odour more pungent than damp earth. It smelt of something rotten and long dead. For the first time Frieda noticed shapes in the other tunnel mouths, and she realised that some of them were human skeletons.

'Cells,' Karnstein said in answer to her unasked question. 'Those who opposed my family and my ancestors have perished down here over the centuries. How amusing would it be to see your Uncle Gustav chained down here with others who have rebelled against my family!'

Frieda managed a thin smile.

'I would happily see Anton Hoffer chained in here, too,' the Count went on. 'Or better still dead – curse him and his interfering ways! If not for him those fools who followed your uncle here would have no idea how to fight us. Their fire would be useless. He is the one who gave them the information they needed to confront us. Where they acquired their courage I have no idea. I doubt it was from your uncle.'

Visible in the sickly yellow torchlight was a large door about ten yards ahead of them, towards which the

Count now moved. He brushed some cobwebs from the lock and slipped his hand into the large metal ring that hung above it. Gritting his teeth, he pulled and the door opened a fraction. The hinges that had not tasted oil for many years screamed in protest, but Karnstein pulled harder and the door opened further.

Beyond it there was a flight of stone steps leading up towards a collection of carved monuments and crypts.

'The graves of my ancestors,' Karnstein said, quietly. 'That is the way we must go.'

He pulled Frieda forward and put his hands on her shoulders, pushing her gently in front of him.

She could see a low curtain of mist over the stairs and the murky graveyard at the top. Gnarled and twisted trees stood like sentinels over the graves and monuments. Most noticeable among the monoliths was a large mausoleum that sported a particularly fearsome-looking stone eagle on its roof. Frieda glared warily at the carving for a moment, as if it were real.

'You must go first,' the Count told her, pointing to the graveyard. 'I'll keep watch.'

Frieda hesitated, then nodded.

'Soon we will be away from them,' Karnstein told her. 'Free of their twisted, misguided morality and beliefs.'

Frieda smiled and moved slowly towards the bottom of the stone steps, pausing again before she began to climb, glancing right and left as she did. It was unnaturally silent in and around the graveyard and she could hear the crackle of fallen leaves beneath her feet as she climbed to the top of the stone flight, the breeze causing her hair and the dress she wore to flutter. She glanced back at Karnstein, who was standing in the doorway of the tunnel, watching her intently.

Frieda reached the top step and smiled triumphantly in the Count's direction.

As she did so a hand shot forward from the shadows to her left and grabbed her hair.

She hissed, trying to turn to see who had seized her long locks, her fangs glistening as she opened her mouth in rage. She managed to turn enough to see Gustav Weil standing before her.

It was his gloved hand that had grabbed her.

He who held the machete high above his head.

He who was glaring at her with a mixture of fury and triumph.

Weil swung the machete down with incredible power. A blow that combined expertise with tremendous strength.

The blade sliced effortlessly through Frieda's neck, severing her head in a single stroke.

Blood erupted from the stump, spewing in huge arcs into the cold air. The headless body swayed uncertainly for a second, then pitched backwards, tumbling down the stone steps, more crimson jetting from the veins and arteries.

Weil held the head in his hand and looked at it, ignoring the blood gushing from it. He stared directly into the still open eyes, noting too that the lips were moving slightly.

He had read once that a severed head could live for up to five seconds after it has been struck from the body, and he wondered now if Frieda was able to see what was going on around her and able to comprehend the terrible fate she had suffered. Were those movements of her lips an attempt at redemption? Was she trying to tell him how sorry she was? Had the good in her finally returned at the point of death, as Anton had said it could? Weil prayed it was the case.

He was interrupted from his musings by the sound of the heavy door at the bottom of the steps being pushed shut once again. Weil shot a wary glance towards the sound of scraping metal against stone and saw Count Karnstein standing in the gap between the door and its frame. He could see that the tall aristocrat was attempting to shut the huge door again and Weil took his chance.

He hurtled down the stone steps with a speed and agility that belied his years, stepped over the body of Frieda and slammed his shoulder into the door in an effort to stop the Count from closing it. However, his efforts were in vain. The weight of the door and the strength of Karnstein prevented entry. The door was slammed shut with a deafening clang and Weil heard the sound of bolts being slid hastily into place on the other side. He grabbed the handle and tugged furiously, but the door refused to budge. Weil kicked at it for a second in rage and frustration, then realised that no amount of physical force was going to allow him through.

He moved back a couple of paces, his breath coming in short gasps as he stood there, his head bowed. Weil looked down at the headless body of Frieda and was suddenly overcome by an unstoppable wave of sadness.

It was an emotion he had not expected to feel, but it came nonetheless and, once more he looked at the severed head of his niece which he still gripped in his hand.

The features had softened and Weil thought he detected an uplifting of the corners of the mouth, as if in a smile. He nodded almost imperceptibly, then hurled the machete away in disgust, watching as it flew through the misty cold air and struck a tree. Weil stood motionless for a moment longer, then with infinite care he laid Frieda's severed head beside her still body, pulled his cloak from his shoulders and draped it over the corpse.

He crossed himself and murmured a prayer softly under his breath, his words interrupted when he heard movement from the top of the steps. He looked up to see that several of the Brotherhood and some villagers were gathered there, looking down at him. They held weapons of various kinds before them, which they lowered when they saw him. One of the Brotherhood pointed to the body beside Weil and was about to speak, but Weil raised a hand and nodded gently.

'It is over for her,' he said, softly. 'Her torment is at an end. Take her to the chapel.'

Forty-Nine

'What will they do to him when they catch him?'
The woman who asked the question was gazing up at the battlements of Karnstein Castle, her body quivering slightly in the chill night air. All along the ancient stone fortifications men from the village were moving back and forth, swarming over the castle like ants. Everywhere she looked there were men with weapons.

'If they catch him, you mean,' another offered. 'He's a crafty one and he has the Devil on his side. They won't find him easily.'

'They'll get him,' Katy Weil said confidently, glancing around the courtyard at the men as they dashed back and forth, weapons brandished as they searched furiously.

'Can you imagine how many places there must be to hide in the castle?' the second woman went on. 'And he'll know every one of them.'

'They will find him,' Katy said again, not sure if she was trying to persuade the woman or herself.

Upon entering the courtyard of the castle, Franz had ensured that the women of the village were safely placed just below the tower that protected the drawbridge, gate and portcullis of the massive edifice. From their vantage point they were able to see the activity before them, but they were also safe from attack. There was nothing but blank stone wall behind them and on two sides here in the gatehouse. No hidden tunnels from which they could be approached. Katy watched as the men ran up the stone steps leading to the battlements, while others headed into the outbuildings off the courtyard. A group of them had already made their way into the main hall in their search for Count Karnstein.

There were a number of archways that led off from the main courtyard, but most had already been searched. A villager or member of the Brotherhood stood outside the ones they had explored so far to show they were clear. Alongside Katy, Maria also watched the men dashing back and forth. She reached for her aunt's hand and squeezed it. Katy smiled reassuringly at the girl and stroked her hair.

'The Devil protects his own,' the first woman said as two men ran past, one of them waving a scythe, the other holding a torch.

'And God guides the righteous,' Katy reminded her. 'God is with us. He will guide our men to Karnstein, and He will protect them when they destroy him.'

'And what of your sister?' the second woman hissed. 'She is with Karnstein now. She is evil like him. How do we know we can trust you? If one of you is evil, then the other might be too.'

Katy shot the woman a furious glance.

'Keep your stupid thoughts to yourself!' she snapped.

'There is only good in this girl.' She slipped a comforting arm around Maria's shoulders.

Maria was about to say something, when she suddenly grabbed at her own neck, her mouth dropping open in surprise and pain. Katy saw the gesture and looked at her with concern.

'What is it child?' she said. 'What's the matter?'

'I don't know,' Maria told her, still massaging her neck. 'I suddenly felt a terrible pain, but . . .' The sentence trailed off and Maria looked around her. 'Something has happened to Frieda! I know it.' She took a step away from Katy who tried to restrain her. 'I must find her!'

'No, you must stay here until Count Karnstein is found,' Katy protested, but Maria was pulling away from her again, looking off into the distance, as if at something that only she could see.

'I must find Frieda!' Maria insisted, and she wrenched herself free of Katy's grip and ran out from the gatehouse into the courtyard, almost colliding with a member of the Brotherhood, who paid her only a cursory glance.

'No! Wait!' Katy called, moving after Maria, desperate to stop her.

Two puritans stepped in front of her, barring her way.

'You must stay inside the gatehouse, Frau Weil,' one of them said. 'It isn't safe until we find Karnstein.'

'But Maria . . .' Katy began.

'Frau Weil.'

Katy turned at the sound of a voice she recognised

and she saw Anton striding towards her, his face slicked with perspiration, a long lance gripped in his right hand.

'Frau Weil,' he said again, now within touching distance of her. 'Frieda's dead.'

Katy closed her eyes tightly and shook her head.

'Are you sure?'

Anton nodded.

'It was the only way,' he told her softly. 'Her soul is at peace now.'

'I hope you're right, Anton,' Katy said.

'You must take Maria back to the village,' he insisted.

'Maria's gone.'

'Where?'

'She went to find her sister.'

Katy drew in a terrified breath and crossed herself.

'Oh God!' she breathed. 'What if he has her, too?'

'We must find her quickly!' Anton snapped. He grabbed two of the villagers nearest to him. 'Look for the girl!' he told them. 'Find Maria!'

'But what about Count Karnstein?' one of them protested.

'There'll be time for him later,' Anton said. 'We must find Maria!'

Fifty

Maria was surprised at how easily she found it to slip out of the castle courtyard, despite the number of villagers and Brotherhood members dashing around. Perhaps, she reasoned, they were simply too concerned with finding Count Karnstein to pay her too much heed and for that she was grateful. She knew she must find Frieda and she needed as few obstacles as possible in the pursuit of that quest.

As she moved towards the archway at one end of the courtyard she shivered, and it was not just a product of the cold night air. It was a chill of foreboding that coursed through her. She had felt this kind of sensation before when she was separated from her sister. It was a kind of sixth sense possessed only of siblings who are so close, and there were none closer than Maria and Frieda. Even though she knew her sister was no longer the girl she had once been, despite the fact that she may be endangering her own life or even her soul trying to find her, Maria had no thoughts in her mind other than to see Frieda. She had to reach her. It was an obsessive thought in her mind, jammed there so deeply in her consciousness it would not budge.

Maria moved on, glancing around to make sure that

none of the men in the courtyard had seen her. Her progress was unhampered as she approached the archway. At the apex of the arch there was a huge carved stone eagle that seemed to look down upon her with its sightless eyes as she paused beneath it for a moment, before moving on towards what looked like a formal garden. High hedges, most of them overgrown and neglected and stumpy gnarled trees were the most immediate feature of this garden. The pathway beneath her feet was cracked, many of the paving stones broken and sticking up like rotten teeth. There were weeds poking through the gaps. Maria paused beside the mould-covered remains of a wooden pagoda, looking around to see which way she should go next. A thin layer of mist covering the ground swirled and billowed around her feet as she walked. There were more stone carvings dotted around, too, but they seemed to have been placed there with no thought of order or symmetry; in fact, to Maria it looked as if they had simply been thrown into the garden by some giant, uncaring hand to land where they fell.

She saw a carved bear towering over some bushes to her right. There was another animal that looked like a boar to the left and, perched on a stone pillar, another eagle. It was like walking through some macabre petrified zoo. Maria moved briskly through the garden, cutting across an overgrown lawn towards another path that twisted and turned down a slight incline, towards some more densely planted and even more overgrown trees and bushes.

Visible among these and about a hundred yards

ahead of her was a simple stone monument about six feet tall that seemed to grow upwards from the sour ground itself. As she drew nearer, Maria could see an inscription on the monument, and when she reached it she traced one of the words with her index finger.

KARNSTEIN.

She stepped back as she realised she was probably standing on a grave. The marker had been placed there to show the resting place of a former resident of the castle. Further ahead of her there were more of the stone monoliths and also the unmistakeable oblong shapes of small crypts. Maria shuddered and looked to her left. There was a high stone wall and set into it were two large wrought-iron gates. They were rusty with age, and as she drew closer to them she could see there was a stout padlock on the chain interwoven around them. Frieda had not left the castle grounds that way, Maria thought, and edged back on to the path that led her into the small cemetery.

Every grave marker she saw now had the word KARNSTEIN on it somewhere, and she realised she was moving among the burial places of the castle's previous inhabitants. The thought made her shudder even more. Maria paused for a moment, checking the ground for any sign of footprints and trying to think which direction Frieda might have gone if she'd left the castle, although for all Maria knew she was still inside with the Count. If that were the case, then she would have to get inside and look around. Even though the prospect of entering the massive edifice alone terrified her, the thought of what might have happened to her sister was even more frightening. She had to find Frieda, even if it meant putting her own life at risk.

Maria saw a flight of stone steps leading down towards a huge metal-braced door and despite her growing fear and unease she moved towards those steps. She stopped when she reached the top, the breath catching in her throat.

There was blood all over the ground here and it had also splashed down several of the steps, coating them crimson. At the bottom of those steps lay a single red shoe, and Maria recognised it immediately as belonging to her sister.

'Frieda,' she whispered and she descended the steps slowly, taking care not to slip, but keeping her gaze fixed firmly on the shoe, as if that simple act would somehow tell her what she needed to know. As if it would magically guide her to Frieda. Maria moved to the bottom of the steps, horrified to see that there was more blood pooled on the dark earth there. Careful to avoid the congealing mess, she reached for the shoe and picked it up, cradling it before her like a child that has just found a long lost doll.

Again she whispered her sister's name, her mind now racing, tortured by images she didn't want to see. Had some terrible accident befallen Frieda? Was this her blood that coloured the ground or did it belong to one of the men hunting her? Maria shook her head, touching her throat again almost unconsciously, remembering the pain she had felt so acutely only a short time earlier. That pain, she was now increasingly certain, was what her sister had felt and the realisation caused her heart to race even faster.

Maria was so concerned with her sister and what had become of her that she barely noticed the door behind her opening slightly. She remained where she was, half-crouching on the dark earth, the shoe held in her hand, wondering where she could look next for Frieda, tormented and appalled by the sight of the blood that had been splashed on the stairs and the dark ground all around her. Again her mind raced, wondering where this life fluid could have come from, and that knot in her stomach tightened until she could concentrate on nothing else. She knew she must get help. She had to find Anton or some of the other men from the village. Even though she had to find Frieda somehow, Maria knew that she could not perform the task alone. She had to have some help from the villagers. She wished Anton were with her now. He would know what to do. She stood motionless, the shoe still clutched in her hand.

Had she been more aware of what was going on around her, she would have heard the faint squeaking as the door was eased open a little further.

Had she turned, she would have seen the face of Count Karnstein looming at her from the darkness within.

But she saw and heard nothing, until he grabbed her and dragged her backwards through that door.

She managed one scream as he pulled her into the enveloping blackness.

Anton Hoffer heard the scream as he ran into the Karnstein cemetery and immediately he swung towards the source of it. Even without seeing, he knew it was Maria who had uttered the cry and he felt his body enveloped by a cold chill as the sound echoed around that mournful place, reverberating in his ears.

'Maria!' he gasped under his breath, then, as he turned in the direction from which the shout had come, he called her name louder still.

He reached the top of the flight of stone steps in time to see her being pulled backwards into the tunnel by Count Karnstein, the tall aristocrat smiling as he jerked Maria off her feet, such was the strength of his embrace. He slammed the huge door behind him as Anton launched himself down the steps in an effort to reach the girl.

Anton slammed into the door, but the impact didn't faze him. He hammered furiously on it, as if the very act would force the Count to admit him.

'Maria!' Anton roared, still slamming his fists against the thick partition.

From the other side of the door he heard her crying in protest, the sound growing fainter as she was dragged further away.

Anton kicked the door impotently, a gesture of despair as much as fury. And, for the first time that night, he was gripped by an overpowering and unshakeable fear that Maria was lost forever. He stood motionless against the door, his forehead pressed to the cold wood and his eyes closed.

On the other side of the door there was now only silence.

Fifty-One

Gustav Weil moved slowly but purposefully along the corridor inside the castle, glancing to right and left, wary of any sounds or movements.

Somewhere in the distance he could hear shouts and curses, but he knew the villagers and other members of the Brotherhood uttered these. He realised they were in some other part of the castle, well away from him, but with the same objective as he: namely, to find Count Karnstein and, once found, to destroy him forever.

Weil felt a combination of rage and sorrow coursing through his veins as he approached the small flight of steps that led towards another corridor a few yards further on. Unlike the passageway he was in, this one had doors leading off on both sides and Weil knew that each would have to be opened and the rooms beyond investigated. There were so many places to hide within the labyrinthine edifice of the castle that it may well take all night or even longer to hunt down Karnstein, but he was prepared to wait. He would take all the time he needed if it meant finally ridding the world of the Count.

Weil knew that he had been responsible for the death of Frieda. Yes, she had sought his company to begin with and she had revelled in the evil the Count had shown her, but she had still been *his* niece. His blood and Karnstein had transformed her from a beautiful young woman into a creature of the night and left but one course of action for any God-fearing and right-minded man. She could not have been allowed to live on, claiming more lives, feeding on the blood of the living and infecting even more people with the vile corruption that had tainted her own system. Karnstein had caused her death when he had infected her. He had condemned her to the eternal quest for blood and he had doomed her to walk the earth, seeking sustenance by murdering others. Weil clenched his teeth as he thought of her headless body lying in the chapel. He knew he had ended her torment and freed her soul, but that did not make the feelings coursing through him any easier to deal with. He had struck off his own niece's head, watched her decapitated body topple and fall, while he held the severed appendage before him.

He would never forget the look in her eyes before he swung the machete. The look of hatred and fury before the blade had sheared through her neck, but then the serenity that had filled her features when the evil had been vanquished. Weil was confident her soul was with God now and for that he was grateful. Were it not for Count Karnstein, she would still be alive and Weil intended to make the aristocrat pay for that once and for all.

He moved towards the nearest door and tried the handle. It was unlocked and he pushed it gently, stepping across the threshold, leaving the door open to allow the candlelight from the corridor to illuminate his progress. The room itself was large with a high ceiling and the light didn't reach every corner, so Weil moved cautiously. The shadows would hide Karnstein. Darkness was his ally and Weil was wary of that. He glanced around the room and saw that it contained little more than a small single bed and a couple of wooden chairs. He wondered if it might have been a servant's room at one time, but the thick layer of dust on the floor would seem to suggest that no one had occupied or even entered this room for a long time. He looked ahead, checking for footprints in the dust, but he saw none. Karnstein had not been inside this room, either. Weil backed into the corridor again, turning his attention to the next door.

This door was also unlocked and Weil turned the handle and walked in, pausing at the threshold this time, relieved to see it was lighter, because of the large windows on the far side of the room. The moonlight pouring in from outside made it much easier to pick out details of what lay inside. The walls were hung with tapestries and portraits and Weil moved inside, studying the faces that leered back at him from inside the ornate frames. There were men and women depicted there, and he guessed they were all ancestors of the present Count Karnstein. Weil paused beside one portrait in particular. It was of a young woman with long blonde hair and piercing blue eyes that the painter had captured perfectly. There was a small plaque at the base of the frame and it bore a name. Weil brushed his finger across it, removing a light film of dust and read the name.

COUNTESS MIRCALLA KARNSTEIN.

He moved further into the room and saw something large and heavy on the floor at the bottom of the four-poster bed. At first he thought it was a coffin, but then he realised it was just a trunk. Not sure why, he decided to open it and lifted the lid.

A nauseating stench rose from within and he stepped back as the rancid miasma filled his nostrils. He waited a moment, waving one hand before his face, then he glanced once again at the contents of the trunk, trying to discover what was causing the vile smell that seemed to be filling the room now, as if flowing from the trunk in invisible noxious waves.

He could see some material that he immediately identified as a woman's dress. Not the dress of a fine elegant woman, but the attire that might be worn by a simple peasant girl. There was also a balled-up linen sheet in there, stuffed over some of the other contents, as if to cover them. He noticed as he pulled the sheet aside that there were women's shoes in the trunk, and Weil was both horrified and disgusted to see that they were caked with dried blood. Everything inside the trunk was stained and coloured with the dark congealed substance. He crossed himself and lowered the lid almost reverentially. Who the clothes had once belonged to he could not begin to imagine. Some of Karnstein's other victims, he mused. Others who had given their lives so that he could live out his foulest and darkest desire. Weil was again overcome with anger.

He moved out of the room back into the corridor, hastening to the next door.

He was about to turn the handle when he heard sounds from close by: voices raised in anger and the unmistakeable sound of crying. A man's voice and then a woman's. But these were not the sounds made by the villagers and the Brotherhood that had reached his ears before. These sounds seemed to be right next to him, and they were coming from up ahead.

At the bottom of the corridor that he now prowled cautiously along there was a small flight of stone steps that rose upwards to some thick velvet curtains, which acted as a screen for what lay beyond. Weil was sure the sounds had come from that direction. He stood still for a moment, straining his ears to hear more, but silence descended once again and for a second he wasn't even sure if he'd heard the sounds to begin with. Perhaps the situation and his own overworked mind was playing tricks on him, God alone knew it would be understandable under the circumstances. He waited a moment longer to see if he could hear the voices again, then he returned his attention to the closed door before him.

Like the others it was unlocked. Weil was surprised at first, as he had been at how easily he'd gained access to the other rooms inside the castle, but why would Karnstein need to keep the doors inside his domain locked? Apart from his servant, no one else ever entered the monolithic building. There was no reason for the Count to be afraid of prying eyes or inquisitive visitors. Not until now. Weil smiled to himself and pushed open the door, allowing it to swing back on rusty hinges.

The room was pitch-black, the heavy curtains at each of the windows drawn shut. Weil moved cautiously into the room wishing he had a candle or torch with him, anything to help banish the tenebrous gloom that filled the room. He stepped back into the corridor and pulled one of the flaming torches from its bracket on the wall near the door, sweeping the object before him as he walked back in, the flame creating a halo of sickly orange light in the blackness.

Illuminated in this newfound glow, Weil saw a large oblong object laying against the far wall of the room.

It was a coffin.

He moved towards it slowly, the torch held before him. The lid of the box was down, hiding whatever might lie within, and Weil was suddenly acutely aware of the fact that he was unarmed. He looked around the room for anything that he might be able to use as a weapon should the need arise, but there was nothing other than a heavy brass candlestick propped on a wooden chest of drawers to his right. He closed his fingers around it and hefted it before him, happy with its considerable weight. Then he moved nearer to the coffin, standing over it, looking down at the box, his eyes scanning its details. The wood it was constructed from was very old and as Weil prodded the coffin with the toe of his boot he wondered if even that gentle contact might splinter the timber.

There were no plaques or markings on the lid, nothing to identify who might have once rested inside the box. He knelt beside it and, placing the candlestick on the floor, he slid his fingers under the lid of the coffin and lifted.

The lid came free with ease and he flipped it open, gazing down at the contents of the box.

A thick, damp, musky scent rose from inside and Weil recoiled from it, peering more closely now to see what lay before him. A thin layer of some dark material that he thought he recognised covered the bottom of the coffin. Slowly he pushed his hand towards it, allowing his fingers to slide into the matter coating the bottom of the coffin. It was earth. Slightly damp and freezing cold earth. Weil frowned. The dirt was about two inches thick. There were long gossamer-like hairs on the soil. Weil shook his head slowly and stood up again, digging one hand inside his jacket. He pulled out a silver crucifix. Weil kissed the holy symbol then laid it on the earth inside the coffin. He knew that vampires must rest in the soil of their birthplace during the hours of daylight, and perhaps this coffin was where Count Karnstein came to seek his shelter. If that were the case then the cross would prevent him from finding sanctuary here, Weil thought with a smile.

He was still enjoying this small victory when he heard voices again and, as before, they were close to him.

The male voice was deep and full of menace.

'Come on!' it snapped. 'Quick! Over here!'

The woman's voice responded with several more sobs and protests.

Weil moved out of the room towards the voices, now

certain they were coming from the top of the short flight of steps ahead of him and from behind the curtains at the top.

On the walls at the bottom of the steps there were a number of weapons displayed, held in place in metal brackets. Knives, swords, maces, spears and axes. Weil grabbed one of the axes and took it down, hefting it before him. The wickedly curved blade was reassuringly heavy and Weil nodded as he thought of the damage such a weapon could cause when wielded correctly.

Again he heard the deep voice of the man, followed by a squeal of discomfort and fear from the woman, and he sucked in a deep breath and gripped the axe more tightly in his hands. He was now certain that the man's voice belonged to Count Karnstein. Who he had with him Weil could only guess, but whoever it was she needed his help and he would not be slow in giving it.

He moved up the stairs towards the thick velvet curtains and whatever lay beyond.

Fifty-Two

More than one of the villagers and members of the Brotherhood froze as they dashed into the main hall of Karnstein Castle.

They stopped, despite the circumstances, and simply gazed almost in awe at the huge room and its contents.

Others, despite the lavishness and opulence of the room, seemed unconcerned with anything except their task, which was to find and destroy Count Karnstein.

'So this is the home of Satan's servant!' one of the Brotherhood snarled, driving his boot angrily into a table near the main entrance. He watched in satisfaction as it overturned, the goblets and glasses that had been standing on it smashing and spinning on the stone floor.

A villager used his sickle to slash at one of the paintings on the wall, the blade tearing through the canvas with ease and shredding a portrait of one of Karnstein's ancestors.

'Burn it!' one of the Brotherhood roared.

'No!' a villager snapped, gripping the man's wrist. 'Find Karnstein first and then we can destroy this place!'

But many others seemed intent only on destruction, and Franz looked around him as those milling about within the great hall set about demolishing everything connected with or belonging to their hated master. Ornaments were smashed, tables split by axe blows, curtains were torn down and trampled, and even the portraits on the walls were pulled from their mountings and either trodden on or smashed to pieces. There was rage and fury on the face of every man in the hall, as if years of pent up fear and anger had finally been released in one night of furious destruction. Even Franz himself overturned a table and kicked out at it angrily, infected by the fury that afflicted his colleagues.

'Search up there!' another of the Brotherhood shouted, urging a handful of villagers towards a flight of steps that led up from one side of the hall towards the first of two galleries high above.

Both these galleries ran around the entire extent of the hall and the villagers moved towards the first of these, weapons and torches in hand, their rage overcoming their fear. They had reached the inner sanctum, the heart of Karnstein's home. They knew that he must be here somewhere and they had no intention of leaving until they found him.

Passageways led off from the hall at ground level, too, and other men hurried towards these in their efforts to find the Count, their need for revenge overcoming all other considerations.

Franz was about to lead a group of Brotherhood members towards one of these passageways when a shout from behind him made him turn.

He spun around to see Anton dashing towards him from the other side of the hall, dodging several villagers in the process, who were busily destroying another painting they'd pulled from the wall.

'We'll find this Devil soon enough and then we'll burn down the castle!' Franz said, triumphantly.

'No!' Anton protested. 'For God's sake tell the men to hold back! He's got Maria!'

The colour drained rapidly from the cheeks of Franz and he took a step back.

'How do you know?' he demanded.

'I saw him take her,' Anton explained.

'Where?'

'He's got her somewhere in the castle. If we burn it now we risk burning Maria along with Karnstein!'

Franz swallowed hard and looked around the great hall, watching momentarily as men continued with their savage bout of destruction, but he shook his head and looked at Anton again, as if seeking guidance from the schoolmaster.

'What can we do?' he asked.

Anton was about to answer when a piercing scream rang out through the hall. The sound was so loud and so strident that it even rose above the sound of the vengeful villagers and Brotherhood members as they went about their task of sacking the castle.

All eyes turned in the direction of the scream and Anton's jaw dropped open as he looked up and saw its source.

In the upper most of the two galleries, Count Karnstein stood defiantly, Maria held in his arms as effortlessly as a child holds a doll. He took a step towards the parapet, pushing Maria towards the rail.

She screamed again as he dangled her over the drop beneath.

'Oh my God!' murmured Anton. He knew that if the Count dropped her she would have no chance. She was thirty feet up, if not more, suspended only by the Count's strong arms. If he allowed her to fall she would plummet straight down on to bare stone. Anton swallowed hard and looked desperately around for something to help her. Other faces looked upwards, too, and the men seemed frozen by the sight before them, all equally helpless before the spectacle, all realising there was little or nothing they could do to help Maria.

Anton took a couple of steps to his right, his eyes fixed on a long spear that was arranged on the wall with two broadswords and a battleaxe. He pulled the spear free and hefted it before him, the razor-sharp point gleaming in the light of so many flaming torches still blazing around him. He took a step forward and raised the spear.

Franz stepped towards him, blocking his way.

'I'm going to kill him!' Anton hissed, his eyes fixed on the Count, who was snarling furiously from his lofty position high above the hall and the men in it.

'No, you can't!' Franz protested. 'She's too close!'

Anton let out a growl of despair and gritted his teeth. Franz was right. If his aim was a foot out one way or the other he could end up skewering Maria with the spear. He gripped the long shaft, his knuckles turning white as he held the wood so tightly.

'There must be some way,' Anton hissed.

'We can only trust in God,' Franz told him, his eyes also fixed on the Count and Maria.

Karnstein extended his arms, so that Maria was suspended over the rail now. One movement and she would fall. Anton gripped the spear more tightly as Karnstein laughed throatily.

He looked at Maria, his eyes burning.

She tried to grab on to his clothes, well aware of what he intended to do with her. She looked down and saw the distance she would fall once he released her. Her heart hammered even more ferociously against her ribs. Her head was spinning now.

'Now,' Karnstein said to her, 'join your sister!'

He thrust his arms even further out, propelling Maria into empty air, only his powerful grip preventing her from falling to certain death. She closed her eyes, waiting for the inevitable.

'No!'

The voice made them both turn.

Karnstein took a step backwards and Maria realised she was no longer dangling over the rail. The Count dropped her to the floor at his feet, stepping contemptuously over her as he moved towards the source of the shout. Maria, too, saw where the sound had come from. She even managed a smile.

With the axe gripped in both hands, his face set in hard lines, Gustav Weil advanced towards Karnstein.

Fifty-Three

When Weil had first heard the voice of the Count so close he had felt a strange combination of sensations course through him. His initial revulsion and anger had been tempered by relief, and then by anticipation and something approaching excitement.

He knew that at last he was within striking distance of the depraved aristocrat, and that knowledge galvanised him. He had moved quickly but warily up the flight of stone steps towards the thick heavy curtains that formed the last flimsy barrier between himself and his quarry and, as he had paused there, peering through the material, he had seen that Karnstein was holding Maria before him. Threatening to drop her over the rail of the gallery like a child would throw away an unwanted doll. Weil had felt his heart thumping even more powerfully as he'd seen that image, and his only thought now was to save his niece.

Then he would be able to deal with Karnstein.

He had stepped from behind the curtains into full view of the Count and everyone gathered below in the great hall, his voice cutting through the air like a knife.

Now he stood only yards from the Count, the axe

gripped in his hands, the curved blade glinting in the candlelight.

'You keep away from her!' Weil hissed, taking a step towards the Count, who held his ground for a moment, perhaps surprised at the vehemence in his opponent's voice.

Maria saw her uncle advancing and she could feel herself shaking. She glanced down into the great hall and saw the sea of faces looking up. Among them she could see Anton and also her aunt.

Katy Weil clasped her hands together in silent prayer as she watched her husband moving towards Karnstein with the axe.

'Oh Gustav,' she murmured.

Beside her, Anton kept his grip on the spear, his teeth gritted as he, too, watched Weil and Karnstein above him facing each other like two gladiators in the arena about to come together for their final conflict. A battle from which only one would emerge with his life.

Weil gripped the handle of the axe more tightly and glared at the Count, who was smiling thinly and mockingly at him.

'I have waited a long time for this moment,' Weil said.

'And I, too,' Karnstein retorted.

But, for all the bravado in his voice, the Count was moving backwards towards a wooden door that stood at the far end of the gallery. Weil sensed the uncertainty in the other man and pressed his advantage, taking another two paces forward as he raised the blade of the axe.

'No one can protect you now,' Weil said, through clenched teeth.

Still Karnstein continued to back off, his arms outstretched as if he intended to embrace his opponent. With his cloak spread wide around him he looked like a gigantic bat standing there, waiting for prey.

His lips slid back to reveal his fangs, but Weil was undaunted by the sight and kept on advancing.

'Just one blow, Weil,' Karnstein chided, pointing to his own throat. 'And it must be here.' Again he touched the flesh beneath his chin with his fingers. 'Have you the strength and the courage? If not, you will join the Devil's souls.'

Weil fixed the Count in an unblinking stare and moved nearer to him.

'Imagine the torments your niece must have gone through,' Karnstein taunted. 'That is what you will endure if you do not strike.'

Weil gripped the axe until his knuckles turned white.

'Strike if you dare!' Karnstein hissed. 'If you have the stomach for it.'

Weil was only a few feet from his quarry now.

'And once I have dealt with you,' the Count went on. 'I will finish my business with her.' He pointed towards Maria. 'Just as I did with your other niece. I wonder if they will taste the same.'

Weil snarled and swung the axe at the Count, who moved swiftly to one side, avoiding the blow by inches. The blade swept past his head, but Weil swung it once more, moving forward this time to add power to his swing.

Again Karnstein ducked to one side and the blade missed his head, but this time it was driven with such force it thudded into the door behind him and stuck there.

Weil tried to tug it free, but Karnstein struck out quickly, catching him with a powerful blow to the face that almost broke his nose. Weil fell backwards, overbalancing and rolling over on the cold floor. He looked around and saw the Count leering down at him and the awful realisation struck him at the same time. The axe was still embedded in the door behind Karnstein. Weil was defenceless now. He shook his head to clear it and scrambled to his feet. He had to reach another weapon, had to get to something to fight the monster with. Even he knew that he had no chance with just his bare hands. Weil noticed two crossed swords mounted on the wall a few yards away. If he could just reach them.

Karnstein saw his opponent get to his feet, watched him turn his back and head for the swords, and he knew what to do. The Count turned and, with one powerful movement, he tore the axe from the door, spinning around to hurl it at Weil.

The weapon hurtled through the air and buried itself in Weil's back, between his shoulder blades.

The impact caused him to stagger and he felt agonising pain shoot up the full length of his spine as the axe blade penetrated. The impact knocked the breath from him and he felt his own blood pouring from the wound, soaking into his tunic, spilling on to the stone floor as he staggered a few more steps, before sagging helplessly against the wall, still somehow remaining upright. He reached back feebly with one hand, but couldn't grip the handle of the axe. Try as he might he could not drag the weapon free. His legs were shaking, the feeling leaving them. An overpowering sensation of cold began to envelop his entire body. And, through a haze of pain he saw Karnstein advancing towards him.

The Count grabbed him by the throat and lifted him an inch or two off the ground.

Weil could smell the foul stink of the Count's breath in his face.

'If I were to bite you, Weil,' he hissed, 'you would become as I am! Would your God save you then?'

Weil's eyes rolled upwards in their sockets, but Karnstein shook him like a dog shaking a rabbit.

'You will die now, Weil,' the Count rasped, 'and your last thought will be that it was I who took your life! Yours and then that of your niece. Think about that Weil. Think about it on your way to hell!'

Karnstein half-dragged and half-carried him towards the rail of the gallery, then, with almost contemptuous ease, he lifted the older man and hurled him over.

For interminable seconds Weil clutched at empty air, then his body plummeted like a stone. He struck the cold floor thirty feet below, his skull shattering upon impact. Several bones were also smashed, but Weil felt nothing now. He was dead the moment he hit the floor. A huge pool of blood began to spread rapidly around his broken body and he flopped over on to his back, his eyes open and gazing blindly at those who gathered around him.

'Oh, Gustav!' Katy Weil whimpered and she ran to kneel beside him, seemingly oblivious to the blood that soaked her dress as she clasped his hand.

Anton looked on helplessly, too, the knot of muscles at the side of his jaw pulsing angrily.

Franz took a step nearer to his dead friend and crossed himself.

Katy Weil brushed the hair back from Weil's forehead, ignoring the blood that was pumping from his pulverised skull. She held him to her like a mother would hold a child, feeling the warmth of his life fluid as it poured on to her hands. She rocked gently back and forth, her lips fluttering soundlessly as she said prayers for the soul of her dead husband. Finally, she leant forward and kissed his forehead, tears now coursing down her cheeks.

High above there was an ear-splitting scream and many turned to see Karnstein once more move towards Maria.

The Count laughed as he looked down at their expectant faces, raising both hands, which were spattered with Weil's blood.

Maria tried to scramble away, but her legs wouldn't support her weight and she sprawled helplessly before the Count. Karnstein smiled down at her, his fangs gleaming.

Below, there were shouts of anger and fear.

Anton saw his chance.

He hurled the spear with all his strength. The long shaft flew through the air, propelled by his anger and desperation and guided by his expertise.

It struck Karnstein squarely in the chest, bursting his heart as it tore through his ribs and penetrated his torso, tearing right through his body, such was the force with which it had been thrown. The point erupted from his back, blood bursting from both entry and exit wounds. He staggered backwards, clutching at the shaft, trying to tug it free, but failing. His hands could gain no purchase, the shaft was so slicked with his own blood. He stumbled against the wall behind him, a huge crimson smear marking the impact. For interminable seconds he stood there, transfixed by the spear, then he opened his mouth to scream in pain, but only produced a muted gurgling sound as blood filled his throat and poured over his lips. He slid down the wall, leaving a bloody smear as he dropped to the ground, his hands still gripping the spear that had killed him. His face contorted in agony as he tried once more to haul the shaft free, but it was useless. His hands slipped from the spear and he lay still, his body twitching as the muscles gradually gave up their hold on life.

Anton sprinted from the great hall up the steps towards the gallery, pausing only momentarily to look down at Karnstein, who fixed him in an unblinking gaze, before his eyes rolled upwards in their sockets.

Anton regarded the Count with disgust as he hurried to Maria and knelt beside her, pulling her closer to him.

She opened her eyes, momentarily dazed by what had happened, and, as she looked about her, she saw Karnstein lying nearby.

Maria shook her head and looked away from the terrible sight, but Anton continued to gaze at the Count almost in wonderment, mesmerised by what he saw.

As Anton watched, the skin began to peel from the Count's face. Great leprous patches of it merely melted away, as if someone had forced his face into a fire. Lumps of flesh curled up like paper in a fire, falling from the visage and exposing the muscles and veins beneath, but then they, too, began to shrivel and rot. Anton winced as he watched the disintegration, the stench reaching his nostrils and almost making him retch.

One of the Count's eyeballs swelled and then burst in its socket, the vitreous liquid pouring down his shrivelled cheek like tears. His fingernails merely crumbled as the flesh on his fingers turned grey, then disintegrated. It was as if the corruption inside him was escaping, searing his flesh as it did so.

By the time Maria looked, his head was little more than a skull, the two canine fangs still prominent in the upper jaw.

She groaned again and turned her head as Anton helped her to her feet.

Below them, the villagers could see that Maria was alive and many smiled. Members of the Brotherhood also joined them in that display of joy, but others were still gathered around the body of Gustav Weil and his wife, who was still rocking gently back and forth as she cradled her husband's body.

Franz leant forward and touched her gently on the shoulder.

'He is with God now,' he murmured.

Katy turned a pair of tear-filled eyes on Franz and nodded.

High above them, Anton and Maria looked down at the scene and she moved nearer to him, tears running down her cheeks.

She managed one glance back at the skeletal body of Count Karnstein, the spear still protruding from his now shrunken body. Anton led her towards the steps that would take them down to the hall. All Maria wanted to do was to leave the castle. She wanted to be away from so much evil, so much death.

As they walked he slipped an arm around her shoulder, almost as if her were guiding her down the stairs towards the waiting horde who watched them with something close to reverence.

More than one member of the Brotherhood nodded deferentially to Anton as he approached.

He returned the gesture, looking a little startled as Maria pulled away from him and ran to her aunt. Katy got to her feet and embraced the girl, and they both stood looking down at the body of Gustav Weil. They crossed themselves, then Maria knelt slowly, bent over the corpse and kissed it tenderly on the forehead.

Anton moved nearer and she turned gladly back into his arms, holding him tightly.

As he passed one of the villagers, Anton took the blazing torch that the man held, accepting it as the man nodded and handed it over, as if it were some kind of peace offering. Still clasping Maria, Anton waved the torch in the air in the direction of the main door of the hall, and those inside began to file out, grateful now to be able to leave this place forever.

Franz and three other members of the Brotherhood

carried Gustav Weil's body from the great hall, and Anton was left standing alone amidst the destruction. He looked around, then walked across to one of the huge tapestries that decorated the walls. He touched the torch to the material and it ignited, the flames spreading rapidly.

Anton retreated, standing for a second to watch the fire as it spread. It was as if he wanted to be certain that this place would truly be incinerated once and for all. He need not have feared. The flames were leaping and dancing everywhere within a matter of seconds. It wouldn't be long before the entire castle was burning.

And as he turned and walked out of the great hall of Karnstein Castle, Anton Hoffer found that a comforting thought.

Wake Wood

K.A. John

Released in 2010, *Wake Wood* was the first of Hammer's new releases

Still grieving after the death of their young daughter Alice in a frenzied dog attack, Patrick and Louise Daley leave the city to try and find some peace in the Irish countryside, and the village of Wake Wood seems like the perfect place to start again.

But the residents are guarding a terrifying secret: they can resurrect the dead. However, the rules are strict, they will bring Alice back only if she has been dead for less than a year; and, after three days, she must be buried.

Desperate to see their daughter again, even for just three days, the Daleys agree to everything. But they have been lying from the start. And by the time the villagers realise, it's too late. Alice is alive and she does not want to go back . . .

The Witches
Peter Curtis

Based on this classic book by Peter Curtis (aka Norah Lofts), *The Witches* was released in 1966 starring Joan Fontaine

Walwyk seemed a dream village to the new schoolteacher, Miss Mayfield. But dreams can turn into nightmares.

When it becomes clear that one of her pupils is being abused, Miss Mayfield is determined to do something about it. But Ethel won't say anything, despite the evidence of Miss Mayfield's own eyes, and someone seems to be actively discouraging her from investigating further. As she tries to get to the truth of the matter, however, Miss Mayfield stumbles on something far more sinister: Walwyk is in the grip of a centuries-old evil, and anybody who questions events in the village does not last long.

Death stalks more than one victim, and Miss Mayfield begins to realise that if she's not careful, she will be the next to die . . .

'Eerie . . . horrific . . . brilliant' *Guardian*

HAMMER

Hammer has been synonymous with legendary British horror films for over half a century. With iconic characters ranging from Quatermass and Van Helsing to Frankenstein, Dracula, and now the Woman in Black, Hammer's productions have been terrifying and thrilling audiences worldwide for generations. And there is more to come.

Leading actors including Daniel Radcliffe, Hilary Swank and Chloe Moretz are now following in the footsteps of Hammer legends Sir Christopher Lee, Peter Cushing and Bette Davis through their involvement in new Hammer films.

Hammer's literary legacy is also being revived through its new Partnership with Arrow Books. This series will feature original tales by some of today's most celebrated authors, as well as classic stories from more than five decades of production.

Hammer is back, and its new incarnation is the home of smart horror – cool, stylish and provocative stories which aim to push audiences out of their comfort zones.

For more information on Hammer,
including details of official merchandise, visit:
www.hammerfilms.com

The Resident
Francis Cottam

A major motion picture starring Hilary Swank

Every year, three million single women in America move into an apartment for the first time. Few of them change the locks.

Juliet Devereau can't believe her luck: after weeks of looking for a place to live, she's found a beautiful spacious apartment overlooking Brooklyn Bridge. It almost seems too good to be true.

It is . . . Over the weeks, a chilling sense of being watched stalks Juliet. Strange sounds wake her in the night, the mirror in the bathroom trembles, and doors she thought shut are open. Then the silhouette of a man standing in her living room makes her realise that she's not alone in there. But what's haunting her is far more terrifying than a malevolent spirit; it's alive, strong and obsessed. Suddenly Juliet is caught up in a deadly game of cat and mouse, and there's no guarantee that she'll come out alive . . .